THE TRUTH ABOUT
AWITI

CP PATRICK

DEDICATION

For my Mother—the perfect chrysalis.

INTRODUCTION

IT IS UNDISPUTED the trans–Atlantic slave trade was a catastrophic moment in history for the continent of Africa, causing social and economic hardship that has endured for generations. The Portuguese first entered Africa in the mid–15th century in search of gold. Shortly thereafter, they began the exploitation of a more readily available source of wealth—slave labor. European empires quickly followed, and by the end of the 19th century, an estimated 11 – 20 million Africans were forced into lives of servitude.[1] There are many repercussions directly linked to the trans–Atlantic slave trade, including the destruction of sacred land boundaries and familial ties, as well as the systemic racism people of the African diaspora presently experience throughout the world.

Traditional folklore within the African American community, particularly in the South, often centers on the belief that the spirits of slaves are not at rest. That the harm done to their African ancestors was so unfathomable, their souls still haunt the places of their transgressions. In *Slave Ghost Stories*[2],

---

1 Trans-Atlantic Slave Database.

2 Nancy Rhyne, Slave Ghost Stories: Tales of Hags, Hants, Ghosts and Diamondback Rattlers (South Carolina: Sandlapper Publishing, 2002), pp. vi – ix.

author Nancy Rhyne shares the narratives of former slaves that were collected during the Great Depression as part of the Federal Writer's Project.

Ms. Rhyne notes, "One of the more interesting questions on the list was 'Do you believe in spirits?' That question resulted in dozens of stories of hags, hants [sic], ghosts, and other frightful luminaries."[3] Many of the interviewees spoke at length with regards to restless slave spirits—they still walk the land rattling their chains, their ghostly faces seen and voices heard as they are forever bound in their misery. And some even seek retribution for their stolen lives.

If one does not believe in spiritual warfare or other forms of supernatural conflict, it is easy to dismiss the narratives surrounding the hauntings of slaves as nonsense. After all, enslavement, while currently considered barbaric in the Western world, was common and acceptable at the time. The most logical conclusion is the Africans who were impacted by the trans–Atlantic slave trade have died, their bodies buried in the earth and the bones of those who perished during the Middle Passage scattered beneath the sea.

But if one believes—or at a minimum has a bit of curiosity—regarding the connection between mind, body, and spirit, specifically as it relates to traumatic experiences, the theory of spiritual retribution is difficult to ignore. It is interesting to note the consistencies surrounding the narratives of particular hauntings that have endured for generations. One such example is the haunting at Igbo Landing in the Georgia Sea Islands (also commonly referenced as Ibo and/or Ebo). The facts are well documented.

---

3 Rhyne, Slave Ghost Stories, pp. vii – viii.

In May 1803, approximately 75 women and men from the Igbo tribe were brought from West Africa to Savannah, Georgia to be auctioned off as slaves.[4] Chained one to the other, they came into port and were led toward the dock. But instead of walking onto the bank into a life of slavery, they all turned and followed their chief into the depths of Dunbar Creek.[5]

Since the Igbo Landing incident, tales of hauntings of the drowned Igbos persevered, their souls disturbing the waters by the clanging of chains and the cries of men. Locals often quote the writings of H.A. Sieber who collected accounts of the drowning as told by the survivors' descendants.[6] So persistent and recounted were the hauntings that on September 2, 2002, almost 100 people "from as far as Nigeria visited the creek to designate the area as holy ground and to give the freed slaves peace."[7] Said one such participant in the two-day ceremony, "They were souls forced here to die without a proper burial. It's a step toward creating rest for us and our ancestors."[8]

Hauntings are by no means unique to the African American community. Many societies where systemic trauma occurred often account for similar stories. Is spiritual

4 Marquetta L. Goodwine, The Legacy of Ibo Landing: Gullah Roots of African American Culture (Georgia: Clarity Press, 2011).

5 Goodwine, The Legacy of Ibo Landing.

6 "Slave legend draws people for two-day remembrance in coastal Georgia," last modified March 5, 2015, http://www.ssiheritagecoalition.org/articles-about-ssaahc.html.

7 "Slave legend".

8 "Slave legend".

retribution possible? Could the souls of those who died at the hands of violence haunt the earth? The spirits of African slaves serve as no better case study for the "what if."

There is lengthy evidence regarding the lasting implications of slavery on people of African ancestry. Connections have been made between well-known topics such as socioeconomic challenges within the African American community and strained race relations, to lesser known areas of study such as health. For example, Harvard Professor Roland G. Fryer explored the notion that slavery may be a causal connection to African Americans having a genetic predisposition to hypertension.

While conducting research on the trans–Atlantic slave trade, Professor Fryer made a shocking discovery—a period illustration portrayed a slave trader licking the face of a prospective slave. The drawing became the focus of Professor Fryer's research on the prevalence of hypertension in the African American community.

The ocean voyage from Africa to America was so gruesome that as many as 15 percent of the Africans died en route, mainly from illnesses that led to dehydration. A person with a higher capacity for salt retention might also retain more water and thus increase his chance of surviving. So it may have been that a slave trader would try to select, with a lick to the cheek, the "saltier" Africans. Whether selected by the slavers or by nature, the Africans who did manage to survive the voyage—and who then formed the gene

pool of modern African-Americans—may
have been disproportionately marked by
hypertension.[9]

The aforementioned research areas are valid topics of study, as they are substantiated with historical evidence. But the theory of spiritual retribution is, after all, just a theory. It is a mystical approach to a tangible event, which is why it is perhaps best to fictionalize the notion of spiritual warfare. *The Truth About Awiti* is a tale of historical fantasy—a chronicle of fact, fiction, and the supernatural intertwined to explore the "what if."

The reader will discover the repeated theme of tropical storms and hurricanes. Are these massive storms the embodiment of restless slaves and their descendants? Hurricanes begin formation off the West Coast of Africa, the very shores where slave raiders sent Africans to their unfortunate fates of servitude and death. Building strength as they pass over the waters of the Middle Passage, the storms send their fury mainly to the South, the very states notorious for their treatment of African Americans both pre– and post–antebellum. Are such occurrences merely happenstance? Perhaps, it's something more…

CP Patrick

---

9 Stephan J. Dubner, "Toward a Unified Theory of Black America," New York Times. March 20, 2005.

"*There was a time when you were not a slave, remember that. You walked alone, full of laughter, you bathed bare-bellied. You say you have lost all recollection of it, remember... You say there are no words to describe this time, you say it does not exist. But remember. Make an effort to remember. Or, failing that, invent.*"

– Monique Wittig

PART I
LIFE

1
IN THE BEGINNING

They say I was born too early. That I came into the world before my time. Father counted the days and watched as his wife's belly became heavy with child. Every movement within her womb a reason to give thanks to the gods. Mother's demanding cravings for odd foods and comforts were cause for celebration. And her dutiful husband gave his wife whatever she wished.

She craved *ugali*, *sukumawiki*, and boiled fish mixed with the hottest peppers. Their bed was often too hard or soft for her liking, but these things amused her husband. Father spent his nights rubbing the taut dark skin of Mother's plump belly as he told stories to me, his first heir.

The pregnancy progressed uneventfully until the day I decided I was ready. That even though it was before my time, I would be born. There was an understanding this was something children should not do. For when children come into the world bringing trouble, they are bound to have a lifetime of such.

There was much concern, as I had not been in Mother's womb for enough days. Her belly was small, round enough to show she was with child. She knew she needed to be much larger before the pains came.

Father had kept track of my growth by marking short, straight lines in neat rows on the birthing wall. When I decided I was ready, Father ran to count his markings. There was nothing he could do but watch, wait, and pray.

And he did pray. Along with Ahenda, the midwife, Father prayed and recounted each dark stroke. There were not enough lines. It was too soon.

They say a storm raged the night I was born. That my birth made the rain fall hard and fierce like the strongest of our warriors beating a thousand drums. Large wet tears pounded our village, flooded the vegetable gardens, and turned the rich soil to thick, dark mud. The ancestors were not pleased with me.

Lightening flashed in long, white streaks, and thunder resounded as though the neighboring mountains were crumbling. Mother grasped her belly and pleaded while I, ever persistent, decided it was time. She tried not to push as I continued to make my entrance into the world. Her legs locked and knees bent in defiance. But I was coming—with or without her assistance.

Ahenda squatted between Mother's legs and waited. Her wrinkled, dark birthing hands open and cupped as if she were scooping water from the river. Lines and creases crossed about the elder's palms. Brown pathways. A fleshy map of unknown destinations. She knew what to do, for this was not her first time delivering a child who decided to come too soon. Familiar with the disobedient ones, Ahenda was stoic. A white cloth draped over her right arm. She was ready to wrap me up lest I be born disfigured or deceased.

Mother's cries could be heard above the drumming rain

and echoing thunder. She was unprepared for the discomfort, the uncertainty of childbirth. Her dark skin was covered with sweat as was the bed where she lay. The cloths soiled and tangled in just as much confusion.

The pain of me coming forth from Mother's womb was unlike anything she had ever experienced. She screamed as though I were trying to kill her. Of course, I was not intent on hurting Mother. I was, quite simply, ready.

And so I came into the world too soon. An ill-timed brown baby with a halo of wispy, black hair adorning my tiny head. Dark, slick curls swirled about and made me look like most newborn children—beautiful, yet disheveled and bewildered.

The air was still as Father, Mother, and Ahenda waited to see if each breath was my last. My lower body lay cradled in the palm of Father's hand, while his long, thin fingers supported my head and neck. I slept while they decided what should be done with me.

"We shall name her Awiti Akoth."

Father decided on Akoth during my birth, for I was born as the rains fell. It was more difficult to choose Awiti. More painful to say the name aloud.

Ahenda comforted Mother as they nodded in agreement. Still weakened from my early arrival, Mother counted my toes, touching each one. Then, with gentle hands, she lifted the swaddling. Seeing my fingers, she counted them as well, kissing each one as she tallied. Mother put one of her fingers in my palm and marveled at her daughter's hand grasping her own.

Awiti. A child to be thrown away. One born after misfortune. It was a common name for a girl child born too soon. They did not expect me to survive.

Had Father and Mother not been through such a terrible

ordeal before my birth, they perhaps would have done just that—thrown me away. Taken me to the edge of our village, said a prayer, and left me to my fate. I would have simply been another life trying to come into the world before its time. A child sure to bring trouble.

But after what Father and Mother endured, I was something they needed. My birth, albeit too soon, gave them hope. Their daughter Awiti was a new life to hold onto and believe in.

Their destiny was altered before I was born. Strange men with brown skin and straight dark hair speaking in foreign tongues attacked their first village. Father and Mother were taken against their will along with many others. Those who were not abducted were killed and their first village destroyed.

The strange men put yokes of wood around their prisoners' necks and led them through the land. It was a sorrowful journey to an unknown place where death was imminent and certain. For who would capture them in such an inhumane way only to treat them fairly once they reached their destination?

Father and Mother were fortunate. After many days in bondage, along with a few others from their first village, they managed to escape their captors. They ran until the strange men were far behind them. After wandering through unfamiliar lands, they came to a village that welcomed them. The village, which they fondly called "second village," became home, and their lives started anew. But many others from their first village were not so fortunate. They were never seen again.

During captivity, Mother was separated from Father, for the strange men thought it necessary to isolate the men, women, and children. I was born with Mother's small dark eyes, brown skin, and the same slick black hair as their captors. It was clear what happened during their time apart.

Father knew without a doubt his wife would never desire to lie with another man. Their love was unyielding, perfect. Childhood friends who grew to understand and conquer life together. Devotion was the foundation of their union. He was certain I came into Mother's belly through force and great suffering.

But there was to be no shame for Mother. No questioning of her loyalty or virtue as his wife. Father blamed himself for being unable to protect her. He was thankful his wife forgave him for failing as her warrior and guardian. It only made him love her more. He loved her for surviving.

I was a byproduct of the pain the strange men inflicted upon his wife. Evidence she was raped by their captors. And yet, just as these facts did not stop Father from loving Mother, they did not preclude Father from adoring me.

In fact, they say it was Father's love that nourished my premature body to health. For seventy-two days he held me close, unable to stop looking at his firstborn daughter with eyes like her Mother. Soon I was healthy and strong as if I had come into the world as planned. Soon, I was just another girl in my village.

A few other children were born after me. My sister, Amondi, with clouds of tight, black curls I enjoyed braiding. Her dark skin was like Mother's flesh. Deep and rich in its blackness. Amondi was the child born with a smile none of her siblings could rival.

There were my brothers Jaramogi, the playful one, and Owino and Onyango, who looked identical to Father. No matter, for everyone knew I was Father's first love. And Mother's too, for she often held me close and told me how blessed I was to be her firstborn.

I was Awiti. A reflection of what Father and Mother survived. And I was also a survivor. For I lived even though I was born too soon.

"You are special," Father would tell me.

"To come to the world through such misfortune. To be born before your time. You were such a small, weak child, we were afraid you would break. At one time you were lighter than a bird's feather. Yet now you are tall and more beautiful than the flowers that cover the fields. You are stronger than a deep-rooted tree by the edge of the river. Yes, you are special, my Awiti."

My childhood was as childhood should be. Simple. One of wonder and exploration of the world around me. There were no worries for necessities. And I had innocent prayers for things I wanted and hoped for. Whenever I was hurt, I ran to Father, for the touches from his hands were powerful. He stroked the ache, and if necessary, wrapped my wounds. All the while comforting and scolding, scolding and comforting. My pain disappeared, and soon I would be back at play.

Whether Father possessed magic or I was a child who healed with ease, I will never know. But I like to believe it was enchantment. For in my early years, I believed Father was the man who controlled the sun.

It was the favorite part of the day for his children. The sun remained high and warm in the sky, drifting in and out of the white clouds and blue heavens until Father was ready to put it to rest. We watched the sun throughout the day. The way our shadows fell on the land determined our responsibilities.

As we tended to our final tasks, we looked forward to the moment Father called for us to gather around him.

Father did not have great wealth, and so we were his only children. Now that I am older, I believe this was intentional. It was not that Father could not achieve abundance. He chose not to pursue affluence, for this ensured he would have just one wife— Mother.

"The day is over," Father would announce. "It is time for the sun to go home."

His children came running toward his open arms, jostling for position, for we all wanted the best view. Amondi often charmed her way into Father's lap. Her brothers would only push her so much, for they were frowned upon if they shoved their sister with too much force. And I was the oldest, and although I wanted to be in Father's lap, it was not really an option, so I crouched at his side.

Father would lift his palms to the sky and enclose them around the sun. Mother smiled as her children clamored around the man who could guide the sun into the earth with his hands and the sound of his voice.

While Father put the sun to rest for all of his children, he made it rise in the morning just for me. He awakened me before my siblings, and together, hand in hand, we walked in silence toward the baobab tree. Long, green blades of grass damp underneath each footstep. We moved quick and purposeful. The pathway familiar. Our feet knew the way without us telling them where to go.

Dark purple billows rolled through the sky at daybreak, providing us little light as the sun waited for Father. We were surrounded by the color of dawn, the sounds of life preparing for a new day. Birds chirped their cheerful songs announcing morning. Insects rubbed their wings together. Nature's music.

The baobab tree stood enormous and forbearing on the horizon. Its branches reaching high before leaning over, wooden limbs stretching toward the earth. Shadows beckoned my youthful imagination, and I believed the tree to be the resting place of hundreds of birds. I knew the branches held gourds of fruit, but I enjoyed pretending the gourds were dark fowl nestled within their own wings, sleeping and swaying in the early morning breeze.

Father called it the tree of life, and near its large trunk, a worn patch of grass revealed our sacred place. I sat in Father's lap as the dark gourds hung on long stems above our heads. Father raised his hands, slow and deliberate. The sun would rise and take its place in the sky.

These moments were for us.

"Remember what makes us special, Awiti," Father reminded me. "I can control the sun. And when your heart desires, you can control the rain."

It was often after Father made the sun rise, he would tell the story of how the rains soaked the village during my birth. The last raindrop fell as I took my first breath.

I know now, of course, it was not true. That Father could not make the sun rise or set. His fictitious display of power was for his children. Young ears and eyes that believed whatever their Father said and showed them. But for many years, I believed him.

Even when I was old enough to question the possibility of it all, I still believed. For he was Father. Perfect in every way.

Our lives were simple then. Gentle breezes carried the smells of meals cooking. Bellies always full with fresh catch.

Vegetables grew abundant in the fertile land. The women braided each other's hair and told stories that made little sense to children's ears but caused much laughter amongst those old enough to understand the tale.

Boys fished in the blue waters with their fathers while the girls and mothers waited on shore for the catch. The younger children watched. Their dark naked bodies splashed about, swimming and playful. When children became aware of their nakedness, the boys went off to become men. And when the men returned, the girls were women. Ready and eager to be wives and mothers.

Sometimes the fathers left the village to trade and hunt, with great fanfare made upon their departure and return. Their travels were filled with stories that enticed the young boys and frightened the girls. Danger abounded outside our village, but the fathers would not be defeated, determined to come home to their wives and children.

Excited to hear of life in other villages and tall tales of adventure, the children loved when their fathers returned. The men often brought small gifts for their offspring and taught us the greetings and common phrases of our neighbors. We laughed at how strange the words sounded, amazed other villages only a few days' travel away spoke a language so different from our own.

As I grew older, I helped Mother, following her movements that would one day be my routine. I learned to cook the meals Father loved. I knew how to tell when the fire was ready and which spices healed sickness. In the mornings, I fetched water from the river and tended to the children. I tilled our garden, giving my siblings and the soil equal amounts of love and attention.

Whenever I looked to the sky, clouds took on the shapes of animals as the sun shined, yellow and resolute. Grass blanketed the land, a vibrant sea of green stems that were sweet when chewed. Flowers with petals of reds, shades of orange and purple dotted the terrain as far as the eye could see. Our village was surrounded by beauty.

There were times when our king called for celebration. Large feasts to honor our ancestors or a successful harvest. Men beat their drums under the night sky while the mothers and older daughters sang and danced around the fire. On these nights the stars in the sky seemed plentiful, glistening and bright against the dark blue heavens. I often tried to count the stars only to awaken the next morning. Father told me I had fallen asleep, but he always encouraged me to try the feat again.

Children scurried about during the village feasts, happy to be awake with the adults after nightfall. I was somewhere in between. Too old to scurry yet too young to dance with the mothers and older daughters, their bodies full of curves from bearing children.

Mother was enchanting in these moments. Her voice strong and harmonious, rising above the others as she sang songs she learned from the women in her second village. Words echoed of courage and bravery. Of joy and forgiveness. Lessons on living and dying interwoven into each melody.

Hips and feet danced to the rhythmic beats of the drums. Father watched Mother, smiling as her dark skin reflected the flames. I dreamed I would grow to dance like Mother. That one day, as I danced and sang, my husband would look at me the way Father looked at Mother.

It was often after our celebratory feasts many of the wives' bellies became swollen.

Love, is what Father said.

Their wombs were swollen with Love.

Much time had passed after the attack on Father and Mother's first village. They were settled and content in their second village. I believe they thought we were safe. If not for my existence—a daughter born with brown skin and dark, slick curls—perhaps they would have thought the strange men to be just a dream.

Their first village was but a distant recollection. Never forgotten, but with each day, memories of the lives they once lived moved further and further away. Father and Mother never imagined the strange men would return. But they did.

Marching boldly, the brown invaders carried yokes of wood to place around the necks of our people. We all saw them coming, as our village sat high above the clearing for times such as these. Women and children ran to places of safety as they waited for the men to protect them. And the fathers and warriors prepared to fight, Father among them.

Before going to engage in battle, Father gathered his children and Mother.

"You must run," he told us. "Run fast and do not look back. Run until you find a new village to call home."

Father promised we would find each other, even if it took a lifetime. And I believed him. I knew no matter what happened, our family would find a way to be together again. I knew I would do whatever it took to ensure our reunion.

And so I ran. I never looked back. And I never saw them again.

2
THE IMMORTAL

Oyo Empire, Yoruba (1693)

When I first heard the faint cries and saw the thin brown legs peeking out from beneath the leaves of the natal guarri tree, I should have turned away. I should have gone in the opposite direction from what was sure to be trouble. But I did not. I could not. For even then, with her body partially hidden, the tree revealing only her long legs, Awiti tempted me.

It was the day the rain came. After thirty-four days of dryness, our prayers were finally answered. The rain began to fall, slow but continuous, the dry dirt eager to soak in the wetness. Raindrops left little circles on the ground where the earth had swallowed them.

I looked up to the pale skies as white clouds moved across the blue with haste. And I thanked Shango, the Sky Father. Then I heard the weak cries, saw the willowy brown legs, and turned toward her. I still remember my first words.

"Báwo ni? Ṣé o lè sọ èdè Yorùbá?"

We were outside the gates of the Kingdom of Oyo, and I needed to know. Was she ours?

Her legs were much too light in color. They had not seen enough sun. She was not black, her skin not saturated with darkness like the women of our kingdom. So she could not possibly be from Oyo. And thus, she could not possibly speak Yorùbá. But she replied,

"Mo lè sọ ọ díẹ." Her voice not much more than a whisper. She could speak a little.

I moved closer so I could see her more clearly. Her thin, awkward frame crumpled amongst the dying leaves at the bottom of the tree. If this was her best effort to hide, she had failed.

Small dark eyes with full lashes blinked back tears. Long, thick hair flowed down her back in deep black waves with rounded curls at the ends. Rain fell on her heart-shaped face. Tiny droplets rested on the dark ringlets of hair. She was beautiful.

"Kí ni orúkọ ẹ?" I asked

Her name might give insight to her village.

"Orúkọ mi ni... Awiti."

Her voice was kind, and if she was afraid of the large, dark man towering over her, she did not show her fear.

"Orúkọ mi ni Ọ̀rányàn."

I reached out my hand to her. I wanted Awiti to know I meant her no harm. That I could never hurt something so beautiful.

Her name was strange. Its meaning and origin foreign to me. Awiti did not reach for my hand in return, and so I crouched down next to her. The rain mixed with dirt, and it created a warm mud that seeped between my toes. But I did not care.

Tears stained the brown face thin from hunger. Although she was famished, her lips were full and pink. New leaves were budding on the branches of the natal guarri, rainfall providing the nourishment they so desperately needed. They were tiny leaves. A pale, gold-tinted green, their true color was not yet rich and deep. Now there was rain. The leaves would darken, yellow flowers would bloom, and berries would grow. I imagined Awiti's full lips tasting the red berries. I was already taken with her.

"Do not worry," I told her, uncertain as to whether she could understand my words. "I will help you."

Awiti only nodded in response.

Her clothing was soiled. All of her unclean and full of evidence of disorder. Her feet, too small for a woman but too large for a girl, were dirty. The petite toenails covered with red, brown, and black stains. There was nothing to protect her hands, and so her fingernails mirrored the feet in their cleanliness. But even with all of these shortcomings, she was perfect.

Her unkempt appearance was meaningless to the brown skin, dark coils of hair, and full pink lips that covered straight white teeth. And nothing, not even the filth that coated her, could detract from her eyes.

The indigo bird's eyes are small and black. And when Awiti looked at me, she seemed a human indigo. I felt as though she could *see* me. The dark eyes searching who I was versus the man I pretended and wished to be. Exposed, I broke our uncanny trance and looked away. I stood up in an effort to compose myself.

The rainfall became more intense. The raindrops large

and warm. Awiti's hair turned darker as the shower soaked the deep, black waves.

"*Ìlú wo l'o ti wá?*" I asked.

Awiti did not answer. She did not tell me the name of her village or people. She just appeared. And that was how it all began. With Awiti appearing outside the palace walls of Oyo, and me rescuing her from whatever she was escaping.

Much time has passed since that day, and each second reminds me of the power of mortality. Soon my life will end. As death becomes more imminent, the mind tends to reflect on life. Chances that were or were not taken. Whether decisions made were right or wrong. And each of my considerations reminds me of Awiti.

All those years ago, although I tried to convince myself I was noble for rescuing a helpless girl, I knew I was being selfish, deviant. Awiti had something I wanted. I knew I could take what I wanted from her. And I did.

I did hurt something so beautiful.

Most will never know the misery of living an indefinite number of years. The reality of immortality is much more burdensome than the fantasy. At first, yes, it was wonderful to take risks and do harm. To live with reckless abandon and know I would never die. But then, and then came much sooner than I imagined, I desired to become old.

I wanted a true life. Many days I longed for a wife and to have children who favored me. There were even times I desired to experience death, for I had become so despondent at the thought of living forever.

And that was why Awiti hiding beneath the natal guarri in the rain, dirty and childlike, was so enticing. Awiti had what I wanted the most. She was mortal.

Often when I reflect on meeting Awiti, I wonder if it was I who was tricked. If all along Awiti had come to Oyo with a purpose. Her spirit searching for someone like me. Waiting for me to bargain with her.

"Come with me," I told her, extending my arms. "Someone so lovely does not belong in the dirt. Will you come with me?"

Our first encounter—Awiti beautiful and vulnerable, and I walking outside the palace walls at that exact moment—well, it was quite fortuitous for us both. And I know from all my years of living such an encounter was rarely happenstance. Could Awiti have known who and what I really was? I have never been certain.

Regardless, that fateful day, I picked Awiti up from beneath the pale, golden-green leaves and cradled her in my arms. Her thin frame was light, and I held her without much effort. She placed her head on my shoulder. Her lips grazed my neck as the dark waves fell over my bare skin.

I took Awiti into Oyo, carrying her past the palace guards, who had never seen someone with such brown skin. The guards' eyes acknowledged her beauty, but they were careful not to disrespect me. I held Awiti as though she were already mine.

"She is injured," I told them as I moved quickly through the large wooden gates. "I must get her to the healers if she is to be saved."

Awiti raised her head so she could take in the magnificence of our kingdom. There was much evidence of our wealth and power. When we passed by the palace of Oba, her dark eyes opened wide. I suspected Oyo was very different from her home.

"Come quick," I yelled, rushing towards the compound

of the Oloogun. The air smelled fragrant, full of incense and musk. I was quite frantic as I pleaded,

"Please help this young woman. Her name is Awiti. That is all I know."

Olujimi, the high priest, prayed for Awiti. And the medicine women tended to her wounds. They fed her well, nourishing her with our finest fruits and vegetables and slaying fresh meat in her honor. Although dehydrated and famished, Awiti was alive.

"She will be fine, Oranyan," Olujimi assured me. "She is in need of nourishment, prayer, and rest."

I continued to linger, watching her.

"Go now," Olujimi commanded. "Let us do our work."

Soon Awiti was in good health, and everyone in Oyo came to see the young woman who had magically appeared outside the palace walls. The medicine women massaged Awiti with the finest oils until her brown skin glistened as honey from a bee's hive. Awiti's thick hair hung down her back, nearly reaching her waist.

"Isn't she so beautiful?"

"Look at her skin. It is though her father is the heavens and her mother is the sun."

"Where is her home?" some men asked. "Could there exist an entire village with women so beautiful?"

Oyo's people worshipped Awiti, stroking her deep coils of hair and not-black-enough skin. We all believed she was blessed. And Awiti was gracious. Even the Alaafin of Oyo came to see Awiti. When I told her his name meant "owner of the palace," she understood his significance. Awiti bowed to thank him for allowing her into his kingdom.

I was pleased Awiti had recovered. For although this

sounds harsh, her successful recovery meant I could take from her what I needed. There existed only one concern. Awiti was anxious. And I was certain it had to do with her past.

I would often inquire, "Awiti, tell me of your village, of your home before you came to Oyo."

"I have told you I cannot, Oranyan," Awiti would say softly. "I cannot allow myself to return to those memories. The weight of what I have lost—it crushes me. When I think of that time, I do not want to live. And so I try not to remember."

"But it is not good to hold in painful memories. Allow me to share in your pain. Allow me to help you heal, Awiti."

"Oranyan, please," she would beg. "Please, can we not discuss such things?"

And often, after we had these conversations, Awiti would cry. Even the sky seemed to share in her misery, dark and gloomy. For many days, Awiti would remain cloaked in sadness.

Because of this, she was not ideal. As an immortal with a troubled spirit, Awiti would live within two worlds. Awiti's body would exist in mortal form. And her restless spirit would walk the earth for eternity. She would be among the living and the dead. But this did not stop me.

She was not perfect, but Awiti was a vessel nonetheless. I told myself numerous times her past affairs were not my concern. But I knew then, as I know now, that was not true.

Many may question my decision to relinquish my immortality, but only I know the true depths of my motivation. Even today I do not regret the decision. But I do somewhat regret choosing Awiti. Perhaps if I had waited for a better host, a less worrisome subject, life would be different. But alas, I cannot turn back the hands of time. It was Awiti who was there that fateful day the rain came. And so it was Awiti I chose.

Even after she settled in Oyo and our relationship grew closer, Awiti never spoke of her past. She refused to answer any questions regarding her people, her village, her not-black-enough skin. While I could have used my powers to find out this information—looked into Awiti's memories and saw what brought her to Oyo—I did not. It was impolite to examine others' pasts without their permission. Although, I often wonder what I would have seen.

Naturally Awiti and I became lovers. And when I say naturally, that was how it came to be. Like a flower must have time to grow and flourish. Its bulb cannot be pried open for fear the blossom be destroyed. We did not force or rush our love. We fell into admiration for each other, and admiration turned into a longing that had to be fulfilled.

There was a current in the air that caused Awiti's nipples to harden and me to rise in my loins. We would look at each other and smile. The anticipation of new love. Nipples hardened more, loins rose higher. It went on this way for some time until we could no longer resist the obvious attraction and desire we had for each other.

"Oranyan, is this what it is to be in love?" she asked. "I feel as though I cannot breathe unless you are near. And then, when you are near me, I am breathless."

"Yes, Awiti, this is love. Well, a small part of the vastness of love. For love is so deep and so wide, it extends beyond the heavens and beneath the earth. It cannot be contained to just this moment, or to us. Or even to life. For even in death, love exists."

"Well, for me, whether to the heavens or beneath the earth, in life or in death, I love you, Oranyan."

"And I love you, Awiti."

When we first lay together, Awiti was not yet a woman. Although I looked not much older than her, I was. By hundreds of years. These were the difficult moments of immortality. In my lifetime I had been with countless women, had many lovers. But even with all of my experience—and Awiti was not the first virgin I had encountered in all my years—she was different. Everything with Awiti was different. More beautiful. More meaningful.

We were beneath Oyo's full moon. The night air a thick blanket of warmth over us. A playful wrestling match had ended with us rolling about the grassland like children. I stroked Awiti's brown skin under the moonlight, held the soft, dark ringlets of hair in my hands. I took Awiti in my arms, and her body relaxed. She was eager for me to please her. She was not afraid. For I was made for Awiti, and she was made for me. That was how we fit together. Awiti and Oranyan.

Our bodies bound together, the closeness continuous. Nothing between us but the longing to please each other. Awiti was the only lover who ever caused me to lose myself. The willowy, brown legs controlling me as they wrapped around my waist. Her dark eyes searching. A simple moan from Awiti's full pink lips, or the deep, dark waves falling over me. Why, even now, the mere memory causes my loins to rise. We were uninhibited lovers. And I relished every moment.

Perhaps it was because I knew of my plan to become mortal. And once I achieved mortality, I would have to choose a respectable life. I would marry, and my wife would come from a family of wealth and influence, and we would have many children. And I would marry more wives who would do the same as my first wife. I would choose wives based on mundane things. What she cooked and whether her figure was one of a woman who could birth many sons. Awiti would be the last lover I would have for passion rather than practicality.

So it did not matter Awiti could not cook as well as the other women in Oyo, or that her hips were not wide enough to bear children with ease. Nor did it matter her skin was so stark against my own black flesh. I did not care that her dark eyes held secrets from her past.

What was of importance was the way Awiti kissed me with her full lips. Her hair falling over my face as she straddled me. Our bodies arched, skin wet with the evidence of our passion and determination to please each other. I loved not knowing where the dark waves would fall next.

We filled our nights with love just as we filled our days with Awiti learning Yoruba, exploring Oyo. Togetherness. We were complete. Always undivided and present with each other.

One night, as Awiti lay in my arms, I decided to tell her I was immortal. This was a great risk. The revealing of a secret I had never shared with another.

"Awiti, I am not the same as you," I began hesitantly.

"What do you mean, Oranyan?"

"I appear as flesh and bones as you do. And I live and breathe. But…" I was uncertain how to continue.

"Yes?" she pressed.

"But I will never die. I am immortal."

At first Awiti did not believe me. She laughed, throwing her head back and opening her mouth wide. The full lips and straight teeth mocked me. Her laugh was always loud for a woman, and I attributed it to her youth. But when Awiti looked into my eyes and saw I was serious, she lay quiet for a moment.

Then she asked, "But how can this be? Everything that is living must die."

"That is not true. There are those who walk among the living with powers bestowed upon them by the Great One. Some are even unaware of their gifts. But I am very much aware. And I assure you I am immortal."

Awiti stroked my arm, as if to test my authenticity.

"I know it is hard to believe, Awiti, but it is true."

I told Awiti of the many times I had tempted death knowing it would never come. That I had lived for centuries. That I would never die.

I fell asleep with Awiti's head on my shoulder, the dark waves cascading over my chest and her breath soft on my skin. The next day when morning awakened us, Awiti said nothing of our conversation. And neither did I.

Initially I thought I would have to entice Awiti with the idea of living forever. But I did not. A few days later when I mentioned to Awiti I wished to part with my immortality, it was she who was quite astounded to learn it could be done.

"This immortality," she questioned, "it is something you can *give* to another?"

"Well, yes. It is called an Exchange. I can exchange my immortality with any mortal who is willing."

"And after the Exchange, that person will never die?"

"Yes."

"And this Exchange," she asked curiously, "is it something you wish to do?"

"Yes. I have lived many lifetimes. And I am quite at peace with the thought of death. But the Exchange is a sacrifice. I have never found anyone who loved me enough."

It was partly true. I had never made the offer to another. I had never found anyone like Awiti.

Awiti thought only for a moment before she told me, "Oranyan, I love you enough to give you the one thing you desire most."

There was a light in Awiti's eyes when she spoke of becoming immortal. The endless benefits of cheating death. Not once did she ask why I was so eager to part with it.

"I look forward to living many lifetimes." Awiti was excited, her young mind racing with possibilities. "It seems we are both getting what our hearts desire. That is the power of fate, Oranyan. And love. I will remember and love you as I live forever."

"And I will love you even after I die."

Before our Exchange, I taught Awiti many things in preparation for her new life. I showed her how to travel throughout the physical realms, to journey to any part of the world she wished. She was always to travel present in history. Never backward to change it or forward to see what was to come. All those who had tried such feats had failed.

I also shared with Awiti one of life's supreme secrets—how to acquire another's gift or power. Initially, she was quite resistant to the idea.

She challenged, "If I am immortal, what would I need to take from another?"

"It is important you understand what it means to acquire the gift of another. It allows you to weaken a man without touching him. To take the strongest, most intelligent being and render him weak and ignorant while granting you strength and intelligence."

The mortal possesses this ability on a smaller scale. Have

you ever spoken with someone or spent time in another's presence and afterward feel drained? Your body weakened as if you have completed some great task? This force is called power absorption. And when performed by someone who understands its true supremacy, it can cause great damage, even death. It was necessary for Awiti's survival, for there would be times in her life when being immortal would not be enough.

I also learned Awiti had a natural gift, although it was undeveloped. She could make the breeze change its course and rain fall from the skies. Perhaps it may have even been Awiti who brought rain the day we met, for it had fallen soft and steady like her tears.

I had heard of this gift of weather manipulation. But in all my years of living I had never met one who possessed it. I knew if not managed, like all gifts, it gave Awiti the ability to bring about much misfortune, especially as an immortal. But this too did not stop me.

Soon I prepared Awiti as well as I could. Taught her all I knew. Once our Exchange was complete, Awiti would have to leave me and leave the Kingdom of Oyo. I told Awiti our separation was mandatory when she agreed to the Exchange, but when the time came, she seemed in disbelief. Awiti thought my love for her would cause me to change my mind. But the rules were not my own.

Awiti acted as though she did not understand. But my words could not have been any clearer. She had to leave.

If she did not depart from Oyo, my vessel would try to regain its immortality. The longer Awiti remained near after our Exchange, she would be a danger to me, and I a threat to her. There was already a strong pull between us.

My body did not like the feeling of impending death.

And Awiti's body would fight to remain immortal. Surely she would grow accustomed to being eternal. If Awiti stayed in Oyo, our two vessels would battle for immortality. We would fight for what bonded and divided us.

"Please, Awiti. Let us have one last moment together. Can I hold you close so you can remember our love?"

"You do not love me, Oranyan," Awiti challenged. "If you loved me, you would stay with me."

"But I cannot, Awiti. Do you not already feel the pull between us growing stronger?" I knew she could feel the pain, the burning in her stomach. She could feel it just as much as I.

"I do not care about the pull. I can live with the pain if it means you stay with me."

"Awiti, we cannot stay together. Come to me before the pull grows too strong for either of us to bear."

Awiti would not look at me, no matter how I begged and pleaded. We still had a small amount of time. A short period for us to say our goodbyes. I needed to hold her one last time.

I longed to stroke the dark waves and kiss the full lips. I needed the not-black-enough skin burning next to mine. I wanted Awiti to remember. To know, despite my decision, I loved her. But she would have nothing to do with me.

"*Fi mí sílè*," Awiti yelled.

Over and over Awiti implored me to leave her alone. With each angry word, the skies grew darker and the sound of thunder closer, threatening. I left Awiti as the storm began to rage. It would be the last time I saw her.

When I came to see Awiti the next morning, wishful her temper had passed, hopeful to have a chance at a proper farewell, she was gone. I picked up one of Awiti's favorite wraps, the silken fabric reminding me of her skin. It still smelled of her, sweet and fragrant. I held it to my face for some time.

There was no pulling from within. My body was adjusting to mortality. I was thankful and full of sadness all at once.

I looked at the fresh dew drops on the grass and remembered how rain fell the day we met. I reminisced on the black waves and small dark eyes that searched me. Awiti, my indigo bird. I thought of the softness of kissing her pink lips and the beauty of her brown skin.

I would never know what would become of her. But I knew of the pain and suffering she would cause and endure. Awiti would forever question my love for her. The truth is, I did and still do love Awiti. And how I did cry that day.

"Yòò dára o, Awiti."

Good luck, Awiti.

3

WHITE FACES,
BLACK FACES

Central Africa (1742)

At first the stories were few. But in time we began to hear of more sightings of White Faces. Wild kinsmen. Evil beings who haunted the land. They did not behave like men. White Faces were always awake, always hunting. They came without warning, day or night. Leaving villages in ruins. Burning every home to the ground with sticks of fire.

They preyed on men and women to cook and eat. To satisfy their insatiable taste for Black flesh. They left the elders and young children only to return when the men were no longer there to protect them.

"White Faces love the fat on children and the bones of the old. They use them to make their favorite stew."

These were the stories we heard from neighboring villages that they had heard from neighboring villages, from those who had seen the destruction of White Faces.

"What do White Faces look like?"

We wanted to know everything about them so we could be prepared.

"They do not look like men," our neighbors warned.

"Their eyes are the color of the sky. And their skin has no color at all, their blackness taken from them for being evil. Even their hair is wicked, unable to curl."

I tried to imagine such a being, but I could not.

"Has any man ever captured one?"

We were told, "Never."

And with strong warnings, we were cautioned not to be the first village to try.

"By the time you see White Faces it is too late. For if you see them, they have seen you. And once they see you, they will feast."

While we did not necessarily believe these stories, they were useful. The children were cautious when fetching water and herding cattle, always concerned White Faces were nearby. Wives lay closer to their husbands at night, scared at the thought of wild creatures who craved Black flesh to eat. Although we were told White Faces hunted all across the land, we never imagined they would come to our village.

The day they arrived, I lay with Leza talking in the early morning. Our bed was large enough for both of us to rest comfortably apart, but we lay in the middle, limbs intertwined. We were always touching, even in our sleep.

I stroked Leza's skin, soft from her nightly ritual of covering her dark flesh with fragrant oils. Her black hair hung in long, tiny braids. And her brown eyes smiled even when she was angry with me. I loved everything about Leza and still could not believe my good fortune. Leza belonged to me.

It was often I imagined her belly full with our first child.

A son. This thought gave me joy, and that morning, unaware White Faces were hunting nearby, I placed my hand on Leza's flat, smooth stomach. Our bodies became one as we prayed our love would create a new life.

And afterward, I shall never forget looking at Leza's beautiful face. The long lashes as her eyelids closed. Sweat on her ebony skin. Her perfect wide nose. Soft lips barely open as she lay in my arms resting.

Then there was a stench in the air. Like something rotting or sour meat. The smell came through the window and filled our home with its putrid odor. I heard the cries of women and children. Shuffling and movement. Sounds of chaos. I jumped up from our bed and looked out the window. And I saw them.

Pale skin. Eyes like the sky. Strange fabric covering their bodies. Their hair hung limp as unbraided twine. White Faces. They were more frightening than our neighbors foretold.

"White Faces are here!" the women yelled. "White Faces are here!"

They carried powerful weapons we had never seen. Loud bangs echoed throughout the village. Birds flew from the trees, and our men fell to the ground with holes in their flesh.

Ropes rattled as White Faces bound their prey. Their voices were possessed with craving. They were eager to feast.

I stood at our window watching in disbelief as White Faces hunted my village. As our neighbors had warned us, they captured the healthy and strongest of our men and women. They ignored our elders and kicked small children out of their way. I imagined White Faces returning to cook them for stew.

Upon seeing the mayhem, Leza screamed.

"Ansa," she cried out. "White Faces!"

Announcing White Faces seemed to be the only words the

women could say. Leza's arms wrapped around me, her nails digging into my skin.

"You must hide, Leza," I told her. "You must hide quickly!"

I realized I had never seen Leza afraid and promised to protect her. And then, understanding what I had to do as a man, Leza ran to hide. I grabbed my weapon and ran outside to save my people.

White Faces were everywhere. We tried our best to defeat them, and many of our men died with honor. But there were too many. Their weapons were greater than our strongest efforts. More and more of our men fell to the ground, and even more were captured, bound in the rattling ropes. I did not know how afraid I was until I felt the hands of White Faces on my skin.

I cried out with my people, our voices filled with the fear of being eaten. White Faces put heavy ropes on our hands and feet and placed thick burdens around our necks. I was bound together with others from my village as White Faces led us away to prepare for their feast.

"Leza!"

I prayed she hid herself well or escaped.

I shouted, "Did White Faces find you?"

But my voice was lost amongst everyone calling out to those they loved.

Perhaps Leza had run to a neighboring village. And their warriors, upon learning White Faces were hunting, would set out to rescue us. We would be forever indebted to them, but that would be a better fate than being eaten.

I imagined my body being cooked over a large fire. It became an all-consuming thought. I did not want White Faces to eat me. I did not want them to eat my village.

We walked for days and nights. Rocks and branches tore at my body. Scratches and welts blistered, hot on my skin. The heavy ropes cut into my flesh. The yoke around my neck grew even heavier, but there was no escaping its burden.

White Faces bound us so if any man fell behind, he was dragged along by the rest of us.

"You must be a man," we encouraged each other.

"We must be strong!"

Each man tried to make the burden lighter for the man behind him. But in time, many men fell. And we were forced to carry them. We listened as their flesh dragged the ground.

I had never been so far from my village. The soil beneath my feet changed many times. Dark brown dirt. Sandy and rocky. Grassy and full. Flowers, trees, and birds I had never seen. But I could not enjoy their beauty.

We passed other villages White Faces had devoured. The land stood abandoned, most everything burned to ashes. Bones littered the ground. Evidence White Faces had feasted.

Our women and girls screamed as White Faces forced themselves upon them. Men went insane, struggling to escape their bonds as they watched the defiling of their family. Seeing White Faces take our womenfolk over and over. Never had I felt so helpless, weak.

I heard Leza's screams rise above the others, her voice calling for me. There are no words to describe this time in my life. Pain, anger, rage—these words are not full enough.

I became wrathful, willing to do anything to save her. Never had I wanted to kill another until White Faces hunted my village. I struggled in my bonds, unable to free myself. I only succeeded in deepening my wounds.

"Ansa, help me!"

My heart beat loudly, pounding within my ears. But not loudly enough to mute Leza's screams as she continued to call out for me.

Leza was mine. I had promised her father and brothers I would always protect her. And I had failed.

We first lay together a few moons before White Faces attacked. My father had told me what to do on our wedding night, but I was not ready. Nothing could have prepared me for the beauty of our union. Leza's breasts were large, and I took her dark nipples in my mouth, kissing them. I put my hands around her waist. There was much confusion, laughter, and joy that day. More joy than I had ever imagined.

Each time we lay together since was more beautiful than the last. Our bodies learned each other. I thought of us, a few mornings ago, praying as we prepared to create our first son or daughter.

That morning seemed distant as I watched White Faces take her. Their hands grabbing her legs, pulling them apart. I could do nothing but listen to Leza's screams. I cried openly as did the other men. We wept for our wives and our sisters, our mothers and daughters.

"When will this end?" Ano asked.

Ano and I had become men together. We endured our rights of passage in what seemed like so many moons ago. He was one of the strongest of us as boys, winning most every test of strength and endurance.

"When will this end?" he repeated. "I cannot take much more."

"I do not know, Ano. I pray for it to end soon." It was the only truth I could offer him.

Not long after our brief talk, Ano fell. His death caused

his father to cry, retching in between sobs. We dragged Ano along with us until Whites Faces removed him, discarding his dead body among the trees as his father wept.

More of our men and women died. When I thought I could not take another step, we stopped. White Faces gave us food and water. They took rags and wiped at our skin. In the distance I could see the White Faces' village.

I understood why our neighbors told us White Faces were half animal. It was not just their desire to eat Black flesh. Their village was carved out of rock, like an open den. There was much movement as people rushed about the land. It was apparent their king did not know how to rule his kingdom.

Behind their village was a large lake. The bright blue water flowed until it reached the sky. The two were separated by a line so thin it was difficult to tell whether it was part of the lake or belonged to the heavens. Large pieces of wood partially covered with white fabric rested atop the water. And the air smelled of salt.

As White Faces took us into their village, I could not believe it. Their land was filled not only with White Faces, but with men and women with Black Faces. Why were the White Faces not eating them?

Our neighbors had not told us this. Perhaps, we still had a chance. Perhaps my village would not be eaten after all.

As Black Faces came toward us, we pleaded for help.

"Please," we cried out. "Please free us!"

We begged them to remove our bonds, to let us return to our village. Instead, Black Faces looked us over as though inspecting goods for trade. A form of payment exchanged hands, and Black Faces began to divide us.

If we were to die, we wished to die together.

We begged, "Cook and eat us all at once, this way we will not miss each other!"

But Black Faces ignored our pleas.

Wives reached for their husbands. Mothers grabbed for their sons and daughters. Black Faces continued to separate us as we stretched for each other, our hands bound in the heavy ropes. Leza reached for me, palms open, yet we were unable to touch.

"Ansa!"

I looked into Leza's brown eyes. I knew they would never smile again. And I could do nothing. I opened my mouth to speak, but there were no words. And I became less of a man that day.

Black Faces took me to a large space, and there, White Faces looked me over to see if I would make a sufficient meal. With rough hands they pried open my mouth. They grabbed parts of me no one had ever touched but my mother and Leza. And when I thought the horror was over, one of the White Faces licked my face to taste me.

I could not understand their words, but I could tell it was agreed I would make a sufficient meal. I prepared myself to be eaten. Like the wild animals they were, White Faces would eat me alive, flesh uncooked. Their eyes watched me hungrily.

I closed my eyes, waiting for White Faces to bite into my flesh. Heat pressed on my shoulder, and I smelled my skin burning. White Faces began to cook me. I only remember falling to my knees.

When I awoke, I was still bound by the heavy ropes. There was no way for me to move, the space so packed with bodies. I longed for fresh air as the odors of blood and human waste were overpowering. Despite my best efforts, I vomited, adding to the stench.

And death. I could smell death swirling and circling, preparing to strike. I tried to speak to other men, but none could understand me. We were from many tribes, speaking in different tongues. I had travelled to other villages for trade and tried to comprehend their words. Still, I imagined their thoughts. They were surely as my own.

I would never return to my village. Never again would I see Leza. I wept beside other men as we cried our fragmented words. All of us not wanting to be eaten.

And when I remember this time, I can still hear the wailing of men in my ears. I can smell the stench of our waste and feel the coldness of the ropes that bound me. The memory returns me to the tight, small space, and it is difficult to breathe.

Black Faces pushed food through an opening, and we were like animals. Our bodies ached for nourishment. We kicked and bit at each other, fighting for the food and water. It was not a good meal. Just a paste made with grains. But we were beyond pride.

We ate the food wherever it lay. Off the ground and off each other. There was not enough for all of us to eat. Only the strongest of us would survive.

Some of the men refused to eat, perhaps hoping by thinning themselves they would appear a less desirable meal. Or even worse, some of the men had given up. Surely, as the smells were so overwhelming, so rancid, there were dead bodies among us. The air was filled with the smell of rotting flesh.

White Faces continued to appear and take men to cook for their feast. Every so often, Black Faces would come and remove dead bodies. When we had enough space to stretch our cramped legs, Black Faces would return and pack the area with more men.

I wondered when I would be selected to be eaten. I began to wish for it to happen.

"We are destroyed," a man said.

Words I could understand. A voice speaking the language of a neighboring village.

He continued, "There is no hope for us now. We are no longer men."

Before White Faces captured us, he and I may have met for trade. We would have exchanged goods, spoken of our villages and families. We would have shared stories of White Faces. Now we were together waiting to be eaten.

"Are you certain?" I asked.

I thought of Leza, and my chest began to ache. My heart again pounding, painful and tight.

"What of the Black Faces?" I asked. "Those with flesh like ours? Will they help us?"

"No."

"Why?" I did not understand why Black Faces were free. We looked the same.

"They will not help us." And then he explained, "White Faces have tricked them so they will not help us. I escaped once. And it was Black Faces who captured me and returned me here."

This man seemed to know a great deal. And he had escaped. Even though he had been recaptured, his bravery was encouraging, admirable. He had done far more than I. Perhaps this man could tell me what I needed to know most.

"Then when will White Faces eat us?"

The anticipation of being eaten was becoming unbearable.

Whenever the door opened, men scampered out of reach, hoping to escape White Faces' hands. We pushed the dead and living in front of us in an effort to save ourselves.

"They will not eat us."

His voice was raspy from crying.

"They will send us into the water," he said.

"Into the water?"

Our neighbors had not mentioned this.

"Did you see the water that touched the sky?" he asked. "We will leave in the wood floating on the water. The water will take us away never to return."

"How do you know this?" I asked.

"I saw," the man explained. "When I escaped, I saw White Faces take men into the wood floating on the water. I met a man who spoke many tongues. He told me if the king does not have enough people with black flesh to send into the water, he gives White Faces his wives. And White Faces send his wives into the water."

I felt the urge to vomit and tried to suppress the bile. I did not want this man to know I was so weak. But a king who would send his own wives into water never to return to him? Surely, such a king would do far worse to me.

"But you escaped before," I reminded him. "Is there no way to escape now?"

I knew it was a futile question. If there was a way, he would already be free. I knew this, but still, I asked.

"There is no way."

And then, he was quiet.

Poor Leza. I felt less of a man knowing I could not save her. Leza would be sent into the water, and I would never see her again. I lost the battle to appear strong. The warm bile rose and forced its way out of my mouth.

White Faces and Black Faces. They removed dead bodies and counted those of us who remained. I thought of dying. But I did not want to leave Leza. I knew White Faces were planning to send us into the water that touched the sky. I tried my best not to sleep lest White Faces or Black Faces catch me unaware. Much to my disappointment, I fell asleep praying to my ancestors.

A cold wind awakened me. Other men began to awaken, and we huddled together for warmth. And then, the earth began to sway and rock. It seemed at any moment the ground would open and swallow us all.

We could not understand each other, but we shared in the fear. In the darkness, it became too much to endure. The tightness of the space filled with bodies. I could see nothing but shadows. Fear sounded more horrifying coming from the mouths of men.

"They are here!"

It was the man who had spoken to me earlier. I had not even thought to ask his name.

"Who?" I asked, my voice shouting.

"The dead!"

And I began to feel them. Cold and spineless as the wind. Spirits brushed up against me, swirling around the tight space. Men twisted and shifted, our bodies pressed against each other, trying to escape.

"Listen!"

The voices of the dead intertwined with the living, all of our many tongues sounding like a child learning to speak. Earnest, determined, but impossible to understand.

And in the darkness, I saw her face. Brown skin and angry, dark eyes. Black hair that swirled in the wind.

She told me, "Run before White Faces take you into the water never to return!"

The ground continued to shake, and walls of rocks crumbled. I saw men moving, fast and determined. They rushed through the darkness, their bonds broken.

"Please," I called out to the woman. "Please, free me too!"

Her dark eyes looked into mine as the bonds broke away from my hands and feet. I did not think. I only ran. I stepped on the bodies of those who had fallen. They screamed as I crushed them beneath my feet. But I could not stop to help them.

White Faces and Black Faces were waiting. But I was determined they would never take me again. I ran through their hands grabbing at me. They wanted to send me into the water that touched the sky so their king would not have to send his wives.

There were others like me, and we ran. I did not turn back. Not even for Leza, I did not stop running until I reached the land that is now my home.

When I first arrived, Black Faces reached out to help. But I did not trust them. I fought anyone who came near. It took the village's strongest men to subdue me. Even after they showed me kindness, fed me, and helped me heal, I did not trust them.

I remembered Black Faces from the White Faces' village. How there, White Faces and Black Faces walked together as friends. And their king sent Leza into the water never to return.

In time, I learned the language of my new village. I

honored their traditions and even took a new wife. And although she was sweet and beautiful, she was not Leza.

I told the people—White Faces are real.

At night the woman who gave me freedom haunts my dreams. My wife says I scream in the darkness. In the mornings our bed is damp and covered with blood. For when the dark hair and dark eyes come to me, I scratch at myself, trying to escape.

"I will make them pay. All involved in this business of selling the lives of my people. They will suffer. And their children will suffer. I promise you, as sure as I will live forever. I promise. All will know the wrath of Awiti."

These are the words she says to me.

"I am coming back, Ansa. For the White Faces and Black Faces. I am coming back."

With every sunrise and sunset, I am afraid. Will today be the day she returns? And if so, what is she planning to do?

4
ABOARD THE
SAINT PHILIPPE

Nantes, France (1769)

23 July

Dear Jean Paul,

I pray this letter finds you in good health. I am pleased to learn of your decision to embark upon life as a seaman. As you know, I find this to be a highly respectable career. If your father were alive, you would surely have his blessing as well. Since his death, you have become like a son to me, and I like a father to you.

This is why I beg of you to abandon this idea of joining the slave trade. While lucrative, there is a side to the endeavor that is evil and dangerous. Such an adventure may seem exciting. At this time in your life, you have cares for none other than yourself. But I beg of you to trust me. The memories of what you witness, the choices you have to make. These recollections will endure a lifetime.

I want to respond to your inquiry about my decision to end my career early and retire from a successful life at sea. You seem on the verge of asking me to reconsider. You mention several times the joys of us conquering the seas together. I imagine this to be your perfect reverie. The two of us sailing side by side.

You are no doubt recalling the times your father and I would return home from our travels, telling you grand stories of life on the sea, the adventures of those who dared to travel the open waters. I must be honest with you now, for you are no longer a lad. We conjured many a story for your little ears. They were to feed your imagination during your father's long absences. We wanted you to believe we were off doing something great and honorable.

I will likely not be able to persuade you with simple words and forewarnings, as I am sure your offer from Monsieur Montaudoin is quite generous. The Montaudoins have mastered the art of the trade and are among the most influential here in Nantes. So I will try to convince you by sharing a personal experience. This is a true account. The few others who know of the details of this affair will undoubtedly take it with them to their graves.

It may help you better understand my decision to sail no more, and even further, my apprehension to you joining the trade. Even Captain Guillaume Denis Hamon himself cannot convince me otherwise. Trust me when I tell you my mind cannot be changed. I will never again return to the seas.

As you know, my final voyage was aboard the Saint Philippe. A historic journey, one for the records. The Saint Philippe is a beautiful vessel, and Captain Hamon a most decorated and moral man, one of whom I have always enjoyed serving. I made the voyage to Saint Domingue many times, but this significant expedition, taking only a record twenty-five days, was truly quite a feat. And while I should be proud it was upon this voyage I ended my career, on such a celebrated endeavor, I am not. And for good reason.

Please note the Jogue brothers paid me well, for like the Montaudoins, they are highly respected and profitable in the trade. But I must say, if I could erase this historic voyage from my memory and return all the funds I received, I would do so today. I have never been as afraid on a trade vessel as I was aboard the Saint Philippe.

I will tell you why. And perhaps, after you learn of what truly happens in the trade, you will give more consideration to Monsieur Montaudoin's offer. I am not certain of your standing, but if debt is an issue, you know I am more than willing to assist you in your financial affairs. But I beg of you, do not embark upon the trade for the money or even for adventure. It is not worth your soul.

Let me begin by saying the African slaves are oft hard to deal with. There are always those among the cargo who resist their inevitable fate. Slaves subjected to captivity for longer periods of time are the easiest to manage, but they resist when encouraged. For no man is born wanting to serve another. But, alas, God has already determined his fate. It is undisputed the Africans are pre-ordained to a life of slavery. Yet still, there are those who continue to resist their lot in life.

You may be surprised to learn I think of the Africans as human. Do you think I have gone mad, as some of my comrades oft testified? The Africans are as human as you and I. Are they not flesh, blood, and bones just as we are? Less cultivated, devoid of religion, and unrefined, yes, this is true. But they are human nonetheless. This cannot be denied.

That being said, I do not believe they are equal to us. But I do believe they could be treated more humanely, especially as such an integral part of the trade. Why, the way the Jogue brothers pack the slaves in the cargo hold, so tightly they cannot move, is unset-tling. The more slaves transported on each voyage, the more money the Jogue brothers can make. The slaves' bodily functions mingle among them, and even when we toss buckets of sea water over them, nothing can wash away the stench.

What of these horrors you will see when it comes to the treatment of slaves? Do you think it is only aboard the vessel? Do you think their horror ends once we reach our destination? It does not.

In Saint Domingue I have seen slaves buried alive. I have seen their masters force them to consume their own feces and drink their own urine. One particularly cruel slave master I saw throw an unruly slave into a cauldron of boiling cane syrup. He invited those of us at dock to witness the event for entertainment, even serving spirits for the occasion. Can you witness such things, my dear Jean? I do not believe you can without it having a lasting effect on you.

I tell you the crying and moaning of the slaves is hard to endure. Day after day, night after night. You do not need to understand their words to know they are suffering. Soon, though, after many weeks at sea, the lot of the slaves becomes resigned to their fate. By the end of the voyage, there is little struggle, and oft-times no resistance. They accept the cruelty, for this is how the mind works. In time, even the strongest willed can be broken.

Slaves new to captivity pose the most danger. They seem quite certain if they bargain with us, beg and plead, we will reconsider their fate of servitude and remove their chains. And when their bargaining does not work, they resort to violence. It is these slaves who, if not properly watched, will kill a seaman with their bare hands. Such slaves provoke the others, even the most obedient, and can start an insurrection. And this is what happened aboard the Saint Philippe.

Everyone has focused on the short duration of the voyage, have they not? Celebrating our historic journey across the Atlantic in twenty-five days instead of the usual several months? They seem to care less about the uprising that left one of our own dead. There is no mention in the papers of those of us who almost lost our lives.

I can still hear the slaves chanting in their savage language. Their words make the skin crawl with fear. They know nothing of God, and you can hear the devil in their voices, feel the evil in the air. Hear me now as I write this. I have experienced many a frightening thing during my lifetime. But aboard the Saint Philippe, it was the first time I believed I might die.

There was a sailor who did indeed perish. A young man named Marceau. A rather good man but he was known to consume spirits heavily. And oft in his drunkenness, he forced himself upon the female slaves. Even some young girls not much older than my own dear Gillette. It is deplorable to even write these words, but this is the culture of life on the sea. No one would ever dare to stop him or any of the others who engage in such ungodly acts. It is merely for sport and pleasure. Simply a way to pass the time.

Those of us who do not condone such behavior would oft try to remove ourselves from the debauchery. But there were those who condoned, and believe me, there are many of our brothers who make allowances for such acts. Oft they would turn from spectator to participant and lay with the same poor slave, until the female or child was ravished unconscious.

The slaves who perish from such affairs are simply thrown into the sea. Indeed, after enduring such abuse, many are worth more dead than alive, for insurance covers such loss. There is an understanding all of the cargo will not survive the journey, which is factored into the cost, like any other commodity. For, again, I am one of the few who view the slave as human and not merely goods.

It is horrid, my dear Jean, but I assure you these words I write are true. I want you to know if you accept the Montaudoin's offer, these are the circumstances you will face.

I have never participated in such ungodly acts with the slaves. Neither with the prostitutes waiting at our ports of entry and departure. As you know, I am faithfully married to my love Marguerite. And neither did your father participate in such sinful affairs, for he loved your mother dearly. But many sailors do. And you, being the son of a decorated seaman, may be forced to participate by your brothers at sea to prove yourself one of them. What will you do when this happens? Will you lay with an African slave child to prove yourself to your fellow brethren?

I shall never forget March 14, for this is the day Marceau went into the hold and selected a slave for the ungodly acts I referenced above. She was browner than the others, for as you know, the Africans' skin can be as black as coal. But this happens from time to time—slaves who have a fairer complexion, most likely due to breeding with the Portuguese during their early explorations of Africa.

The mixing of the races is ungodly and oft results in slaves who looked like this female. Her skin was the color of honey, and her dark hair like silk, such as ours. These fairer slaves are always the most favored to be taken by our brothers.

When Marceau emerged from the hold with her, the other raucous sailors cheered. They were about to embark on one of their drunken escapades, and I knew this poor slave would be had by the lot of them. I could not bear to watch, and so I went to seek refuge in my cabin.

When I walked by, I made eye contact with the slave. This was something I rarely did, for I learned early in the trade it does something to your soul to look into the eyes of those you enslave.

But I did look at her. And I will admit this only to you—she was quite beautiful.

This may all sound maddening, to hear me speak of a slave as beautiful. But I assure you this happens with all seamen from time to time. We are, after all, men. And beauty is beauty. And this slave, when I walked past her, and I am sure she could sense me admiring her, smiled at me. Hear me when I tell you the look in her eyes and smile was one of pure evil.

For some strange reason, even now unbeknownst to me, I could not remove myself from the setting. I stood and watched as they removed her chains and Marceau set upon her while the others cheered. She continued to smile as Marceau ravished her. And all the while, the sea rose and the waters became choppy. The skies darkened as a storm appeared out of nowhere.

And then, because he had removed her chains so he could be free with her, she attacked Marceau. Like a wild savage, she scratched and bit at him, handling him with unimaginable strength. Below in the hold there was chanting and disruption as the waves tossed the Saint Philippe. The skies opened, and dark clouds released torrential rain. Fear and panic set in among us all.

We were at all points on deck. Some were trying to pry Marceau from her grasp. Others were struggling to man the sails and keep the Saint Philippe afloat. We tried to protect ourselves from slaves who had somehow escaped. They rushed the deck, trying to kill us.

The Africans and their pagan beliefs. I would not believe it if I had not seen it time and time again. But when they pray to their devil gods, they are stronger than the average man. It is madness!

Eventually, we did regain control of the ship, but Marceau did not survive. His body was so badly damaged, it looked as though he had been mauled to death. The honey-colored slave was *thrown into the sea along with the other slaves who had attempted insurrection. They were no doubt devoured by the sharks that oft followed our vessels. We fed them well with the bodies of the dead and defiant.*

I must tell you, when we reached the shores of Saint Domingue, I could not wait to return to my dear Nantes. I longed for my lovely wife and darling, sweet daughter. I promised the good Lord if I were to return home safely, I would abandon this treacherous business of the trade forever.

And so now you know the reason I have retired. It is not because of an illness or because I have gone mad, or any of the other motives you may have heard through gossip and falsehoods. I learned firsthand no amount of money is worth one's soul. There are times I cannot sleep when I think of the Saint Philippe. I oft dream of Marceau's mangled body. I see the honey-colored slave's smile as they tossed her into the sea.

The memories haunt me day and night. Even as I write this letter to you, I am perspiring and my hands are shaking. So I ask you, beg of you, for my sake and so your father's soul can rest in peace. Reject the Montaudoin's offer, and find a trade you can be proud of. One you can retire from with honor and not out of fear.

When you come to visit for the holiday, we can discuss this further. Do write back to me soon, my dear Jean. Do let me know of your decision.

Believe me yours faithfully,

Jacques

5

THE PACOTILLEUR

Le Cap, St. Domingue (1794)

I was eleven years of age when the *pacotilleur* came to the Vergennes Plantation. I had heard of these peculiar folk, freed slaves who travelled about the island. *Pacotilleurs* went from plantation to plantation, selling trinkets one could only acquire from Europe. When I opened the door, she asked,

"Might your mother be available?"

The *pacotilleur's* dress was long and white, the hem embroidered with delicate lace. Polished black shoes peeked out from beneath the flowery stitching. The small, round buttons down the center of each shoe reminded me of hard licorice candies. She wore a large white hat, tilted so part of her face was hidden beneath the brim.

"Yes, missus," I replied. And I ran to get my mother.

"Hello, pleased to meet your acquaintance," my mother greeted the *pacotilleur*. Then she asked her directly,

"Do tell why you've come calling."

"I have some things I'd like to show you. Nice things you

might fancy. You're not obliged to purchase a thing at all. Take a look and see if any of my possessions might suit you."

"Well, all right. Come in then," my mother said.

The *pacotilleur* was fancy, her black case filled with shiny gems none on our plantation could afford. I took in every detail of her visit—the trinkets and her speech, which was proper as if she were one of the French. I could not wait to tell Cécile I had seen an actual *pacotilleur*.

Cécile and I played together since I could remember. She would come to the main house and take me away from my chores, walking boldly past her father to announce, "Francine and I are going to play now."

Then Cécile would grab my hand and pull me toward her playroom. Master Vergennes smiled and said nothing, for his darling Cécile did whatever she wished.

Now we met in secret. I was a house slave, and Cécile the daughter of Master Vergennes. Our families told us to end the friendship, but our bond could not be broken. Cécile left her room, and I snuck out from the slave quarters. We met in the cane fields and talked most every night.

Cécile told me of girls and boys at her school. She shared stories of how other masters treated their slaves, always reaching the same conclusion:

"My father treats his slaves the best."

I believed her, for Master Vergennes could be kind. Still, he did not want us to be friends.

My mother said Master Vergennes was my father too. That was the reason we worked in the main house. It was true Cécile and I had the same blonde curly hair. Her eyes were bright blue, mine a warm brown. My skin was a smidgen darker than her pale complexion.

But I was never to tell Cécile we were sisters, although we often called and treated each other as such.

"Don't we look like sisters, Francine?" Cécile would ask.

"Yes. Let's pretend we are sisters."

Cécile tied her ribbons in my hair, my blonde tresses braided in two pigtails. We twirled in circles until we were dizzy with laughter.

Mother told me never to speak on the matter with Cécile or anyone else. And so, I said nothing, although I wanted nothing more than for Cécile to know I was her true sister. We belonged to each other, as sisters should.

When the *pacotilleur* returned the next day, I had a real good look at her. She was a beautiful woman, her complexion fair like my mother. Her eyes were the darkest brown I had ever seen, almost black. She watched me from behind the brim of her hat before asking my mother to speak in private. They walked to the front parlor room and closed the door.

Although I knew it was wrong to eavesdrop, I sat outside the large wooden doors and put my ear to the crack. My mother and the *pacotilleur* spoke in hushed whispers. The *pacotilleur* had no intention to sell her trinkets. She had a message for the slaves at the Vergennes Plantation.

"If slaves desire freedom, they must fight for it. Freedom will never be given to them," the *pacotilleur* said.

"Of course there are many who wish to be free," my mother responded, "but how do we begin to fight?"

"It has already begun. Mackendal is preparing for battle, and he will lead the slaves on Saint Domingue to freedom."

I was surprised when I heard the name Mackendal. It was just the other day while serving Master Vergennes and our neighbor, Mr. James Mouge, the men had spoken of him.

"The authorities still have not captured this Mackendal," Master Vergennes had said. "He is causing much trouble about the island. He continues to incite many of the slaves. They believe he possesses a magic that can free them."

Master Vergennes' last statement caused both men to laugh.

"Seriously, James, this may soon be no laughing matter," he continued. "Many slaves have already escaped to join this Mackendal in the mountains. And they continue to flee by the day. Andrè Bandeaux lost five slaves last week."

Master Vergennes looked at me and smiled as I poured his tea. There were times such as these where I believed he knew he was my father. He often looked at Cécile with the same adoration.

"These types like Mackendal—they are a real threat us," Mr. Mouge agreed. "I am amazed none have been able to capture him, especially with the bounty so high."

It was a warm day, and Mr. Mouge started to sweat. I fanned him so I could continue listening to their conversation.

He nodded in approval as he said to Master Vergennes, "We have to be careful. We must remember slaves are uncivilized and therefore dangerous. Especially since they outnumber us here on the island."

This was news to me. Until that moment I had believed the French outnumbered us, for they controlled us.

Neither man showed any real concern for their own plantation. They believed none of their slaves would dare leave and join this wild Mackendal in the mountains.

At night I told my mother everything I heard that day. And she shared words with me.

"The *pacotilleur* did not come to sell trinkets," my mother confirmed. "Her name is Awiti. And she will return in a few days. Mackendal is planning a *révolution*. Our lives on Saint Domingue are about to change."

Awiti was lucky my mother was available the day she came calling. Had it been one of the others, such as Marion or Colette, they would have gone straight to Master Vergennes. They were loyal slaves to their master. But not my mother. There was nothing my mother wanted more than her freedom.

Awiti's timing was fortuitous. Master Vergennes had recently purchased a new slave, François. He was tall, his physique strong and muscular. When he arrived, I could not help but stare, for his skin was as dark as the night itself. If not for his kind demeanor, François was frightening.

François told us horrible accounts of abuse throughout the island. It was nothing for slaves to be hung upside down until they died, blood pouring from their ears. He told us of friends who had tried to escape. When captured, their master put them inside barrels with sharp spikes and rolled them down the mountainside to their deaths.

"What sort of life is this?" François questioned. "We work for the French, and they do nothing but mistreat us, torture us. I have seen slaves eaten alive by dogs as their masters stood by and laughed."

François showed us his scars from burns and whips. He exposed his left hand, which was missing two fingers, taken by a cruel master when he was a boy. It was hard to believe François had endured so much. He looked stronger than two men. But even at my young age, I knew slaves were not ruled by strength. We were governed by fear.

Although we tried to assure François that Master

Vergennes never treated his slaves so cruelly, he could not be convinced.

"It is only a matter of time before evil reaches the Vergennes Plantation," François told us. "And I will not be here when it does. I will be with Mackendal."

François did not wait for Awiti to return. He escaped a few days after he arrived.

At the time, the name Mackendal was somewhat foreign to us, but the injustices slaves endured were not. François was not the first slave to tell us of such horrific abuse. On Saint Domingue we knew some slaves suffered more than others. But suffering, more or less, was still suffering.

Master Vergennes had means to discipline us, with whips and such. But we never experienced the brutality we heard occurred on other plantations. And this Mackendal. We had not heard of him until the *pacotilleur* came to sell her trinkets, Master Vergennes mentioned him over tea, and François escaped to join him in the mountains. Collectively, this made many of the slaves curious to hear what Mackendal had to say.

Whenever Awiti came to visit, I pretended to be interested in her trinkets. Her black case contained nothing extraordinary, but I asked to see the baubles. I held them carefully and inquired of their origin.

Awiti knew I was not interested in her goods. I wanted to be close to the woman who brought messages from Mackendal. Awiti was the mysterious *pacotilleur* who caused the slaves to whisper for hours at night about freedom.

One day, Awiti told my mother, "You should let Francine come to the meeting to hear Mackendal speak. She is old enough and smart. We need her. The youth will help lead Saint Domingue to freedom."

Mother was concerned, but she trusted Awiti. Unfortunately, my mother could not come with us. Her duties were many, and Master Vergennes might notice her absence.

We snuck out under the darkness of the night. The trees along the pathway to Bois Caiman were marked with various symbols. The full moon shined on the freshly carved wooden markings guiding us toward Mackendal. I walked in silence with my father who was not really my father. He held my hand tightly as we travelled through the dense forest.

When we arrived at Bois Caiman, many slaves were already present. Shadows of mostly men and older children filled the area. We had risked our lives to learn about the *révolution*. Based on our numbers, there were countless slaves who desired their freedom.

Mackendal was charismatic, and he easily captured our attention and trust. He began by teaching us of our past. I learned the French had stolen us from Africa. Our people had once been free. Kings and queens, nations of great wealth. We were not meant to live in servitude. But there was no way for us to return to Africa. So if we were to live here on Saint Domingue, Mackendal was determined we would live as free people.

"If you do not want to be slaves, you must join the *révolution*," Mackendal demanded.

Awiti stood with the others in Mackendal's army. She was bold and fearless, and I desired to be like her. I was determined to become a female warrior who would fight for the rights of slaves.

Mackendal shared his plan to bring about our freedom. First, we would kill the French with poison, mixing it into their food and drink. Those of us who worked in the main houses were in the best position to enact the first part of his plan. We would start the *révolution*.

Then, once the French were weakened, Mackendal's army would leave the mountains. They would fight until the French agreed to end slavery. And we would live as we had once before—free.

At the end of his speech, Mackendal held up a dark vase. He called the vase Saint Domingue. As he pulled out a yellow scarf, he asked the crowd,

"Do you know what this yellow scarf represents?"

He did not wait for us to respond.

"The yellow skin of the Indian. This island was once their home. They walked this land freely as we once did in Africa. And where are they now? All but a few are dead. Their blood is on the hands of the Spanish."

Then Mackendal pulled out a white scarf and said,

"And this is the skin of the wicked French. Forcing us to labor in their fields. Raping and killing, even our children. And yet they call us animals? But soon, my French, soon you will see. You will fall from power. We will rise again!"

Cheers sounded around Bois Caiman. They were quiet praises, for we were away from our plantations—a serious offense if captured. Then Mackendal pulled a black scarf out of the Saint Domingue vase.

"This is us," Mackendal told us, waving the black scarf high above his head and twirling it wildly. "We will be free!"

I could not help but wonder, what if Awiti had not come to the Vergennes Plantation? Suppose I had not been playing in the foyer the day she came calling? I might have grown to be a slave forever.

But I had a new goal and purpose in life—to become

a warrior in Mackendal's army. I would become a part of the *révolution*. I would help bring freedom to the slaves on Saint Domingue.

After the meeting at Bois Caiman, Cécile and I grew apart. I was no longer interested in being her pretend sister who was her real sister. I had no desire to be best friends in secret. Cécile was one of *them*, the French. And Cécile too pulled away.

Our conversations were brief, and Cécile dismissive. Soon we barely spoke at all. This did not bother me, for I was focused on my role as a warrior in Mackendal's army. So when Cécile came to the slave quarters to confront me, I was quite surprised.

"Francine, we are no longer friends," she said.

She stood as her mother did when she ordered the slaves to their duties: hands on her hips, an air of authority in her stance. It was clear this would not be a discussion, and so I let Cécile speak.

"Do you know why we look so much alike?"

Although I knew the answer, I knew how best to respond.

"No, Cécile."

"Of course you don't!"

Cécile's blue eyes squinted as she held back tears. I knew it was best to be still. I looked downward as I had seen other slaves behave when being disciplined, whether they had committed a wrong or were innocent.

"Well, I will tell you," Cécile said matter-of-factly. "Your mother tricked my father. Used her African magic on him. She made my father come to her."

Cécile sounded as though she were repeating a story. Most likely one told to her by her mother.

"And of that wicked union, she made *you*."

Cécile stopped in front of me. The word "you" was laced with hate, sadness, anger, and confusion. My eyes remained on the floor. I focused on the scuff marks on Cécile's leather shoes.

"Look at me," Cécile commanded.

I looked up and tried to feign meekness. But I knew my gaze was strong and intense.

My mother did not trick Master Vergennes. Many brown and fair-skinned slaves lived on our plantation. It was clear Master Vergennes did what he wished. Thankfully, I would be free before he came to my slave quarters seeking to do the same.

"We are not friends," Cécile repeated. "And we are not sisters. You disgust me."

Cécile spit in my face as her mother often did to the slaves. It was a poor attempt. A few speckles of her saliva landed on my arm. Another drop or two fell on my right cheek. I wanted to laugh in Cécile's face. But I knew it was best do nothing.

"From this day forward, you are a slave, and I am your master, you hear?"

And before I could respond, Cécile slapped me across the face.

I felt myself warm as she walked away. There was much I wanted to say, but I remained quiet. What Cécile had spoken was the truth—I was a slave, and she was my master. Her words made me even more determined to be a part of the *révolution*.

When I told my mother about the incident, she was not surprised. Her only astonishment was the confrontation had not occurred sooner.

"Perfect timing," my mother told me. "You need to focus. The *révolution* has begun."

I could not afford to be distracted by my childhood friend and sister. When the time came, killing Cécile would be easy.

Like many house slaves, I had easy access to the kitchen. Part of my duties included serving Master Vergennes and his guests. I was so proud when Awiti chose me to distribute the poison. With great care, I added the packets of powder to the meals of Master Vergennes' guests.

"Do not poison Master Vergennes," Awiti instructed. Then she added, "Not yet."

Throughout the island, house slaves poisoned the food and drinks of the French. *Pacotilleurs* continued to visit plantations, their black cases filled with cheap gold and small packets of poison—a deadly mixture of ground herbs and roots concocted by Mackendal.

At first the French believed an illness had come upon the island. A disease spreading among the French as their men, women, and children fell ill. With each report of a French death, slaves celebrated in silence, and our desire for freedom grew stronger. It was some time before the French realized the *révolution* had begun.

More and more slaves began to escape to the mountains. Those who were captured were put to death publicly as a warning to the rest of us. But their deaths did nothing but fuel the *révolution*. I could not wait to poison the Vergennes family. It was hard being so close to freedom.

The kill order could not come soon enough. I hated my pale skin and blonde curls. My reflection in mirrors or water was troubling. My appearance was a constant reminder of the harm done to my mother and other slaves throughout the island. I longed to live in the mountains, to leave my life of slavery forever.

Finally, I received Awiti's command. I poisoned Master Vergennes who was really my father. I stirred deadly herbs into the tea of my once best friend, Cécile, who was really my sister. I gave an extra dose to Madame Vergennes who spread lies about my mother and spit in the face of slaves. Their illness came swiftly.

"They are dying," I told Awiti. "Can I leave now?"

Although I hated the Vergennes for keeping us as slaves, I could not bear the thought of watching them die. The effects of the poison caused vomiting and intense pain. The Vergennes would suffer, and while I wanted it to happen, I did not want to see it. But Awiti would not let me leave.

"You cannot be a warrior without looking death in the face," Awiti told me. "Especially of those you care about. When the last of the Vergennes' eyes have closed, when they have taken their final breaths, then you may come."

Slaves fled our plantation, my mother among them. But I stayed as Awiti instructed. I listened as the Vergennes called out for me to help them. I heard each retch and cry from the deadly herbs. I watched as Master Vergennes closed his eyes, the last member of the Vergennes family to die.

After his death, Awiti led me to the mountains. It was wonderful to reunite with those from the Vergennes' Plantation, especially my mother. She cried as she hugged me and said,

"Cécile! We are finally free!"

I looked the same as the young girl who had stood at Bois Caiman, but I was different. I was no longer simply a slave girl mixed with the blood of the French. I was a warrior focused on the freedom of my people. I had looked death in the face and survived. And I knew I could do it again.

The mountain was inaccessible except to those who knew the secret routes. As Awiti led me through the treacherous terrain, we were surrounded by the stench of dead bodies—the French, Awiti told me. Mackendal wanted their bodies to remain where they fell. A reminder to any White man who tried to retrieve his runaway slaves.

Awiti had told me of the thousands of slaves who lived in the mountains. They were from many different nations in Africa. But on Saint Domingue, they were united by their black skin and desire for freedom.

To see us together was unlike anything I could have ever imagined. The mountains were like the Africa Mackendal described. The Africa stolen from us. The Africa we would never see again.

Under the tutelage of Awiti, I became a decorated soldier with poison and weaponry. We fought for many years against the French, the *révolution* long and arduous. I lost my mother and many friends to the war, although I knew their deaths were not in vain. I held on to hope, believing I would see them again. Like Mackendal, their spirits would live forever.

"If the French ever capture me, do not fear," Mackendal often told us. "Even if it appears the French have killed me, you must know I am not dead.

"I will return," Mackendal promised. "I will come to Saint Domingue as a deadly insect, a wild beast. Forever, I, and those like me, will cause great suffering. We will toss men about in the wind. We will make the ground shake and mountains crumble.

"Whenever you hear of such things happening, you will know I have returned."

And indeed, Mackendal came again. He appeared as a massive plague. Mosquitos with yellow fever attacked the British and French troops. Hundreds of their soldiers were stricken with illness. Mackendal killed them while we remained in the mountains, healthy and strong. And Awiti and I celebrated every one of their deaths.

"Do you see, Francine?" Awiti asked me one day. "The *révolution* is not just for Saint Domingue. It is for every life stolen from Africa. For my Father and Mother. For my siblings. For your mother. For the friends we have lost."

"Yes, Awiti. I know. The *révolution* is for all of us."

"It is for those who are living and those who have died. Will you continue the fight, Francine? Even in death?"

I knew what I was capable of while I was living. I could only imagine the depth of my destruction once I was among the dead. To join Awiti, Mackendal, and so many others. To fight alongside my mother once again. It gave me great pleasure to know I would send my torment and wrath for eternity.

"Of course I will, Awiti."

6
STILL MAY

Sea Islands, Georgia (1803)

When Ms. Susie come home for Easter, she left me this here little book to write in. She say it's called a diary, and I loves it. It's the only place I can speak my feelings without somebody telling me I'm right or wrong. It's a place for me to keep secrets too. And the good Lord know Denton Plantation got lots of secrets.

Master Denton don't know I can read and write. Ms. Susie, his own daughter, the one who teach me. Me and Ms. Susie around the same age. She started teaching me when I was small, right 'round the time I started to serve her. And even though she grown up some, every time she see me, we practice. And when Ms. Susie not here, I still practice my letters and words. I wants to make sure I don't never forget.

I dream of running away. Wonder if I'm ever gon' get the nerve to do it. Don't know where I would go. Might end up running some place worse than here. So guess I gon' stay put for now.

Still April

Things about to change. Not sure if the change gon' be good or bad. But things changing anyhow. I been working in the big house since Ms. Susie was little. But now Ms. Susie gone away to help her uncle who sick.

Master Denton say he don't need me in the big house no more. Say he wants me to learn a real special job. He know it make Ms. Susie real happy if I learned something. So I gon' learn to catch all the slave babies.

Still April

Today I start learning about babies with Nan. She been catching babies for a long time, but soon she gon' be too old. I gots to learn while she can still teach me. Nan the one help me come into the world from my own mammy. And she watched after me when Master Denton sold my mammy away. Nan like my only family I guess.

Still April

It's so much I want to write. I'm afraid I might run out of paper if I writes something every day. So I try and write only about important stuff.

Sam say Ms. Susie gon' be home soon. I'm gon' keep the paper in my diary so I can write when she come home.

May

Ms. Susie home! I so excited to see her. She ask me if I been reading and writing. I says yes. Then she sneak me books from her uncle's house.

She say her uncle real sick now. His wife died a few years back, and he don't got no children to help him. That's why

Master Denton sent Ms. Susie to take care of him. Guess I should feel bad getting books from a man set to die. But I don't.

Ms. Susie say she keen on the slaves on her uncle's plantation. She wish I could meet some 'cause she think we'd make good friends. Wish I could too. The overseer real mean. He thinks Ms. Susie too nice to the slaves. I believes it. That's why I love her so.

Still May

I so happy Ms. Susie bring me more books. I wish I could teach Nan to read and write. But I'm afraid. Master Denton might kill me if he find out. He might whip me and send me down the river to some place worse than here. Then I'd never see Ms. Susie again.

I love Ms. Susie so. She the sweetest girl. Master Denton don't whip the slaves as much when she home. She don't like whippings, and she always been busy enough to tell her pappy so. Nan say Ms. Susie been soft for slaves ever since she was a child.

When I was young, Ms. Susie treat me like one of her baby dolls. We play school, and that's how she teach me. I so glad Ms. Susie home. I wish she don't have to help her sick uncle. I wish she stay here with me.

Still May

I been learning to catch babies. Nan say I'm real good. When she die I gon' be the one to catch babies all by myself. I hope Nan don't die no time soon. Catching babies still scary to me.

Every day me and Nan checks on slaves with babies in they belly. Some slave bellies big. They babies set to meet the world any day now. Some mammys got a little belly. They babies not ready yet. Nan always say the babies in little bellies still cooking.

Today Nan taught me how to tell if a baby ready or if he playing 'round. Lacie's belly real big. Her baby start twisting and turning soon as Nan touch Lacie's belly. Nan say Lacie's baby not playing around. He gon' meet the world soon.

Still May

Today I learn something called helping the baby come. Nan had me put my hand up inside Lacie and turn it all 'round. She ask me what it feel like. I told her, and she say Lacie's baby coming tomorrow.

When Nan walk away, Lacie say she glad it was me help her baby come. Lacie laugh and say Nan hands so big. Then Nan yell out they not as big as Sam's hands. And all the women laugh and laugh. They always got jokes I don't understand. But they laughs make me happy.

Still May

Lacie's baby come today. Just like Nan say. First everybody happy. Then things turn bad. So bad I wish I could wake up and it never happen at all. Be nice if it was a bad dream.

Lacie sure did enough hollering. Her baby boy act like he change his mind about coming to the world. He gave us such a fuss. First he lay still in her belly like he sleep. Then he come all quick. Change his mind and slide on out.

He come out so fast I'm glad my hands was there to catch him. Nan say I always got to have my hands ready. Soon as Lacie's baby come out everybody real quiet.

Lacie start asking what's wrong. Nobody speak, so I hold Lacie's baby boy up for her to see. He hollering and wiggling and making a fuss. He wants his mammy's milk. Lacie see that red face and straight brown hair and she scream. Her baby look like Master Denton.

Lacie scream like nothing I ever heard before. Even when I see folks get whipped, they don't scream like that. Nan went over to Lacie. She say some words real soft in her ear. Nan tried to calm Lacie down. But Lacie keep crying and screaming.

Sam come knocking at the door, but no one wants to open it. His White baby still hollering and wiggling in my arms. I don't know what to do. This my first time ever seeing a Black mammy have a White baby.

Nan don't make it to the door in time. Sam seen me holding his White baby, and he run. Make Lacie cry even more.

Still May

Yesterday seem to stay on my mind. So today I ask Nan. Why Lacie's baby don't look like Sam? Nan told me it's time I learnt some things. She say Master Denton, overseer, and any White man in the whole world can have a slave any time they wants to.

Nan say Lacie love Sam. She lay with him to make a baby. But one day Master Denton must of come and lay with her too. Even though Lacie didn't want him to. And that's why the baby look like Master Denton. That's his pappy. Everybody wants that boy to be Sam's baby. But he won't ever be.

Nan say we safe. Master Denton needs us to catch his slave babies, so he never gon' come lay with us. Won't let his friends lay with us neither.

One thing Nan say make me sad. She say never let a man touch on me and tell me I'm nice. No man can love me and lay me down. That's the only way to keep a baby out my belly. That's the only way I stay safe.

The rest of the slaves have to worry. When they baby come, they never know if it's gon' look like the man they love or the man they hate.

Still May

Lacie don't want nothing to do with her baby. Nan try and tell Lacie the baby a part of her too. But Lacie say no. That's not her baby. She say it over and over. Won't even give her baby a name.

Nan say we got to give Lacie time. She gon' come around to loving on her baby. Just not yet. I took him to the wet nurse so he can eat. Lacie won't even feed him. Today a sad day.

Still May

Ms. Susie tell me a secret today. She found a man she wants to marry. His name Peter Fitzgerald. Funny last name. Ms. Susie show me how to write it.

Peter live 'round near her uncle on a real big plantation. She say her and Peter thinks the same way about life. And he love to read like she do. They sit in the grass on her uncle's plantation and read together from time to time. Sound nice.

Still May

Ms. Susie say she kiss Peter. Now she know what love feel like. She say you feel funny good inside. Like you swallowed a dozen butterflies and they all flapping they wings. Then she tickle me so I know what it feel like.

Ms. Susie say love make you feel safe. You wants nothing in the world except for you and the one you love together.

Ms. Susie ask, don't I want to feel that way? Don't I want

love? I think about what Nan told me. Love sound like something land me with a baby in my belly. If I feel love, I could end up gone crazy like Lacie. She not the same since she had Master Denton's baby. So I tell Ms. Susie no. I don't want no parts of love.

Still May

Ms. Susie's soon to be husband come visit today. They makes a fine match. Peter easy to look at. He got dark hair and big blue eyes. He smile at me like he means to be nice. I can tell he good.

Nan say Peter come from money. That's why Master Denton had Betsy and Mainy pull out the best of everything for his visit. Poor Betsy and Mainy had to wash and clean all night. Then they cook all day. Good food too. We got us some good scraps today.

Still May

Ms. Susie and Peter come see me tonight. Peter say he want to meet me proper since Ms. Susie talk about me all the time. Then Peter say something that shock me. He don't believe in slavery. Say he think everybody got the right to be free.

Peter say one day him and Ms. Susie gon' get married. They gon' head up North and change the law so slaves can be free. And they want me to go with them. Made my heart so happy. I got something to look forward to in life.

Peter read to us from one of his books. My word! His book full of stories about all types of folks and places. And Peter read so nice. He change his voice so we know different folks talking. Stories seem more special since we was sneaking and whispering together.

Ms. Susie and Peter leaving to go back to Macon soon. I gon' miss them when they gone.

Still May

Lacie done went mad. Master Denton told Lacie she gots to mind her child. Say a baby needs his mammy. Everybody know Lacie don't like her baby. But we never thought she kill him. Lacie did though. Drowned her baby right where she supposed to be washing.

Everybody try and say it was an accident. We say Lacie's baby slipped out her hands. But Lacie look at Master Denton straight. Told him she killed the baby because he wasn't hers. Master Denton got so angry. He whip poor Lacie till she almost dead.

Master Denton say she got no rights to be killing his property. Only one don't have to watch the whipping was Nan. She went off with the baby boy. She bury him some place private. Baby's name was John. Wasn't John's fault he born. Now he dead.

Still May

Some days I feel like dying. Feel like giving up and asking the good Lord to take me home. Sometimes I even wonder if God real like the preacher say. Why God let us live this way if He love us? Don't seem fair since God supposed to love us all the same.

I told Nan my feelings about God. She say not to talk that way. Say the good Lord gon' be angry at me. Seem like He angry enough already. I won't tell nobody else what I'm feeling. I gon' write it in my diary.

Still May

May sunshine is hot. Days seem to go on forever. It's so hot I can see heat dancing in the air. Like the devil and his friends throwing themselves a party.

Catching babies not easy. I do loves it though. Nothing like seeing babies being born. They bright eyes and making them sweet noises. Babies skin smell so nice, and they curls so soft. Nothing like seeing they new little faces.

Some babies funny. Soon as they born they open they eyes. Looking around trying to figure out where they at. Some keep they eyes closed long as they can. They don't want no parts of this world.

I like babies who smile when they born. I put them on they mammy's breast, and they get to eating right away. Some babies cry. Like they about to work on they first day of life. Those be the funny ones. They got no worries yet. No idea about the life they gon' have. I always ask them babies, what you crying for? You don't know nothing hard yet, child!

Still May

I still don't forgive Master Denton for making Lacie crazy. Sam gone crazy too. Master Denton whipped him for not wanting to do no work. How Sam supposed to work? Man found out the baby from the woman he love not his. Then his woman gets whipped for killing it. Poor Sam.

Wish I could be like Nan. Nothing move her. She strong. She the only one Lacie talk to after she gone crazy. Nan make everything right 'round here.

Don't know how I gon' ever be like Nan. I see it's more than catching babies. I got to be here for these slaves. They gon' need me. I hope to be like Nan when it's time.

Still May

Scary thing happen today. Mainy told me she might have one of Master Denton's babies inside of her. Say he lay with her sometimes, and now she not bleeding when she supposed to. She say she know the baby gon' be White. She never lay with no one else.

Mainy ask me to help her. Say she need to get rid of Master Denton's baby before it come. First I told Mainy no. I didn't want no parts of killing a baby, White or not. Mainy cried and begged. I knew I had to help her. She afraid of going crazy like Lacie. Finally I told her yes. I gon' help her.

Still May

Mainy boiling the special roots tonight. When they cool, I'm gon' put them up in her real deep. She say she might die, the roots so strong. But Mainy don't care nothing about dying. Say she rather be dead than have Master Denton's baby.

Still May

Seem like Mainy's roots did the trick. She started to bleed today. Real bad bleeding too. She was crying, the bleeding hurt so bad. Master Denton ask me and Nan to check on Mainy. Nan took one look at Mainy, and then she look at me like she know what we done.

Soon as Master Denton leave, Nan ask me straight. Did I help Mainy kill her baby? She say if I did, it's a sin and the good Lord gon' strike me dead. I told Nan no. Told her it seem like Mainy bleeding start later than usual. Don't know if Nan believe me. I do feel bad for lying. First time I ever lie to Nan in my life.

Now me and Mainy shares a secret. I know Mainy not

gon' be the last slave to ask for my help. No way I can get to heaven now. I done killed the Lord's most sweetest thing. Keep telling myself it don't matter no how. The slave's part of heaven probably like hell anyhow.

Still May

Don't know how I'm even writing these words. Today I seen something I won't never forget.

Master Denton had me and Nan go down to the creek this morning. A ship was coming with slaves on it. Master Denton say a couple of them slaves set to have babies, and he want me and Nan there to catch them.

Me and Nan stand on the bank waiting. Then we see the ship coming. We see the name. The Schooner York. So we knows this the right ship. Closer the ship got, we see all sorts of fighting going on. White men jumping off the ship trying to escape slaves. Them slaves real black too. Tell they come straight from Africa.

It's a boy on the bank named George. He say the slaves on the ship his people. Say they I-G-B-O. George say Igbo the only word he know how to spell. George understand them slaves' words. The slaves was singing. The sea brought me here, and the sea gon' bring me home.

Nan told George to run get Master Denton quick. A few masters down by the creek waiting for they slaves. Can tell they want to help. We all see the White men trying to swim to land. But they as scared as we is. I'm scared writing it. I'm gon' finish later.

Still May

I cannot stop thinking about yesterday. Slaves on the ship was being led by an old man and woman. They singing and fighting. Whatever them two say, all the slaves repeat. The old man leading the slaves looked like George. His skin was black as a pot. The woman looked young. Had pretty brown skin like Mainy. Her long black hair was flying all 'round her head. She looked wild.

I tried to look past the fighting. I wanted to find the slaves about to have they babies. I kept thinking of the babies. I didn't want them in that mess. But I couldn't see nothing but fighting. Didn't hear nothing but singing.

Right when the ship was set to run up on the bank, the old man and the young girl jumped right in the water. Rest of them slaves jumped in the water too. Don't try to swim neither. Just let the water pull them under.

By the time Master Denton got down to the creek, most of them slaves dead. White men who jumped from the ship dead too. All them bodies was floating in the water. Master Denton was real quiet. Him and the other masters pulled them dead bodies out the water.

When they pulled out the slaves with babies in they bellies, I cried. They bellies was so big. They babies was set to come any day. Now they dead, and they mammys dead too. Nan cried with me. I never seen Nan cry about nothing.

George say the slaves not dead. He said come night, they gon' rise up from the holes they buried in. Some of them gon' walk on the water right back to Africa. And the others? Well, he say they gon' stay and haunt this land forever.

Still May

Past few days the worst of my life. Killing Mainy's baby. Seeing slaves with babies in they bellies drowned and dead. Pray Peter and Ms. Susie get married soon. Pray they go North like they say and I can go too.

Pray what George say is true. That them dead slaves gon' haunt this world and make folks suffer for what was done. For making them drown in chains. For those babies who died in they mammy's belly before they even had a chance at life.

These the times I don't believe in God. Why He allow these things to happen? And if He is real, He gon' have to strike me dead. I just don't believe in no God who's not fair.

7

HEADS ON POLES

Destrehan Plantation, German Coast, LA (1811)

W hen you staring death in the face, it makes you think about life. Not just your own life, but the lives of those around you. Lives you touched or hurt. The lives you value most. And lives you almost forgot until death looked you straight in the eyes and said, "Remember."

Death is not kind or patient with its memories. They come flooding. Suffocating and drowning you until it is difficult to breathe. Filling you up with recollections as you gasp for a few more moments.

More time. That's what looking at death feels like. Death is watching the phases of your life tick away. Whether fast or slow, easy or difficult. Don't matter. Anyone about to die wants more time.

Everyone's sleeping but me. Peaceful too. As if death isn't right around the corner coming to snatch us up. Like death isn't standing there, right outside the door, waiting. Won't even knock. It will walk right in, pick us up off the floor, and say, "Time's up."

We waiting for trial. All of us guilty of the same thing—not wanting to be slaves. Guilty of wanting to be free. We rebelled against the men claiming they own us, and we set to pay a hefty price. Seems like the fact our trial is in a few hours, that death will be there waiting to determine our sentence, don't mean nothing. Guess they know like I know. Death will find us all guilty. We all gon' die.

"You have broken the laws of this land, and you will pay for your crimes," Master Destrehan said.

It's supposed to be a trial. But no such thing as a trial if you got one drop of Negro blood in you. Having that one drop means you don't have a voice. It means yes, you live and walk and breathe like a man, but you not a man. You not equal to men who don't have that one drop. You tainted by that drop of Negro blood. Dirty. And tainted, dirty men don't get a fair trial.

I want to believe I might somehow be saved. That death will change its mind and give me more time. I want death to whisper in Master Destrehan's ear. Remind him I was a good slave. I served his family for years with nary an ounce of trouble. I need death to make Master Destrehan understand. All I wanted was my freedom. But I know it won't happen. Death has no reason to fight for me.

"I don't know what came over you, Petit."

Master Destrehan's disappointed I joined the revolt.

"Didn't I treat you well all these years?" he asked me. "Wasn't I a good master to you?"

It's not that he wasn't a good master. Him and the Missus was all right as far as masters go. It's just I wasn't supposed to have someone owning me. I'm a man same way he's a man. I deserve to be free. No way to make Master Destrehan understand, though.

Soon Master Destrehan will come through the door walking side by side with death. Holding hands. He will tell us it's time for the trial, but what he's really saying is,

"Get up now, because it's time to die!"

He's keeping us in the storage room. We in here right along with all the other things Master Destrehan wants out of sight. Things he's holding on to but knows he needs to get rid of.

Storage room used to be the slave's secret place. Lots of us came here to be with someone we love. I remember the first time I was here with Celestine.

"I'm scared, Petit," Celestine said.

I lifted her dress, moved extra slow. I wanted to show her I loved her enough not to rush. I was her first. Not even her master had taken her yet. I was going to be one of those memories she had when death came calling. I wanted it to be special.

"Don't be scared," I told her. "I love you."

She trusted me and lay real still as I showed her how much.

Now death is near, and I can't help but wonder,

Did I show Celestine enough? Does she know how much I love her? Have I given her enough love to leave her in this life alone?

Memories start rushing. Like the waters of the Mississippi after rainfall. The memories rise higher and higher as death reminds me I have no more time with Celestine. The moments we shared will have to do.

"You all right, Petit?" Charles asks.

I didn't even notice Charles was awake.

Charles doesn't fear death. Wish I was more like him. The march for freedom was his idea, and he stands firm on his decision. Even if it will cost us our lives.

When death comes through the door, Charles might try to fight it. And he has a good shot at winning, at least for a few extra moments. He's mulatto, looks near White. But he got one drop of Negro blood. So he's tainted like the rest of us.

"What they gon' do to us, Charles?"

Even though I know death is coming, I need to talk to about it.

"Well, Petit," Charles begins, "first thing is, not all of us will die. I'm not saying you will be one of the lucky ones. I'm just saying they won't kill us all."

More men start to rise, moving slowly. As if they realize death's coming today. No need to rush nothing.

Sun is up. Shines enough light for us to see where we are. Enough light to remind us although we were free for a brief moment in our lives, we still slaves.

"They will let some of us live," Charles continues. "Because one, it will make the masters feel good about themselves. And you know masters like to feel good about themselves."

His words upset Koock. He's the most wild of us all, having killed a White man with his bare hands. Koock mumbles inaudible words before punching his right fist into the palm of his left hand. The sound causes me to jump. I try to make my movements seem unrelated to his actions.

"Two," Charles says, "they need some of us to tell the story. You know, so no other slaves ever think about fighting back."

This makes sense. I know if Master Destrehan lets me live, I will never try again to get my freedom. I will be the best slave Master Destrehan ever seen. I don't say this out loud, of course. If I do, Charles might kill me himself. But I know I'm not the only one in the room thinking it.

Somehow, I can feel it. I will not be one of the slaves who gets to live. They won't choose me to tell the story of how freedom's not worth it. I saw it in Master Destrehan's eyes. Disappointment. Then anger. He's set to kill me for sure.

Charles continues, "Now those of us who will die—and I am certain as your leader I will be one of the first—we know it will be a painful death. They will make us suffer…"

"Suffering is no matter, for suffering is temporary," a voice interrupts.

Awiti appears as she always does.

Charles looks at her with admiration. Together, they planned one of the biggest slave revolts ever seen in these parts. What they feel is more than love for each other. They share a hatred. A rage far deeper than the average slave. For Charles and Awiti, what they share is worth dying for.

"Awiti…," Charles whispers.

"Those who endure the greatest suffering, your spirits find a way to seek retribution," Awiti says. "For after death, there is no fear. The biggest fear is right now. Living the rest of your life as a slave. Fear of dying. Imagining the horrible things they plan to do to you. Wondering what death feels like. I say to you, don't worry. For only in death are you truly free."

I know I am living my greatest fear. Knowing death is coming. I can't stop worrying. What will it be like when my life is no more? And what will my death do to Celestine?

"I've heard their plans."

Awiti sits on the floor next to Charles. Both of them, upright and proud, unafraid of death.

"Charles is right," Awiti continues. "They will leave a few of you alive to tell a cautionary tale. But most of you will die. They want to ensure this will never happen again. And once they kill you, your heads will be cut off and placed on poles."

James lets out a long sigh. For certain, he is thinking of his wife and son. They will see his dead body on the ground and his head on the end of a stick. And that will be the memory that floods them.

I sit still thinking of my head on a pole.

"That's right, I heard them talking," Awiti continues in a hushed whisper. "Once they cut off your heads and place them on poles, they will line the streets from here to New Orleans. They plan to even place your heads atop the levees so all can see what is done to slaves who disobey."

Footsteps shuffle outside the door.

"Remember," Awiti promises us, "I will make them pay. For every one of your heads placed upon poles, I will make them suffer a hundred fold."

And then Awiti leaves us as she always does.

Death is finally here, and nobody dares to move or talk. Our memories are flooding.

The footsteps stop, and a familiar voice calls out to us.

"I am here to get your stories. Trial startin' soon, so you've got to be quick. Who's tellin' first?"

I need Celestine to know. Even though it was but a few hours of my life, I was free. I walked where I wanted to. Said what I wanted to say. Lifted my hands for what I wanted and not for Master Destrehan. I need Celestine to know when I die, even if they put my head on a pole, it was worth my moment of freedom.

Death is calling. Not much time left.

"Me," I say, moving closer to the door.

I crouch down so my mouth is near the crack. I see Griot's brown ear waiting, listening for my story. And I tell him.

* * * * *

The oral tradition is our way of keeping track of history here in the Parish. Many Negroes cannot read or write. Griots capture the stories of the people so we can retell them later. This is the story of Petit Lindor. He told me these things as he awaited trial for his involvement in the insurrection. As is the tradition, I begin at the past and come to the present. These are Petit Lindor's final words told to me at the Destrehan Plantation on January 13.

So much I want to tell you, my dearest Celestine, but Griot got to collect stories from the others, so I can only end with these words—I love you.

Know I love you more than the life I lived until I died. Do not weep for what they do to my body. If what they say is true, I'm set to die a terrible death.

Believe I will always be with you. Watching over and protecting you as best I can. If you ever get the chance to flee to freedom, do so. Don't be scared as we once were. Run away so your life won't end here in this Parish.

I'm sad we will never marry or have children. I'm sad I will never see you again, at least not touching skin to skin. Don't think I have gone mad, Celestine. I promise something within me is at peace.

Whether true or not, the thought of me living on after I die helps. For if I believe I can still live on, even as a spirit, well then, I don't care what they do to my body.

As Charles and Awiti always say, the body ain't nothing but a vessel for the spirit. The body is capable of breaking, of being tortured and buried. It is the spirit that cannot be tamed.

Some people, when they die, their spirits don't pass on. No heaven or hell. They stay right here among the living. That's what I hope to do.

Do you believe that, Celestine? Once they kill me, do you believe I can stay? That I can be near you, watching over you and loving you, but you won't be able to see me? Won't that be something?

Do you remember when we planned to run away, Celestine? Go off the coast of the Mississippi River? We could have made it. Swam there and been free. I remember being so scared. The fear of getting caught. The punishment.

Now I wish we would have tried. At least we would be together, whether in death or in life as freed slaves. Now, all I have are memories of you. And all you gon' have are memories of me.

I believe James, Thomas, Hypolite, and Koock—all of us—will be found guilty. Guiau, Nede, and Etienne and Amar might too. And surely Charles will die. In the eyes of the law, no matter what I say, I am guilty. My dearest Celestine, I know they will kill me. So I tell these words to Griot only for you. I love you.

8
MARSH V. MARSH

PLAINTIFF: James Thomas Marsh III
DEFENDANT: Sarah Marsh
CASE NUMBER: 1857-112377
FILED: July 30, 1857
COURT: South Carolina District Court
OFFICE: Florence
COUNTY: Charleston
PRESIDING JUDGE: The Honorable Joseph Duce, Jr.
REFERRING JUDGE: The Honorable William Singleton
NATURE OF SUIT: Criminal
JURY DEMANDED BY: Plaintiff
ATTORNEY FOR THE PLAINTIFF: James Paul Myruth, Esq.
ATTORNEY FOR THE DEFENDANT: Charles Roycee, Esq.

WITNESS TESTIMONY OF VIRGINIA TRIPP

JUDGE DUCE: We are preparing for the witness testimony of Virginia Tripp. Mrs. Tripp, do you understand the crimes being brought against the Defendant?

A: Yes.

JUDGE DUCE: Very well. We will start day two of this trial with the witness testimony and cross examination of Mrs. Virginia Tripp. Please remember you are under oath, Mrs. Tripp. Your witness, Counselor.

ATTORNEY ROYCEE: Thank you, Your Honor. Please state your name and residence for the record.

A: My name is Virginia Tripp. Wife of Mr. William Tripp. I reside at 425 King Street. Charleston. With my husband. At the Tripp Plantation.

Q: Thank you, Mrs. Tripp. May I call you Virginia?

A: Yes. Yes you may.

Q: Thank you, Virginia. Can you please state your relationship to the Defendant?

A: She is my younger sister. My only sister.

Q: Thank you, Virginia. I know this must be difficult for you.

A: It is. Indeed it is. Thank you.

Q: Can you please confirm for the record whether you received a letter from the Defendant on June 18? "Defendant" sounds so harsh. Let's call her by her name, shall we? Did you receive a letter from your sister Sarah?

A: Yes. Yes, I did receive a letter from Sarah.

Q: And what did you do once you received the letter?

A: Well, I opened it and read it, of course.

Q: And after you read it?

A: I showed it to my husband, William. And well, he thought it best we take the matter straight to the sheriff.

Q: Okay. Thank you. We can discuss your visit to the sheriff later. And this letter I am holding, is this the letter you received from Sarah?

A: Yes, it is.

Q: Thank you, Virginia. I am going to ask you to do something. And it will be difficult. But I want you to be strong. Think about the duty you have, not only for Charleston, but all of South Carolina and other Confederate states where a respectable Christian woman may find herself in a similar situation.

ATTORNEY MYRUTH: Objection, Your Honor!

JUDGE DUCE: Sustained. Please refrain from such talk, Counselor.

ROYCEE: I apologize, Your Honor. Virginia, I am going to ask you to read your sister's letter to the court. And I know it will be difficult for you. Please remember you are under oath.

MYRUTH: Objection, Your Honor! Does the court need to hear the letter read in its entirety as part of the witness' testimony? Its contents are private and extremely prejudicial to the Defendant. They are merely my client's thoughts at the time she wrote the letter. Not evidence of her planning to commit the crimes for which she is being accused. Perhaps the letter may be summarized by the witness?

JUDGE DUCE: Overruled. I believe the court, especially the jury, has a right to hear the entire contents of the letter. It has been properly entered into evidence. It may aid the jury in returning their judgment.

ROYCEE: Thank you, Your Honor. Virginia, can you please read the letter to the court?

A: Yes. It begins, "My dearest Virginia. I write this letter to you with a broken heart. I know you and Mother told me the day might come where James would show affection for one of the slaves."

MYRUTH: Objection, Your Honor. This was merely an interpretation of the Defendant's beliefs about her husband's actions regarding one of the slaves.

ROYCEE: You cannot object on a document that has been

entered into evidence. Counselor, if I may ask, where did you obtain your license to practice law?

JUDGE DUCE: Order in the court. Counselors, please approach the bench.

(Short recess)

JUDGE DUCE: Please continue with the letter, Mrs. Tripp.

A: It continues, "I know you and Mother told me the day might come where James would show affection for one of the slaves. I thought I had avoided the likelihood of this happening. I made sure attractive wenches were sold before they came of age. But it was not enough. I believe James has an eye for one of the slaves. And dare I say, I believe he loves her."

(Murmurs)

JUDGE DUCE: Order. Order in the court, please.

ROYCEE: Please continue, Virginia.

A: "I have seen it time and time again on the plantation of our friends. Even with you, my dear sister. The pickaninny running about your plantation looking like William."

(Witness is emotional.)

Q: It is okay, Virginia. Can we please allow the witness a moment to compose herself? Take my handkerchief, please.

A: Thank you. And for the record, my husband is a respectable man here in Charleston. He most certainly does not love any of our wenches. And there are absolutely no slaves looking like William running about our plantation.

Q: Thank you, Virginia. That will be noted for the record. Please continue with the contents of the letter.

A: Then she wrote, "It begins with favoritism toward a wench who is easy on the eyes. Then, before you know it, he is sneaking out of bed at night. Well, I will not stand for it!"

MYRUTH: Objection, Your Honor!

ROYCEE: On what grounds? Your Honor, this is ridiculous. The witness so much as utters two words, and Mr. Myruth seeks to object.

JUDGE DUCE: Counselor, there will be no further objections during the reading of this piece of evidence. Another unsubstantiated objection from you, Mr. Myruth, and I will hold you in contempt. The witness is to finish reading the letter in its entirety. Is that understood?

MYRUTH: Understood, Your Honor.

JUDGE DUCE: You may continue, Mrs. Tripp.

A: The letter continues, "My problems began when James and the Nicholas brothers went to the Old Slave Mart a few months back. We were in need of two young bucks and an older wench to replace Abigail. I am sure you remember Abigail went blind and could no longer serve as a chambermaid. I was quite clear to James the wench he selected needed to be older, for as you know, I have taken great care regarding this matter. As Mother warned us, a young wench can cast a spell, making their masters want them. I know now this is true."

(Witness pauses.)

ROYCEE: You are doing great, Virginia. Please continue.

A: "Do you know James returned home with the two Negro boys as agreed and an old wench to serve as the chambermaid? And he purchased a young wench. Not any young wench. A mulatto! Those known to cast their spell! She could not have been cheap. I could tell she was well kept. Her breasts were firm and upright under her dress, tempting James. It angered me so much! And do you know James was fawning over her? He showed her around the plantation like he was giving a tour to Mayor Charles Macbeth himself."

(Murmurs)

JUDGE DUCE: Order, order in the court, I say.

A: "I knew then she would be a problem. I told James we had all the help we needed in the house. That the young wench could work in the field picking cotton. Nonsense, James said. She was a trained chambermaid and would serve as such. But he had purchased an old wench to serve as the chambermaid, so what was the young wench going to do? Her name is Ah-wee-tee (court note: unsure of proper spelling). Is that not such a God-awful name? And James refused to change her name. Said he liked the way Ah-wee-tee sounds."

(Witness pauses again.)

ROYCEE: Please continue, Virginia.

A: I am sorry. This is all so hard for me. Although, in my heart of hearts, I do believe I am doing the right thing.

Q: I understand, Virginia. You may continue.

A: Okay. "Do you know he assigned her to Palmetto? The only wing with the covered passageway leading to the main house. As if I were too naïve to know what that implied. She barely does any work. Only light work like running errands. When James started leaving out of bed at night, I knew he was going to her. He would come back and sleep soundly. The way I used to make him sleep when we first got married."

(Witness pauses again.)

Q: Please continue, Virginia.

A: "One day, I slapped Ah-wee-tee, for I could hardly stand the sight of her prancing around as if she were the lady of the house. And you will not believe this, dear sister, but the wench slapped me right back."

(Reactions from the court)

JUDGE DUCE: Order! Order in the court, I say!

A: "She looked me right in the eyes and asked me, didn't I know who she was? Said she was someone special. Virginia, never in all my years have I experienced something like this. That wench said she was going to make me pay for what I've done. For my people keeping slaves. Said that I and everyone I love was going to suffer in the worst way."

(Murmurs)

JUDGE DUCE: Order!

A: "Well, I took her words as a threat and went straight to James."

(Witness pauses again.)

JUDGE DUCE: Please continue.

A: I'm sorry, Your Honor. I just cannot believe it. Every time I read these words.

MYRUTH: Objection, Your Honor.

JUDGE DUCE: Counselor?

MYRUTH: I am sorry to interrupt the Court, Your Honor,

but I do believe I am making a sound objection. Mrs. Tripp's outburst is prejudicial to the Defendant. Her task is to read the letter, not to comment on its contents.

JUDGE DUCE: Sustained. You may continue, Mrs. Tripp.

A: Well, I wasn't commenting on its contents. I was saying…

JUDGE DUCE: Mrs. Tripp, please continue with the reading of the letter.

A: Well, all right. "Do you know James defended her? He said I had no right to go about slapping slaves for nothing. That's when I knew Ah-wee-tee had cast her spell on him." (Stops reading) I'm sorry. The next part of this letter is so hard for me, Your Honor. I am sorry I keep crying.

JUDGE DUCE: The court understands, Mrs. Tripp, as this is a delicate matter. Please continue when you have composed yourself.

A: Okay, I am sorry. So sorry. It goes on, "Oh, Virginia, this horrible thing I have done. You must rip up this letter and discard of it once you are done reading it. We are sisters and best friends, so I know I can trust you. I was so angry at James. And so, while he was away on travel, well, I did the most unthinkable thing. I went to the slave quarters and got Thomas—a tall, healthy young buck with the blackest skin. And well, I made him lay with me."

(Reactions from the court. Shouts of profanity.)

JUDGE DUCE: Order! Order in the court, I say! Order!

ROYCEE: Please continue, Virginia.

A: Oh I cannot! It is too horrid! I just cannot!

Q: Virginia, you must.

A: I will try. To see justice done in this matter, I will try. The letter continues, "At first it was awkward, but then I quite came to enjoy it. Thomas' arms were so strong, and he did everything I told him to. I believe he came to enjoy it, for he was determined to please me. I know you have seen your bucks without clothing, so you know male slaves are quite well-endowed."

(Reactions from the court. Woman faints.)

JUDGE DUCE: Order! Order in the court!

A: "Well, I will tell you this, dear sister. Thomas did pleasure me more than James ever has."

(Reactions from the court. Outbursts of profanity. Several husbands and wives leave the courtroom.)

JUDGE DUCE: Order in the court, I say!

A: "I made Thomas come to me every night until James

returned home. It was intended as revenge. Oh, but Virginia, it has an irreversible consequence. Virginia, I am with child. And I cannot be certain if the father is James or Thomas."

(Reactions from the court. Shouts of threats.)

JUDGE DUCE: Order in the court. Order. Order!

A: Oh, let me get through the reading of this letter, please dear God!

JUDGE DUCE: There shall be no more outbursts from the galley until this letter is concluded, or I shall have you all removed!

ROYCEE: Go ahead and continue, Virginia. I believe you are almost done. You are doing a fine job.

A: Then Sarah wrote, "And that horrible wench. Every time Ah-wee-tee sees me, she smiles at my growing belly as if she knows my secret. Oh Virginia! I have made a horrible mistake. James rubs my belly every night. He's taken with the idea of having a son. I cannot imagine what he would do if he finds out what I've done. I must somehow kill this child before it is born."

(Reactions from the court. Women in courtroom are emotional.)

JUDGE DUCE: Order! I will have order in this court!

A: "I know it's such an awful thing to say. Killing a child.

But I have no choice. Can you imagine the talk? Our family name would be ruined and known throughout the entire territory. No one would buy our cotton or sugar, and we would become poor, something I do not wish to experience. Oh Virginia, please forgive me. I know this secret is a heavy burden, but I had to tell someone. I promise I have learned from my mistake. If only the dear Lord would take this child from my womb. I had to tell you, my dear sister. Surely you understand and will pray for me. Please discard of this letter after reading. And please, please, come visit me soon. Love. Your dear sister. Sarah."

ROYCEE: Thank you, Virginia. You did a great job. We all know how difficult this must be for you.

A: Thank you. Thank you. Yes, it is by far the hardest thing I have ever done in my life.

Q: I am almost done with my questions, Virginia. So upon receiving this letter from the Defendant, your sister Sarah, what did you do next?

A: Well, naturally I was horrified. I mean, to have slept with a slave? Why, I cannot understand what possessed her! She could have gone to our pastor for prayer before doing such an unforgivable, deplorable thing. So I read the letter to my husband. I knew something had to be done.

Q: But you were too late, correct?

A: Yes. Before we could fully inform the sheriff of the

matter, we heard Sarah had fallen down the stairs and lost the child.

MYRUTH: Objection, Your Honor! He is leading the witness to convince the jury the Defendant did not truly fall, that the fall was intentional.

JUDGE DUCE: Sustained.

A: Why is that sustained? Sarah said in the letter she wanted the child gone. And then she happens to fall down the stairs? Seriously, even a blind man can see through that lie. Sarah fell on purpose. Threw herself down the stairs so she could keep her slave love child a secret. We all know that!

(Murmurs)

JUDGE DUCE: Order! Mrs. Tripp, you are to act honorably while in this court.

A: And now Ah-wee-tee is on the run. No one can find her. Who's to say she won't try to kill me because I am Sarah's sister? She said she was going to hurt everyone Sarah loved! My life is in danger! This court must do something!

JUDGE DUCE: Mrs. Tripp, please control yourself and only respond to the questions asked by Mr. Roycee.

A: I can say what I please. She did it! Slept with a slave and knew she was going to have that slave's baby. And James had the right to kill him. I'd say the same if he killed Sarah too. She brought shame on our family name. Sarah deserves what's coming to her. You hear what I say? She is no longer my sister!

JUDGE DUCE: You are not to speak to me in that manner, Mrs. Tripp. Even in your anger and shame, you are to respect this court. One more outburst, and you will be held in contempt of court.

ROYCEE: Thank you. I have no further questions. Your witness, Counselor.

9
THE OTHER IMMORTAL

New York City, NY (1847)

When I first encountered the other immortal in Bowling Green Park, I was intrigued. Her walk was precocious. She seemed to float, unlike so many of the mortals nearby—those with burdens. The indigent shuffle their feet as though the very act of walking was an intense struggle. But even before I observed her floating walk, I felt the pull.

The young woman appeared to be an ordinary human— yet another defense mechanism to conceal us. Her skin was a lovely complexion, and for some offbeat reason, her coloring made me think of a warm cup of tea. I admired the elegance of her dark hair pulled into a proper bun, the hem of her mauve skirt hovering above the grass. Her attire was neat and fashionable. She seemed oblivious to those who passed by admiring her beauty.

She walked about the manicured lawn enjoying the crisp New York day, and then she too began to feel the pull. Knotting, twisting, and burning from within—the warning.

The other immortal looked around in anticipation, searching. But I was well hidden. She placed her right hand across her belly to massage the pain.

There were more mortals than usual in the park. They were no doubt pleased the grounds were available for recreation while Central Park remained under repair. Mothers watched over their little ones, attempting to catch their children before they fell or stumbled, wanting to shield them from the pains of life for as long as possible.

I always found their efforts amusing. Mortals went about life not knowing if each day was their last. They busied themselves with mundane tasks and responsibilities that were quite meaningless, since one day they would perish. The younger mortals were filled with curiosity and hope, while the older mortals wore faces laden with wrinkles, regret. What an unfortunate destiny. How thankful I was to not be one of them.

It was a chilly spring day. The air cool and brisk. But the light warmth from the sun made the day bearable, perfect even. I continued to watch as the other immortal strolled about the park, one hand on her abdomen trying to ease the pain from the pulling. It was time for me to reveal myself.

I walked across the lawn, trying to make eye contact so she would know I meant her no harm. We needed to become familiar, to ease the pulling. But she looked right past me. As I came closer, she began to grab at her stomach in pain, the burning intensifying. This was a good sign. I was the stronger of us.

"Hello," I said as I approached her cautiously. "I am Semya, one of the progeny of my creator Semyazza."

Again, I tried to make eye contact. If she would just allow

our vessels to acknowledge each other, it would ease the pain of the pulling.

"May we acknowledge each other?" I asked. "I have no intentions of harming you. Look at me."

The other immortal stared into my eyes, her facial expression a strange dichotomy of disbelief and happiness. Her small dark eyes seemed bottomless, black, as though she had no pupils. The pull between us grew stronger until both our vessels acknowledged we were not enemies. Not friends, but not enemies. Kindred beings. Only then did the pulling of unfamiliarity pass. And she fell into my arms.

She clung to me, her head resting on my shoulder as she wept.

I asked, "What is your name?"

All immortals are named. Their name bears some reference to their creator.

"My name is Awiti."

"Awiti, you say? That is odd."

I was not being rude. I was not familiar with any of the descendants of the Nephilim of that origin. My creator Semyazza taught me the history of Creation, including the names of all the Nephilim and their progeny. I was quite certain the name Awiti was not discussed.

"Tell me about your coven."

"Coven?" Awiti asked. She seemed genuinely puzzled.

"Yes. You know, that to which you belong. Or as the mortals say, your family." I smiled, quite pleased at my witticism. But Awiti still seemed confused.

"I have no family. No coven, as you say."

"Impossible," I replied. "Who created you?"

"Oranyan." Awiti smiled when she said his name.

"Did you say *Oranyan*?" I needed to be certain.

"Yes," Awiti said proudly. Then she asked, "Do you know him?"

There was no mistaking the hopefulness in her voice.

"No, I do not know him," I said. I chose my words carefully. I knew *of* him. So I was not telling Awiti a lie. But for clarification, I added, "I have never met him."

Awiti looked disappointed. She smoothed her hair with her hands. There were no strands out of place. It was just something for her hands to do.

"Well, I am pleased to meet you, Semya. I have been alone for so long. Since my Exchange with Oranyan, I have never met another immortal."

And when Awiti said those words, I was certain. Immortals must always be a part of a coven, under the guidance of the Watchers. There were a few immortals who, for various injustices, were banished. Designated to live their eternity in isolation. Their evils so great, they were a threat to all. And Oranyan was one of the transgressors.

"I need you to wait here," I told Awiti.

I tried to hide my thoughts. I did not want her to read me. For if she saw what I was intending to do, she would not be pleased.

"Trust me, Awiti. I will be right back."

"Promise me," she said firmly.

"Promise." I only hoped she would wait for me to return.

When I arrived at our coven, one of the Watchers stood reading the Rules of the Order. The large red book appeared blank, full of empty pages. Its contents remained visible to only those designated by the Nephilim in the beginning of time. The Watcher's long robe draped about the ground, creating a thick black train of fabric behind Him.

Even though He had heard me enter and could feel my presence, the Watcher did not acknowledge me. I hated to interrupt Him, but it was necessary. It was my duty to protect the coven, to ensure the protection of the descendants of the Nephilim.

"Most Honorable One," I began, "I am sorry to disturb you. But I have met one who is like us, except, she is not like us. I cannot explain it. But I believe she is a creation of one of the banished."

And then, to make certain He would understand the urgency of the matter, I added, "She said she was created by Oranyan."

The Watcher lifted His gaze from the Rules of the Order, and the book closed. He walked over to me and placed His hands on my head. I bowed, closing my eyes as He read me.

When He was finished, the Watcher replied, "Take me to her."

We arrived at Bowling Green Park moments later. I was afraid Awiti wouldn't be there, but she was—sitting in the grass, picking at the long green blades like a small child. Strands of dark hair had escaped the bun, and they blew around her face in the gentle breeze.

The Watcher's presence made Awiti double over in pain. He was far stronger than I, and He exerted His powers without apology. She screamed as the pull grew stronger. He was testing her, challenging her. He needed to know the extent of her power.

Awiti seemed defenseless. She rolled onto her side, holding her stomach with both hands. A passerby looked upon the scene with interest. And then, after sizing up the statuesque figure of the Watcher, the young man decided to walk away from a matter that did not concern him.

When the Watcher was certain Awiti's discomfort was not an elaborate performance, He released His pull. She looked at me, her eyes pleading. But I could do nothing.

"I need you to tell me," the Watcher commanded, "how did you come to be?" His voice was deep, the words laden with His obvious supremacy. Out of fear, Awiti vacillated in responding, and He demanded,

"Speak!"

"My name is Awiti. I...," she began, her voice hesitant. "I was in my village. Father told me to run, so I did. Because strange men came to enslave us. And then I met Oranyan. He said I could become immortal. That if we did an Exchange, I could live forever. I loved him, so I said yes. And because I wanted to find my family. Then Oranyan did the Exchange. And then I..."

She rambled like a criminal pleading her innocence. She shared fragments of her story, the important and mundane facts jumbled together. But the Watcher heard the most important piece of evidence. Oranyan.

"Fear not," the Watcher said to Awiti. "I will not hurt you." He took a few steps closer, and Awiti recoiled.

"Come now," He said, reaching out His hand to help her stand to her feet. "Let me read you. This will tell me everything I need to know."

The Watcher rubbed His hands together, preparing to read into Awiti's past. As she stood, the mauve skirt gathered about her tiny frame. It created a muddle of pink fabric, wrinkled and bunched. Awiti seemed more child than woman, messy and adorable in her innocence. She did not smooth her skirt, as women do, or tidy her appearance.

The Watcher put His hands to Awiti's head and instructed, "Close your eyes and take a deep breath."

The Watcher held Awiti's head in His hands for a few moments. He closed His eyes and nodded. Within a short time, He released her.

"Awiti, I have seen how your troubles first began," the Watcher reflected. "It is most unfortunate what happened to your village, your family. You were but a child when Oranyan tricked you. But you are no longer innocent. You have lived for many years now, experienced life."

Awiti opened her mouth to defend herself, but the Watcher continued.

"Do not interrupt when I am speaking. I have seen the harm you have done. You have caused others so much pain. Destroying the innocent because you are unable to deal with your loss. This must end today."

He did not wait for Awiti to respond. The Watcher was unrelenting as He admonished her.

"You cannot live among the mortals, pretending to be one of them while you exact your revenge. Do you understand, Awiti?"

There was a long pause as He waited for Awiti to acknowledge His instructions.

"Yes," Awiti responded. "But..."

"I am certain Oranyan did not tell you of the burden of immortality. Surely he focused on the benefits most enticing to you. But it was still your decision, was it not?" The Watcher implored, "It was your choice to become immortal. You wanted an opportunity to find your family. You were willing to give someone your life without asking detailed questions. And for that, you can only blame yourself, not Oranyan."

Awiti looked at the Watcher, her anger evident as the skies darkened.

"I know what you are capable of, but you are no match for me, Awiti. I suggest you control your temper lest I show you true wrath. Your storms are nothing compared to what I can do."

And to remind her of His supremacy, without moving, the Watcher began to pull her. Awiti screamed from the burning pain.

"Is it fair to say someone tricked you if you did not inquire before making your decision?" the Watcher asked.

"No," Awiti responded. "But if I had only known what it meant to become immortal, I would have never agreed."

"That is because you are not a descendant of one of the Nephilim," the Watcher informed her. "If you were, you would understand that immortality is a supreme gift. But you were created by one of the banished. And so the immortality you experience is not what was intended.

"Oranyan should have never created you," the Watcher told Awiti. "It is unfortunate he tricked you with the strongest of human emotions. Love."

The Watcher continued.

"You will question what you and Oranyan shared. I will tell you so you do not waste time on such trivial matters. Oranyan did not love you. He tricked you to relieve himself from an unfortunate situation. I am certain Oranyan was malcontent with his life as a banished immortal. This is why he selected you. Not because he loved *you*. Oranyan was in love with your mortality."

Awiti began to cry, but her reaction did not affect the Watcher. His only duty was to speak truth. His words were harsh and swift, but honest.

"Oranyan did not consider how his decisions would impact you for eternity. And that is not the way of human love, Awiti.

"There exists a great heaviness in your spirit. No doubt from the loss of your family. The slave raiders attacking your village. During the Exchange, your spirit was not at peace, and it did not cross over. And so you exist in an immortal body still bound to your spiritual self.

"You are not accepted among the descendants of the Nephilim," the Watcher concluded. "And it is for these reasons I must banish you."

"But where will I go?" Awiti asked.

"I have a place in mind. A land where there are few mortals. This is for your protection."

"Why?" Awiti asked. "Why can I not be around mortals? I must remain alone? Forever?" She was a child in this moment, fearful at the thought of being lonely.

"Just as you are not welcome among the descendants of the Nephilim, you will not be accepted among mortals," the Watcher said. "They cannot know what you truly are. And the more you interact with them, the more you will want to become like them."

He reminded Awiti, "This is what happened to Oranyan. He left his place of banishment. His desire to become mortal was so great, it led him to deceive you."

Awiti nodded in acknowledgment.

"You must stay in your place of banishment," the Watcher instructed. "Do not try to find your village or the land that was once the Oyo Kingdom. Stop seeking to harm the descendants of the White Faces and Black Faces, as you call them. You must abandon your quest to seek retribution for those enslaved."

Then He warned her, "What I am asking is a great sacrifice. But you must heed my words, Awiti. There will be no Watcher to guide and instruct you. Once you are banished, it will be your responsibility to adhere to these rules. And they are just as much for your benefit as they are for the safety of others."

"Is there no other way?" she pleaded.

"There is no other way. It is regrettable this happened to you. While you will suffer, be certain to never do this to another. No matter how tempting. Remember what you are feeling in this moment."

"I will never do this to another," Awiti said. "Never."

"Good," the Watcher encouraged. "Reach out to those in the spiritual realm. They will share in your pain and sorrow. But again, you must be careful. For you may find yourself wanting to become like them. Spirits, once they find peace, can cross over. But you must remember, your spirit will never cross over.

"Your task as a banished immortal is to find peace simply for the sake of finding peace. To make your infinite years on this earth bearable. And this will not be easy."

Awiti nodded.

"I will record your name in the Order so the descendants of the Nephilim shall know of your misfortune," the Watcher advised. "Awiti, I can only encourage you to find peace. It is my hope you comply. If not, you will learn a most difficult lesson. No matter the extent of your persistence, damaging others will not heal you."

10

IN TIME

Tristan da Cunha (1872)

I now know since Creation others have been banished. The Watchers record their names in the Rules of the Order to document their tribulation. And now, my name is among them. Awiti Akoth. A child born of misfortune as the rains fell on her village. One who should have been thrown away, for she was a girl sure to bring trouble. How I have lived up to Father's naming of me.

"Do you know what I think when I say your name?" Father once asked me.

"No, Father. What is it? What do you think of?"

"That you were once destined for death. How you grew from a tiny child I could hold in one hand to a young girl who captured my heart."

I try not to think of Father and my family, of the love we shared with each other. I do not like to remember my village. To wonder what became of my people once the strange men with brown skin bound and led them away. I know they faced untimely deaths and unimaginable suffering. Days and nights within the confines of stone castles; shackles around their hands, necks, and feet, packed aboard slave ships. Torture as they were sold into lives of servitude.

I especially try not to think of Amondi. But her smile and the soft puffs of black hair haunt me.

"Do you like being the oldest?" This was a frequent question Amondi asked of me. "Do you enjoy being the first?"

"Sometimes." My answer was always the same.

"I wish I was the first."

"Why? You are perfect, Amondi. You are the youngest. It's not always who is first who is best. Sometimes it is she who is last." I was always surprised whenever I found myself repeating proverbs told to me by Mother.

"But..." Amondi thought for a moment.

"But what, my little sister?"

"Well, if I were the oldest, there would have been a time when I had Father and Mother all to myself."

I smiled.

"Do you remember that time, Awiti?" she asked. "What was it like to be the only child they loved?"

We were selfish in that way. Guilty of wanting all of Father and Mother's love from time to time. Not that we were children who didn't love each other. We shared the type of love siblings possess. Only we were allowed to annoy and taunt each other, to be self-centered in wanting attention. We were individuals, but we were nothing without each other.

I hear Amondi's voice.

"Do you remember, Awiti? What was it like to be the only one they loved?"

My memories are a swirling pot, boiling over with love,

grief, and anguish. Recollections so tormented, I am no longer certain whether they are real or imagined.

"Yes, I remember, Amondi," I tell her.

Mother teaching me to braid. The softness of her hands as she showed me how to till the garden. Father holding me in his arms, naming me. Sitting beneath the baobab tree. Times that were just for us. Those moments when they loved only me.

I often imagine Father and Oranyan wrestling for my heart. In my dreams, Oranyan is still handsome and I am honored he has chosen to fight for my love. And yet, Father knows the truth. He can see Oranyan does not want the vastness of my heart, just my life. Both of them, the two men I loved most, dark skin sweating and fighting. Each man determined to win. My value to them, though the rationales are different, is priceless.

"You cannot have her," Father says.

And then, just as he did when the men with brown skin appeared, Father turns to me and says,

"Run, Awiti. Run and don't look back. Run until you find a new village to call home."

But there is no place to run. I am banished. Living with the heartache and memories of a time long past. Dreams that are mixed with reality and fantasy. Imaginings to sustain me.

Before meeting Semya, I thought I was alone. For many years I had never encountered another. Oranyan told me there were other immortals, but as with most things, he failed to tell me the whole truth. Just fragments sure to entice.

"You must be comfortable being alone, Awiti," Oranyan instructed me before the Exchange.

I remember that day, his words. Our lives were complete the morning he whispered those words to me. I had just oiled

Oranyan's skin, washed his hair. I loved him, and I was enamored with his beauty, his intelligence. And while I thought he was also besotted with me, for he looked at me with love, it was my mortality that he held in high regard.

"You must realize as an immortal you will be different. What mortal would feel comfortable being friends with someone they know will live forever?"

"But I am comfortable, Oranyan."

I was beyond comfort. I was taken with him and his words.

"Ah, but you became comfortable with me *before* you knew."

"Yes, but…"

"Did you not feel fear the night I told you I was immortal?" Oranyan asked. "I remember your eyes, Awiti. You wanted to run."

"But I did not run."

"Only because I wouldn't let you," he said with a smile.

Then he grabbed me, pulling me close to him. His lips touched mine. I still remember his eyes and full, dark lips whispering sweet words, promising to love me forever. But did he ever love me? Didn't he know I would one day be banished?

Although I am exiled here on Tristan da Cunha, I am not alone. It is a place of refuge for those in the spiritual realm. A gathering place for the dead who wish to remain among the living. Watching and longing. Loving.

The spiritual world is vast and infinite. A never-ending stream of consciousness. Some are anxious at their misfortune and lot in life. Others simply refuse to let go. Their lives were complete and full. Spirits with lifetimes one might define as wonderful. Yet, they are unable to leave this earth. The thought of being separated forever is incomprehensible.

"How can I leave them?" Marisol once asked.

She could not bear the thought of leaving her children on this earth alone. Motherless and fatherless on the count of an unnecessary war.

She rationalized, "I have to watch them. To protect them. Sometimes they hear me. Sometimes they do not. But at least I am here. At least I can be near them."

It is not uncommon after death that spirits remain. In the shadows and within the breeze. They hover around that which they cannot leave behind. Spirits are felt, even seen at times. But the human mind possesses great strength. It can convince itself of anything it wishes. So many simply pretend the spirits of the dead do not exist.

I am so thankful. For while I find myself alone in the physical sense, I am never lonely. I have taken great interest in spirits' past lives, their reasoning for refusing to cross over. And of all of the spirits I have encountered thus far, I have most enjoyed my time with Seraphina.

"I am thankful to be among the dead," Seraphina once told me. "I lived a long life, one that was not easy, but not as difficult as others. And in my lifetime I learned a lot. By watching and listening. My family taught me everything there is to know about life and death. About the afterlife. And I prefer to stay between. As long as I am in between, I know what to expect."

Gracious in her knowledge and wisdom, Seraphina is the mother I never had the chance to fully know. To her, life is simple.

"All of life is a balance," Seraphina explained. "Light cannot exist without darkness. Wet is nothing if there is no dry. One cannot only acknowledge good and say evil does not exist. Just as one cannot only recognize the spirits of the living and say the dead are not present. That is not the way of the Great One. For if there is one, there always exists the other— the contradictory.

"This is why it is essential to respect both good and evil, whether alive or dead. This is where so many of the living often make their biggest mistake. If they would acknowledge the dead, they could learn so much."

Whenever I lament about my lot in life, Seraphina admonishes me. I chose to become immortal. And thus, the fault is mine.

Seraphina's words echo the sentiments of the Watcher. "You cannot be angry at Oranyan for not telling you everything there was to know about immortality. He did not owe you the truth. Man owes another man nothing."

"But had I known, I would have chosen otherwise," I argue. Living in isolation. The burden of living alone indefinitely. The unlikely possibility I would ever find my family. I would have never chosen such a life.

"This is true, but would you still be here?" Seraphina asks. "If you had not chosen immortality, would your spirit still be here, unable to cross over? Angry and unable to forget the life taken from you?"

"Perhaps."

"This, my dear Awiti, is what the Great One intended with free will. Choices. And consequences."

I know Seraphina is right. Even if I had not chosen immortality, I would still exist in the spiritual realm. Mourning with so many others.

So hidden and deceiving is Tristan da Cunha, mortals who spot the island from a distance believe it to be a mirage. A figment of their imagination, the mind wanting so desperately to see land after being enclosed by nothing but water. People come to the island and believe themselves to be the first, or among the first, of the few inhabitants. They claim the land, believing because they found it, they own it.

"One of man's biggest failures is his need to possess," Seraphina admonishes. "Not everything is meant to be a possession. No one can own the island, for the earth does not belong to any one man. Likewise, man is not meant to control another man. All things—in the land, the air, the sea, both good and evil, whether alive or dead—belong to the Great One."

The Great One is All. I suspect had the strange men not come to my village, I would have learned my people's version of the Great One. I am certain my family taught me of this omnipotent being. I try to remember words from Mother and Father, songs from our village. But it was too long ago. And so, everything I know about the Great One I learned from Seraphina.

In the beginning, the Great One breathed life into many. She called Her creations the Living. The Living were not only humans, those with flesh and coherency. All of the Great One's creations, even the earth itself, were among the Living.

She took joy in creating plants and animals, from the most minuscule to the mighty. Her creations were of varying degrees of beauty and competency. The Great One desired Her creations to dwell together in harmony, no matter their standing.

Some of the Living needed no governing, their purpose for existing modest. The Great One did not create in them a complex system of thinking and being. These Living simply were. Rooted in the ground, swimming in the waters, or existing in the air. They served their ordained purposes to purify and cleanse, or even as sources of food for other Living. They remained where the Great One destined for them, and She allowed them to govern themselves.

This was a success for some and a great failure for others. They were not intellectuals. They did not have adaptability, and so many did not survive. And this too was the way of the Great One. For there cannot be life if there is no death.

And yet some of the Living needed much governing. The Great One constructed within them a system of intelligence and creativity. They were dominant beings capable of great things. These Living were curious and daring. And the Great One, although powerful, could not watch them all. So She designated Watchers to govern the most influential of Her creations— humans and animals with infinite potential. Living that were blessed with free will.

The Watchers were tasked with authority to oversee those among the Living who were intellectuals. Their responsibilities were to encourage the Living to heed the advice and precautions of the Great One. For this would ensure the Living coexisted in harmony.

Watchers were more protector than dictator. They had no control over the Living. Because the Great One had blessed the most influential of Her creations with free will, the lives they chose were ultimately their decision. And the repercussions theirs as well.

Those among the Living that were animals and plants proved themselves to be the most obedient. They remained where the Watchers told them to stay—in the air, land, or sea. Even if it meant their extinction, they did not leave.

But many of those among the Living who were human proved themselves to be disobedient. They did not stay on the lands the Great One designated for them, their gifts of curiosity and free will often too enticing to ignore.

Humans became more authoritative, confident in their hierarchy among the Living. Each generation posed a greater threat. They questioned and defied the authority of the Watchers. In time, there were humans who even began to challenge the Great One. And it was written these humans were called the Defiant.

The Defiant began to go about and challenge all of the Living. Many of the Defiant did not survive. They tried to dwell in places the Great One had not prepared for them. They did not have wings to fly in the air. Some could not withstand extreme cold and heat. But some of the Defiant, although not properly equipped, did survive due to their resourcefulness.

And the Defiant who were disobedient have altered the plan of the Great One forever.

"So the strange men who came to my village, they were among the Defiant?" I ask Seraphina.

"Why, yes, of course. They were away from the land the Great One designated for them."

"But why?" I ask. "Why could they not behave like my people? Why didn't they stay on their own land?"

"As I have told you: the need to possess. The desire to explore and challenge is one of the Living's greatest failures. It is difficult to understand, but this is also the way of the Great One. There will always exist a contrary. She knew that given free will, some of Her creations would choose to be defiant. Even though your people were obedient, this does not mean all people will be obedient."

"But it makes me so angry!" I feel a storm brewing as the skies darken. "Because of their defiance, they altered not only their lives, but mine!"

"Yes, this is true," Seraphina agrees.

"What if I did the same? What if I was disobedient and left my place of banishment? What if I continued my wrath? Destroying the descendants of the White Faces and Black Faces?"

"The choice is yours, Awiti, to do what you wish."

"I want to return to Africa. I want to make the Defiant suffer for disobeying the Great One. I want them to pay for coming to my country."

"So go, Awiti," Seraphina encourages. "Go and do what you feel you need to do. I will be here waiting for you to return. You have my blessing."

"Seraphina..."

"Tell me, Awiti, what is stopping you?" Seraphina asks.

"Because I know it is wrong. It is a direct violation of the orders given by the Watcher."

"So?" Seraphina is unapologetic in her questioning. She explains, "Awiti, you must make the choice to do what *you* wish. Whether you stay or whether you go, you will suffer consequences. But, if *you* decide, the choice of where and how you will suffer is yours."

11
ATMO

Goree Island, Africa (1874)

Bàbá named me Ajulo Daren. A strong and purpose-ful name for his second son born in the night. On the eve of my birth, *Bàbá* heard thunder, the sounds of a great storm. He ran outside to see if Orunmila was sending an omen.

Rain was falling only on our home. The rest of the village sat dry in the moonlight. A small white haze hovered above our roof. It released droplets of rain, slow and continuous. *Bàbá* ran back inside, stood beside his wife, and said,

"Orunmila has blessed us."

Mama put me to her breast, and I began to suckle. My family knew what had to be done. Our tribe was careful to acknowledge the gifts that reside within every living being.

Gifts are most apparent when babies first enter the world. Whatever is happening around them a direct reflection of their blessing. And I had been born with a most impressive talent.

Although *Mama* was thankful Orunmila had chosen our family, she cried. *Mama* knew she would have a short time with her newborn son. I could not stay with my family. Each day, as I grew older, my gift would mature and develop. And in time they would be unable to control me.

It was necessary for me to dwell with those who could teach me to manage the gift Orunmila had bestowed upon me. I would spend my life with the Awo. They would raise and protect me. This was the way of our people.

At sunrise, *Bàbá* took me to the Awo. There, on the outskirts of my village, along with all the others who had been born with great talents, I would learn to master my gift.

The Awo assigned a *babalawo* to every child, a mentor who possessed the same talents. I simply called my mentor "Babalowo," for my speech during my formative years was troublesome. I liked the name. It reminded me of the word *Bàbá*. And Babalawo was like a father to me.

His frame was slim, but muscular. And his face and skin youthful. But perhaps Babalawo's most striking feature was his height. He was taller than any man I had ever seen. Babalawo's hair hung in long, twisted locks. Thick black and gray tresses intertwined like thread.

Babalawo's appearance was misleading. He was old. He taught many over the years and took great pride in teaching me. I slept on Babalawo's floor, my body stretched out on a special mat woven of feathers and lion's hair. I was not an ordinary child, and so I could not sleep as ordinary children do. The hair from the lion calmed my spirit while I slept. And the bird's feathers made certain I had pleasant dreams.

We went to the river every morning, cleansing ourselves in the healing waters. Babalawo prayed to the spirits to guide him. It was essential he taught me to find the balance between power and control. Once we were cleansed and had eaten a proper meal, I would begin my training.

"You know, Ajulo," Babalawo would often remind me, "not all are chosen. Many come to acquire the gift of Atmokinesis through other means. Ways that anger Orunmila. But you are one of the elect. As long as you do the work She desires, you will be blessed.

"Your body. Your mind. All of you is sacred."

Babalawo taught me to cup my hands as I focused my thoughts on developing a storm within my palms. As I expanded my hands slowly, the small clouds of rainfall grew large and powerful. I sent it over the tops of the trees and past the hills, where it dwindled until it was no more than a gust of wind.

As I grew older, I controlled the wind and rain with little effort, always cupping my hands to control the elements. Under the guidance of Babalawo, I became highly skilled. Often, I was called upon to do tasks Orunmila requested.

In times of war, I unleashed storms with winds so strong, trees fell to the earth. My torrential rains made the land full of wet patches, our enemies unable to reach our village due to the flooding. During droughts, when we needed water for harvest, I made certain to send enough rainfall for crops to grow and flourish.

I was never to use my gift to kill or for amusement. This was not why Orunmila chose me. I was chosen to do great things.

If only the slave raiders had not arrived by the element of surprise. I would have unleashed a mighty calamity. I could have trapped them in the wind and drowned them with rain. But they used their evil ways to hide themselves. They knew where the Awo protected the most gifted. And so the slave raiders attacked us first.

I tried to run, but I was captured. Babalawo was also seized, and we made eye contact, both of us bound as chaos ensued around us. The slave raiders constrained every man, woman, and child. They restricted our hands and feet so we could not defend ourselves.

Babalawo called out to me, "You do not need your hands, Ajulo. Send a storm from within. Call on Orunmila to guide you, and I will do the same."

At first I felt nothing. But soon, for the first time in my life, I could feel a storm developing not within my hands, but inside of me. The elements churned within my body, growing strong and anxious, waiting to be unleashed. The winds began to blow. Rainfall followed.

As I looked to Babalawo for guidance, one of the slave raiders ran toward him with a long, sharp black knife. With one blow, he cut off Babalawo's head. I watched as my mentor's blood rushed over the dirt. Babalawo's eyes remained opened as he watched the horror occurring all around us. I began to cry, and my world went dark.

I was but a few years away from becoming a man when I was taken from the Awo. If not for the slave raiders' thievery, I would have completed my rights of passage. Orunmila was firm boys should not learn certain things until they became men. Who knows what great works I would have done?

To the slave raiders, I appeared youthful and healthy. But they were looking only at my body. My mind never recovered from seeing the death of Babalawo. There was not a single memory of my life that did not include him.

Aboard the slave raider's vessel, I thought only of

Babalawo. With each memory, I developed a sickness. A disease of heartache and loss. My body began to wretch and heave. One of the slave raiders came to inspect me as I continued to vomit. The bitter white bile covered my body. I tried, but I could not control it. The sickness was the memories of Babalawo's death rising inside me, forcing their way out.

The slave raider called for one of his comrades, and together, they determined the best course of action for me. One took hold of my shoulders while the other took hold of my feet. They hoisted me over the side of the ship and tossed me into the sea.

The impact of my body hitting the salt water was painful. My wounds and broken skin stung and burned. Chains still bound my feet and hands as I began to sink beneath the waves. But even if I could, I would not have tried to keep my head above water.

I had no reason to live. No will to survive. I sank into the ocean, drifting beneath the water as my lungs filled with the cold blue. Soon I was looking down from above. I watched my body fade into the darkness of the sea.

Pain disappeared the moment my flesh died. But not the sorrow. The sadness remained, all encompassing, filled with memories of my life before the slave raiders arrived. The destruction of the Awo. The murder of Babalawo. My spirit continued to grieve long after my death in the sea.

I believe these memories forever bound my spirit to Goree. The land was beautiful. Green trees, mountainous coast, and the air filled with the scent of salt water. The blue ocean flowed on until it met for a conversation with the sky.

What were the sea and heavens discussing? The horror that occurred along this Western coast? Were they counting the number of African bones scattered about the land? Did they know the number of bodies buried at the bottom of the sea?

The slave port on Goree Island was not as active as the others, like Lagos, Jakin, and Grand-Popo. After my death, I visited them all, the visions of the destruction of people with black skin adding to my sorrow. Yet it was on Goree where my spirit felt most connected.

Goree was the last place I saw those from my village. Those who did not cross over remained at Goree, our spirits restive and intense. But those who did survive, those from my village who went aboard the slave raiders' ships, I never knew what happened to them. Until Awiti arrived.

We all sensed her presence, but there was much confusion. We saw a woman walking about alive, with flesh and breath. Yet we could feel and hear her in the spiritual realm as though she were with us, among the dead. We had never known anyone with this ability. She was our first encounter with an immortal.

Awiti possessed much knowledge of the world. She had walked amongst the living and witnessed what became of our people once they left the shores of Africa. Their fate. This is what Awiti wished to share with us. And we did not like what she revealed.

Awiti asked, "Do you think sorrow and suffering is confined to these shores? That grief remains only among you dwelling here in the slave castles? Do you think you are the ones with the most misery?

"You who are dead, you are the fortunate ones. Those of our people who survived, they have endured the real horror.

"Many of you know of the wickedness in the slave castles,

for you were there. And many of you suffered on the slave ships before dying. Let me tell you the fate of those who remained aboard the ships.

"They embarked on a long journey at sea, and many died, for the conditions were so inhumane. The slave raiders did horrible things to our men, women, and children. And many of our people met with death this way."

The elements within me began to stir, and the wind started to blow through the trees.

"Many of our people died or rebelled. The slave raiders threw their bodies overboard to be eaten by sharks or to drown in the ocean. But those who died at sea, they were the lucky ones."

The fact the dead fared better than the living was impossible for us to imagine.

"Those who survived the treacherous journey were in for a worse fate. The ships would dock at ports all over the world. And from there, more suffering, as the slave raiders sold our people to the highest bidder.

"Our people were sold into a life of slavery, but the White man's slavery is not like our slavery. They have constructed a system governed by evil and unnecessary abuse. It was there, in slavery, in a life of bondage and servitude, the true misery began. And it still remains today, for our descendants continue to suffer.

"Just as our country tries to rebuild from the stolen lives, our people who were enslaved have tried to rebuild. The slave trade is ending, but I believe its lasting effects will never end," Awiti concluded.

This was what had become of our ancestors who went into

the sea. Death and destruction. A torment that would endure for generations.

We were incited. Our collective force rose and swelled. The rains began to fall, and white streaks of lightening flashed throughout the sky, bright and blinding. Thunder sounded like the beating hearts of our people.

We gathered off the Western coast, calling out for other spirits to join us. Finally, we had places to send our indignation. We would direct the storms' momentum at the lands where Awiti had seen the injustice of our people.

Our fury could not be contained to Goree. We unleashed it in varying degrees of strength and vengefulness. And for many years, across the world, there would be great suffering.

PART II
DEATH
(AND WHAT LIES BETWEEN)

12
SPLIT IN TWO

Isle Derniére, LA (1856)

Louisiana," Awiti said. "Send it to Louisiana."

Awiti had spent much time in Louisiana, and her memories called her there often.

She often said, "I believe a slave ship took my people to Louisiana."

Perhaps my loved ones had endured the same fate. I looked forward to meeting Louisiana with my fury. So I demanded of Awiti,

"Take me."

Louisiana was where Awiti saw the heads of our people placed on poles. The land was filled with the presence of many like me. Those who died with a sorrow so great, they were destined to remain in the spiritual realm forever.

Yet nothing Awiti shared prepared me for Louisiana. I listened to the spirits of slaves, each story of hardship more horrific than the last. But the spirits all agreed—1140 Royal Street, at the Corner of Royal Street and Hospital Street, was a place of great suffering.

The building was a large residence of sorts. It stood abandoned and clearly devastated by an unforgiving fire. Charred, burned wooden beams littered the ground. Broken glass lay scattered about, fallen from the large windows that were once picturesque. But even the burned, impoverished condition of the home could not mask the abuse that occurred there.

Evidence of torture remained among the debris. Chains sat among the blackened wood and soot. And the slave spirits of those who were unfortunate enough to reside there while they were among the living, their presence filled the entire dwelling. The house resounded with lamenting as they all cried out.

"Madame LaLaurie loves to whip me. She whips me simply to see wounds appear on my skin. Then, once my skin is broken and there is blood coming from my wounds, she rubs salt into them," the spirit of a young woman told me.

"Do not go to the upper room in the left wing. For no one who goes there ever returns," an older spirit warned.

"Madame LaLaurie gouged out Pierre's eyes. He will never see again! And he has done nothing! Nothing!"

"Leah fell from the roof! Madame LaLaurie done killed her! We must tell her mother. Someone run get Delphine! Quick!"

The spirits continued to resonate their stories, their voices filled with fear as they remained trapped in their greatest moments of torment. They echoed throughout the burned dwelling as Awiti walked about the ruins, stroking chains that once bound wrists and ankles.

"Leah is here," Awiti said. She called out to her, "Leah?"

"Yes, ma'am."

Leah appeared before us, hazy and soft as smoke coming

from a pipe. She was a young slave girl. No more than twelve or thirteen years of age. Her white dress was shabby, full of holes and tears. Her dark hair disheveled. And her youthful body mangled, limbs broken and bashed.

She looked as she did the day she died. Her appearance evidence of the harm done to her. Some spirits choose not to show themselves for this reason, preferring only to be heard. But Leah wanted us to see her.

"What happened to you?" Awiti asked.

I also inquired, "Who would hurt a young girl in a cruel way?"

"Madame LaLaurie," Leah replied. "I was brushing her hair when I caught a knot and the brush snagged. Her head jerked a bit, and she screamed at me. I tried to tell her it was an accident, but she chased me with a whip. She whipped me as I ran. See these cuts? Here and here? I ran to the roof, and there was no other way to escape her but to jump."

Leah paused before continuing.

"And so I jumped."

The charred mansion grew quiet.

"But I am free now." Leah's mangled form faded away.

The spirits began to speak in earnest as Leah disappeared.

"Madam LaLaurie chained Jean to the stove. She wanted her to cook on command. Wouldn't let her leave the kitchen. Any business she had to do, she had to do right at that stove. Had her baby right there," an older man said.

"In the torture room, Madame LaLaurie hung slaves. Stretched them out till their arms and legs broke right off their bodies. It was in the papers. Lots of folks was angry, but nothing was done to Madame LaLaurie."

I could stand it no longer. I imagined my sons being

stretched. And my wives! What if Madame LaLaurie forced them to jump to their deaths?

"Where can I find this Madame LaLaurie?" I asked, my anger evident.

"She is gone. Escaped on the ferry. You will never find her. No matter where you go in the world. Many spirits have tried. Wanted her to pay for what she done to 'em. She gone, but there's plenty more like her."

"And where can I find those like her?" I demanded.

"The Isle Derniére. That's where those like Madame LaLaurie like to go," one of the spirits said with certainty. "I will show you where."

We came upon a small island off the coast of Louisiana. It looked like any other island. Light sand, dotted with green trees, surrounded by blue waters. White people walked about the island. They swam in the waters as the descendants of my people watched over their children and fixed meals.

The Isle Derniére was an obvious place of happiness for those like Madame LaLaurie. Their contentment rose above the clouds and filled the atmosphere. It made me even angrier. How I wished to be content. I knew what I had to do. I had never been so certain.

Awiti felt the same as she said to me, "Let's destroy them."

Awiti and I returned to the shores of Western Africa. We followed the routes of the slave ships, moving slowly and deliberately across the Atlantic. We called out to the stolen lives who had died at sea. The storm grew as they joined us, our winds and rain gaining momentum with each restless spirit.

Beyond a storm, we became a hurricane. Deadly and furious as we focused on the Isle Derniére. We came upon the island with the element of surprise, just as the slave raiders had attacked our villages.

Awiti and I were not impartial with our wrath. We did not mind watching the descendants of our people drown as they tried to save their masters' children and things. Their suffering was necessary.

Death would afford them freedom. If they chose to cross over, they would forever be free from a life of bondage. And if their spirit would not allow it, if the lives they lived were filled with unforgivable abuse, they would stay with us in the spiritual realm.

I took great pleasure in destroying the Isle Derniére, the force of our hurricane so great we split the island in two. With our heavy rain, we submerged the island and watched the faces of men, women, and children suffering. They screamed as my children had screamed. I watched them drown in the waves. Just as my people had drowned when thrown off the slave ships. I felt nothing but joy.

At the end of our wrath, once our hurricane winds and the rain ended, nothing remained of the Isle Derniére. All of it submerged in the water. It ceased to exist.

What I felt was not a total and complete happiness. The obliteration of their island did not bring back my family. Death and destruction did not return me to the life I had before the slave raiders came to my village. I waited for my spirit to cross over. But it never did. And I know why.

Louisiana still existed. As did other lands where my people suffered. The destruction of the Isle Derniére was nothing more than a small victory. But it helped me come to understand my destiny. I realized a new purpose with those in the spiritual realm. And together, we continued the wrath of our retribution.

13

PEACE

Effingham County, GA (1881)

From the outside, 447 McGregor Street looked like the home of Walter and Mable Lee. Red shutters framed the windows. The small two-bedroom house was a perfect square—framed weather-worn wood topped with a tin roof that sounded like pennies were falling on it whenever it rained. A small vegetable garden sat full of tall stalks of corn and patches of ripe greens. But on the inside, the house was still.

Walter sat in one of the chairs in the kitchen. His elbows rested on the round table, which served multiple purposes, more than the builder had intended. He had on the same clothes as the day before—a wrinkled white shirt rolled up at the sleeves and ill-fitted tan pants caked with mud.

Walter didn't move.

In fact, Walter hadn't said a word since he came home yesterday. He had thrown his work bag on the floor, sat down at the table, and assumed the position he was currently sitting in.

Mable hadn't finished setting the table for dinner. It was still covered with the ears of corn Mable planned on shucking.

Mable wanted to clear off the table, but she wouldn't touch a thing. She was afraid to come near her husband.

Walter could feel Mable staring at him. His wife's eyes were searching, questioning, *What the hell happened?*

Walter wanted to talk to Mable about it. They had shared a lot over the years. Everything, actually. They knew everything there was to know about each other. Like Mable growing up the only girl child in a house full of boys becoming men. There was no father to tell them not to force open the legs of their sister. And so Mable learned to be strong, to fight and hide. And when those tactics no longer worked, she ran away.

Mable's mother made certain her children went to church every Sunday. She talked to God, the preacher, and anyone else who was willing to help her raise four children. She spent plenty of time warning Mable to be wary of men with dreamy eyes. To watch out for tall brown-skinned men with deep voices full of empty promises. But she never thought to warn Mable of her brothers.

The siblings shared the only bedroom in the small house, while Mable's mother slept in whatever spot she could find. Often this was in the main room on a bed made of straw covered with thick blankets. She worked day and night to support her children, taking small naps in between. And so Mable often found herself alone with her brothers.

Although their mother gave strict instructions for the boys to take care of their sister, they did everything but. Those early, dark years of Mable's life were a secret, one she only shared with her husband. Walter kept his promise and never told a soul.

And Walter had shared with Mable his fear of being lynched. The choking thoughts of having a noose around his neck, his body hanging and swaying in the wind. Memories of hiding in the bushes with his father always present in his mind.

They watched the Klan kill his Uncle Jon. The men in white enjoyed it. Laughing and taunting Walter's favorite uncle as they tied a noose around his neck and hanged him from a cypress tree.

Walter tried to escape the memory. But it was always so fresh, so real. He could smell the damp air, feel the bushes scratching at his skin. Walter felt bugs crawling up his legs, biting him. His father's eyes staring with a look that said,

"No matter what, son, don't make a sound."

And because they had been so still, Walter remembered Uncle Jon's gasping last breaths. He watched his uncle sway back and forth, the weight of his lifeless body making the branch creak. They waited until the threat of the Klan was gone. Only then did Walter's father cut down Uncle Jon.

Walter often had terrible dreams about Uncle Jon's murder, accompanied by loud screaming and night sweats. Mable always consoled him, never made him feel ashamed. She stayed awake and talked with him if he wished. And when he wanted to lie in silence, she stroked his back and said nothing.

So it wasn't Walter couldn't tell Mable what happened on his way home. He didn't know *how*.

"I saw ghosts at Ebenezer Creek," he could say.

Or perhaps, even better,

"I saw ghosts at Ebenezer Creek, and they spoke to me."

Mable would think he'd gone mad. Walter didn't know how to begin to tell her. So he simply said nothing.

Walter hadn't seen one or two haunts. There were many. They had called out, reaching for him with their bloated limbs and swollen faces.

Mable walked over to the stove. She was relentless, determined. Walter both loved and hated that about her.

"Want to talk about it?" Mable asked as she poured water into the kettle and lit the stovetop.

It was her relentless way of saying, "We *will* talk about it. Wherever you're ready, of course."

But would he ever be ready?

Ebenezer Creek was plagued by rumors, tales of ghosts who haunted the water and cried whenever the creek rose. The stories were always conflicting. The only thing certain was many Negroes died in the waters of Ebenezer Creek. Old folks said it was best to stay away.

Walter had listened to the warnings all of his life, carefully avoiding the creek, taking the longer route wherever he needed to go. But the older he became, the sillier it all seemed. In fact, it was downright ridiculous.

He was a man. Married with a wife and young child. It seemed so foolish to take a detour to avoid an old creek. Walter wanted to get home as soon as possible. And the extra time spent traveling to and from work was wearing on him.

Walter had started counting the time he spent traveling. Time felt like money he was wasting, precious. Walter knew exactly how he would spend each minute. More time playing with his baby girl when he got home. Extra time with Mable in the evening. They could sit out back and talk like they used to. All the time he was wasting. It frustrated him.

"C'mon, honey," Mable said. "You know you can tell me anything."

Mable was pleading now. She had stayed in the kitchen with him all night. Walter opened his mouth to speak, but his words were trapped. Just like the bodies.

It had been a long day at the Adams' picking cotton and chopping wood. Unlike most employers, Mr. Adams paid his field hands a fair wage at the end of each week. He was the most respectable share cropper in Springfield, and Walter had been lucky to get the job. After collecting his pay, he was eager to get home.

Walter came to the familiar fork in the road—the path on the right leading to the long route home, and the left pathway leading toward Ebenezer Creek. He did something he had never done before. Walter turned left onto the dirt road.

He made quick strides, following the pathway a few feet away from the bank. The walk was easy, peaceful even. Lofty trees with full foliage shaded the edge of the creek. Their roots were exposed, coming out of the water to form little woven huts at the base. Walter was all too familiar with cypress trees.

Walter's pace began to slow. His feet and mind were in disagreement about what to do next. He heard the words as plain as day.

"Come here, Walter."

It did not take long for them to show themselves.

Swollen, bloated faces emerged from the murky water. Their voices filled the air. Screeching, deafening and piercing.

Walter fell to his knees. What he was feeling was heavier than watching Uncle Jon hang from the tree. He remained on the ground, listening to the cries of the swollen spirits in the still water.

Walter had no words, just sounds from a voice that sounded like it didn't belong to him. He was hoarse, as if he had been crying. Had he been crying? Walter hadn't even noticed the tears on his face.

A young woman drifted toward him. Her blue dress was tattered. A red headscarf scarcely covered her dark, kinky hair. Her feet were bare, and like the rest of her body, bloated. She reminded Walter of a dead animal left in the sun.

Two children held each of her hands, a young boy on the right, and an even younger girl on the left. They were of the same tattered and engorged appearance as the woman. The girl looked to be no older than five or six, and the little boy perhaps a year her senior. Their eyes were full of sadness as they clung to the woman Walter assumed was their mother.

"They lied," she said to Walter. "Said they was gon' help us, but they drowned us. That's what they did."

Walter sat still, as unmoving as the day he hid in the bush with his father. His mind refused to believe what he was experiencing.

The woman realized Walter was of no use to her. She turned from him, her children in tow, and returned to the murky water.

Uncle Jon was everywhere. In the reflections in the water. Hanging from the cypress trees. Walter could not escape the staring eyes. They reminded him of Uncle Jon's eyes when death had set in. Dark and wet. Still and final in their gaze.

Although Walter wanted to run from the cypress trees and the memories, he couldn't move. He seemed stuck to the bank. He sat there in the mud. Green leaves touched the surface of the dark water. There were so many cypress trees. So many faces with eyes like Uncle Jon.

Walter stared as a young man appeared from amongst the trees. His wet eyes were a bluish-green. Dusty reddish-brown curls peaked out from beneath his gray cap. The young man's body, while hazy, was not bloated and puffed. His feet were bare, and his simple clothing torn and nearly ripped apart from an apparent struggle.

"She tellin' the truth, she is," the young man said.

He told the story in one long, continuous sentence, hurried.

"We was followin' the Union soldiers after they freed us. Tryin' to help 'em any way we could. Walked 'cross Georgia makin' our way North. Then we come to this creek here. Ain't no bridge to cross over, so we helps the soldiers build one. General tell his soldiers to go over first. Say once the last soldier over safe, then we can come. But when the last soldier cross, General tell his men to destroy the bridge. We don't know what to do. We trapped. Can't cross if it ain't no bridge. Can't turn around, 'cause Confederates not far behind."

"So what happened?" Walter asked.

The question was unnecessary. Walter knew what happened. He was surrounded by swollen bodies in Ebenezer Creek.

"Folks start to panic," the young man continued. "Try to swim 'cross, but they can't. Other folks pushed by the folks behind them. They tryin' to get away from them Confederates. It's December, so the water real cold. Feel like ice. Folks drowned. Union supposed to help us. That was they job. To help us. But they didn't."

The young man paused.

"I fought through all them bodies and got out the river," he said. "Made it to the trees. Thought I was gon' make it. But Confederates found me and shot me dead."

The wet blue-green eyes searched Walter. They wanted something Walter couldn't give.

Walter's memories were interrupted by knocking. Mable ran to the front door and flung it open as though whoever was on the other side was there to rescue them. Walter saw the silhouette of their visitor. It was his granny.

"What you done did, Walter?" she asked.

Like when he was a child, her tone implied she already knew Walter had done *something*.

"Went down by dat creek, didn't you?" she demanded. "I see it in ya' eyes. Somethin' told me one day, 'Walter is gon' go down by da creek.' You never did mind!"

Granny opened the kitchen cupboard and grabbed the salt dish. She began to sprinkle salt all over the house, praying as the salt fell from her fingers. Mable watched the entire scene, disconnected as if it wasn't taking place right there in her home.

"Seen dem spirits?" Granny asked.

Walter nodded his head. Mable sat down on the chair opposite Walter. She put her head on the table, next to the ears of unshucked corn, and began to cry.

"What dey tell ya'?" Granny asked. "Spirits told you something, didn't dey? What dey tell ya'!"

Walter closed his eyes. He was back on the banks of Ebenezer Creek.

He remembered the beautiful young woman coming forth from the dark waters. She wore a white robe and looked as alive as Walter. She seemed like a rising angel from amongst the dead.

The brown woman came and stood right across from him. Her dark hair flowed down her back. Walter found himself staring into her small dark pupils. He felt her breath on his face as she asked him,

"You see what has happened here?"

"Yes," Walter responded.

"I have to make it right. Help these folks find peace."

"Okay." Walter wasn't certain of what else he should say.

"You know what I'm going to do? To make it right?"

"No, ma'am." Walter tried not to scream. He was talking to a spirit. A real live haunt.

"All of us here, we going to gather up our memories, the wrongs done to us. And we will send a storm to rain down on this land. And when it comes, and it's coming soon, you are to tell everyone it's the wrath of the dead at Ebenezer Creek."

Walter wished he could collect his memories of Uncle Jon. His anger at his father's cowardice. His frustration over being a boy, unable to do anything as Uncle Jon's body hung from the cypress tree. Like the spirits in Ebenezer Creek, Walter wanted to find peace.

Walter looked at Mable. He watched as Granny continued to sprinkle salt all over the house. Both women were looking at him, their heads cocked, waiting for answers. His tongue felt heavy, as if someone had control of it, making it thick and unable to move. Walter tried to speak. But his words were trapped. Like the bodies.

Walter closed his eyes. He didn't want to see Granny's blue-gray eyes staring at him like wet marbles. Or Mable's gaze burning him like hot coals. If only they could see what he saw, hear what he heard.

"Do you know what it's like to drown, Walter?" the woman asked. "To feel cold water rushing into your lungs as you gasp for air?"

"No, ma'am."

"Can you imagine reaching for your child, hearing your baby scream for you and you can't help? Everybody's trying to survive. Pulling, pushing, reaching. Drowning."

Walter didn't know what to say.

"These people didn't deserve to die that way. Hundreds and hundreds. So many, their bloated bodies formed a make-shift dam for weeks while they lay dead."

"It's a shame, is what it is."

"It's more than a shame, Walter," the woman said as she walked to the river's edge, her hands outstretched to a ghostly figure. They didn't touch, as there was no way for them to embrace. "It's not right. But that's what I intend to do. Make it right. Need some folks to know that drowning feeling. Need them to know what loss feels like."

Walter opened his eyes. Granny and Mable were still there, staring at him, their eyes looking like they could set the wooden table on fire if they tried. Granny's wet eyes burned the most as she yelled,

"Answer me, boy!"

He wanted to tell them what he had seen. How all those bodies at Ebenezer Creek had called out to him. That the woman in white was going to make it right. But the only words Walter could say were,

"Hurricane coming."

14
EVERYONE ELSE
IS GONE

Laforche, Terrebonne, LA (1893)

Whenever I hear rain falling or know a storm is coming, I feel sick. There's no tonic that can make the illness go away. Most times I vomit. Even if the rainfall is light, more of a shower than a downpour, it doesn't matter. The sound of rain takes me back to that day.

We moved to the beautiful island of Cheniere Caminada on September 26, 1893. My folks hoped to start a new life for us. But by October 7, 1893, the island was gone. The dream Francisco Caminada envisioned and that my parents believed in was washed away.

Father had wanted to move for the work opportunities. Cheniere Caminada was becoming a tourist town, and that meant more money for fishermen. Mother, ever the optimist, believed the coastal waters would cure the rheumatism that plagued her. She could not contain her excitement.

"We are moving to Cheniere Caminada! There we will live

like those on the Grand Isle. The sun, the sand, the beaches. Why, I can hear them calling my name!"

"Calling my name" was one of Mother's favorite phrases. When something was calling her name, it meant she was excited.

Sammy and I dreamed of endless days spent swimming and searching for crabs. We were young, so a move for us meant another adventure. New experiences and friends. We were eager to leave our old lives behind.

And life on Cheniere Caminada was good. Plenty of fresh catch, new faces as lots of folks visited and met with Francisco to discuss his plans. As short-lived as it was, it was the best few weeks of my childhood. That is, before the storm.

No one thought the storm would be as bad as it was. The people of Cheniere Caminada believed this storm would be like all the others. There would be violent wind and rain. And of course damage, and perhaps even a small loss of life. But we believed the island would survive. We were wrong.

The storm was unlike anything we had ever seen. A few of us lived to tell about it. Everyone else is gone.

The bodies of our mother and father were never found. Or perhaps they were, but whoever found them thought it best to shield me and Sammy from their deaths. To let us remember our parents healthy and strong. Vibrant and full of life.

Had they stayed with us at the Archambaults, perhaps they would have survived. But Father had wanted to return home to gather a few last minute supplies.

"We will be right back, Sebastian," Father told me. "Watch over Sammy until we return."

I wish they'd never left.

When they walked out the door, the wind was starting to pick up speed. It blew with a seriousness that let us know a hurricane was coming. When they did not return by the time the first rain began to fall, I was only slightly worried. Light rainfall was always the beginning. Many people were still outside boarding up their windows and doors. There was still time.

"Don't worry, Sebastian," Mr. Archambault encouraged me. "They'll be back in time."

The rainfall became more intense, and the winds blew harder. Debris began to scrape against the sides of the Archambaults' storm shelter. I panicked, anxious for my parents to return.

"Is that them?" I asked. Every bump against the shelter sounded like my parents knocking to get inside.

"No, Sebastian. It's just loose items outside hitting the shelter. Try not to worry," Mr. Archambault added. "I promise to leave the deadbolt unlocked as long as possible."

A few moments later, when the wind caused the shelter to sway slightly, Mr. Archambault went and locked the door, shutting us all in tight. Our parents were locked out for good.

I didn't blame Mr. Archambault. He had a wife and three small children to protect as well as two other families who sought refuge with us. And the D'Aubignes had a newborn baby girl. I understood everyone's lives could not be risked on the account of our parents. But I was still sad.

The shelter rattled as the wind blew against the wooden boards, trying to find a way in. It was a frightening sound, but not as frightening as the screams of the people who remained outside. Those who didn't make it to their places of refuge. I prayed my parents were not among them, that they had found a safe haven somewhere.

"I know what you're thinkin', Sebastain," Mr. Archambault

said. "Your father is smart. I am certain they realized they wouldn't make it back in time and hunkered down where they were."

I knew they would not make it back to the Archambaults until the storm subsided. All I could do was hope they survived.

The hurricane thrashed about violently, attacking the Archambault's storm shelter from every angle. I had been in other storms, but I had never heard rain come down so hard and the winds howl so loud. We were inside the eye of the hurricane. Father always called it the belly of the beast. We could feel its power as it devoured our island.

Mr. Archambault worried the shelter might rip apart at any moment.

"Gather close together," he instructed. He sat on the floor next to his wife as his children assembled close to their father. Even though they were afraid, being with their father made them feel safe. It made me long for Father even more.

"Do not go near the door, Sebastian," Mr. Archambault said to me sharply. Perhaps he was afraid I would try to open it for my parents in a moment of desperation. But I would do no such thing. I was afraid to move.

We listened to the ocean crashing against the shores. The hurricane seemed angry with us. The sounds of the wind and rain were interwoven with the fervent screaming of those stranded outside. Cries circled around the Archambault's storm shelter as the wind tossed about our friends and neighbors. Trees, wood from houses, anything not bolted to the ground or built to withstand the wind flew about the island, hitting the shelter randomly.

Each bump and thud caused us to jump and the women and children to scream. The wind wailed like a frightened woman. It howled and whistled as its wrath rained down on Cheniere Caminada.

It seemed the hurricane would never end Would the screaming never cease? Sammy covered his ears with his hands and rocked back and forth. The storm shelter rattled and swayed in the wind, and the roof buckled as the wives clung to their husbands and the children clung to their mothers.

And because we only had each other, Sammy and I held each other close. I longed for our parents to be with us, to hear my mother's calming voice. I tried my best to comfort him.

"There, there, Sammy," I said repeatedly. "Everything is going to be all right."

But everything wasn't all right. The inside of the storm shelter grew darker until we were encased in blackness. We could make out the forms of each other and hear the cries of the children, so we knew were still alive. In time, we seemed to tolerate the darkness. Even the children grew silent as we listened to the storm swirling around us. And I believed we would have been fine. Until we saw her face.

"Look there, Sebastian," Sammy whispered to me. "Look there above!"

If he was gesturing, I could not see his hands, and so I looked up. And there on the storm shelter's ceiling was the face of a Negro woman.

"My Lord," Mr. Archambault called out.

The women began to scream as the Negro woman looked down at us. Her dark eyes were angry, and as she opened her mouth, she howled with the storm winds. The shelter grew cold, and I could feel Sammy shivering in my arms.

"In the name of Jesus, leave this place," Mr. D'Aubigne

shouted. He ordered her to leave us, to take fear in Jesus and return to Hell where she belonged. But she remained.

"Close your eyes, Sammy," I whispered. "Just close your eyes!" I did the same, peeking periodically only to see the Negro woman still looking down on us with angry eyes, her voice wailing with the winds.

Eventually, the winds ceased, and the rainfall became slow and steady before ending all together. As abruptly as it had begun, the hurricane was over. Still, we were afraid for Mr. Archambault to open the door. His storm shelter was beaten with wind and rain and seemed a bit unstable. One wrong move might cause the entire dwelling to collapse on us.

We were also afraid of what we would see. Once the howling wind moved on, we could hear more clearly the cries for help, the moaning of people. Some were calling out the names of those who they had become separated from during the swirling, wet madness. Our parent's voices were not among them.

Of course we could not stay in the storm shelter forever, so Mr. Archambault went to open the door. Only, it would not budge. He was a strong man, and he pushed with all his might, but still the door refused to open.

"Come and help me," Mr. Archambault said to Mr. D'Aubigne.

Stepping away from his wife and children, Mr. D'Aubigne went to help him open the door. They grunted as they pushed with their shoulders and hands, their voices showing the extent of their effort. Neither man mentioned the Negro woman. And I knew better than to ask.

Finally, the door pushed open. It was a small crack, but the sunlight came rushing in, the bright light blinding us. We could feel the fresh air, and through the crack, we discovered what made opening the door such a challenging effort. Dead bodies were piled amongst the trees and debris. They fell into the storm shelter as the door opened further.

An island that yesterday was a bustling, thriving community was now gone. There were a few structures barely standing. The rest were fallen to the ground or blown away as if they had never existed at all. On the dwellings that still remained, the roofs were caved in, the sides of houses collapsed, like a ramshackle deck of cards.

Dead bodies lay all about the island— men, women, children, and young infants. The storm had not been kind or courteous to the young or old. Those near death cried out for our help, but we could not move, over feet cemented to the ground in shock. The sand was littered with the dead, like human seaweed washed ashore. Many of their eyes and mouths were open. They looked surprised the storm had taken their lives.

Those of us who were living could only stare at the destruction, not knowing what to do first. The hurricane had leveled the land. God had wiped away the island with His omnipotent hands, and there was nothing left. And Cheniere Caminada was so far away from the other parishes, we wondered if anyone would ever learn of our devastation and come help us.

The men recovered from their shock before the women and the children. Samuel and I stood and watched helplessly as the men began to take action. I wanted to look for our parents, and yet I did not want to look for our parents. As my eyes adjusted to the carnage, I could see how terrible of a hurricane this had been. I knew our parents did not survive.

As we ventured outside of the storm shelter, not only were bodies strewn all over the sandy beaches, but the dead and barely living seemed to be everywhere. They were floating in the ocean where they had been washed out to sea.

Trees leaned toward the earth from being battered by the wind, their trunks and branches bent and broken and tangled with the bodies of our neighbors. The branches held the people of Cheniere Caminada by their hair and clothing.

It was too much carnage for the adults to see, let alone children. Samuel cried as I held him close.

"There, there, Sammy," I said.

I tried to comfort him and sound like our mother.

"Everything will be fine."

But would things ever be fine for me and Samuel? Our parents were gone, among the sand, ocean, or trees.

The men were stacking the bodies of the dead, trying to distinguish them from the survivors. I heard Mr. Archambault say, "I know they are children, but we need their help. They can help us dig graves."

My eyes caught his, and I knew he needed us. The people of Cheniere Caminada needed us.

Mr. D'Aubigne handed me and Samuel large sticks and told us to dig shallow holes in the ground. The men moved body after body, stacking them next to the shallow graves and throwing them inside as soon as we were finished.

Burying the dead was necessary to prevent the spreading of disease and sickness. It was painful, sad work, and we cried as we dug graves and listened to the moans and weeping all around us.

"Mr. Beauchamp," Mr. Archambault said.

He was standing over the dead body of a tall, thin man dressed rather smartly. The man's navy blue suit fit precisely over a crisp white shirt. It was the kind of suit my father only wore to church and funerals.

Mr. Beauchamp's shiny black shoes were only outdone by his shimmering gold jewelry. There were gold chains about his neck, and rings of gold sat on his fingers. Mr. Beauchamp appeared to be in a deep, peaceful sleep. But I knew he was not sleeping. I knew he was dead.

Mr. Archambault said to Mr. D'Aubigne, "Come over and help me now. No need to bury these good things. Like they say, you can't take your possessions with ya'."

Sammy and I watched as the men stripped Mr. Beauchamp of his clothing, shoes, and jewelry before throwing his naked body into a shallow grave. This scene was repeated many times on any man, woman, or child who wore something of value.

Time passed slowly, so painstakingly, many of those who had survived the hurricane were now among the dead. We started to believe the neighboring parishes were also destroyed and that no one would ever come to our aid.

People rationed food and water and continued to dig holes, larger ones, for the dead were beginning to decay, and it was easier to dig large graves for many bodies. We needed to bury them before disease infected us all.

My mind and body were numb as I helped throw bodies into shallow mass graves. I was certain someone had found our parents' bodies. They had buried them quickly so Samuel and I would not be subjected to the memory of our parents among the dead. Still, as I touched the dead bodies, I could imagine my parents laid along the beach or their bodies hanging from the trees.

At night, it was hard to sleep. The sound of the hurricane still howled in my ears. Would it return and take the rest of us away in a swirl of wind and rain? I wondered if the screaming I had heard during the storm was the wind, or the cries of my parents being washed out to sea. Sammy remained at my side, and understandably so. We only had each other.

When we saw the relief boat on the horizon, we all cheered. News of our disaster had reached New Orleans, and the Picayune sent a steamer to aid us, *The Emma McSweeny*. Never was I so thankful for food and fresh water.

The doctors checked us to make certain we were healthy, and while Sammy and I were fine physically, mentally we would never be the same. Reporters took sketches of us at the scene and asked us questions.

"What was it like?" one reporter asked me. "Can you tell us what the hurricane was like?"

"The winds howled and screamed as if they were angry with us. The rain came down as if the heavens had opened."

"You have survived quite a storm, young man," the reporter encouraged. "You are lucky to be alive. Do tell, if you can, what was the worst part of the storm?"

I was quiet while I thought of my response. And then, I spoke of what I remembered the most.

"Well I suppose when we first opened the storm shelter door and I saw all of the dead bodies. That was something awful. And losing my parents. Knowing they are dead and that I will never see them again. And the Negro woman. Perhaps the worst part of the storm was the Negro woman who watched us and screamed as the hurricane almost washed us away. Even now that we are safe, I cannot forget her face."

15

I SHOWED MYSELF

Beaufort, South Carolina (1893)

Some places just filled with more hate than others. Cities and towns where soon as you step on the land you can feel hate creeping up through the soles of your feet. Burning hatred. Pulsing through your body and causing tiny hairs to rise on the small of your back. Next thing you know, you so hot that your body turns cold. Those tiny hairs freeze up on your skin like early morning frost.

Hot. Then cold. That's the sign. It's funny how the body knows where it ain't wanted. Folks need to learn to watch for that hot-cold feeling. They need to listen to that voice inside saying,

"Run quick now. Your kind ain't welcome here."

Might save them some trouble.

At the Davis Plantation, hate lived in the soil. Crops grew hate, and folks ate it right up. White bellies full of hatred for Black skin. Slaves wishing they could peel off each layer of flesh in the hopes they would turn White and be free. Trees grew strong and tall, their big green leaves helping the wind blow hate all across the land.

I used to think the Davis Plantation was the only place hate lived. It seemed to sprout out from the ground and cover the fields. It lived in the air of the slave quarters and dripped from the moans of slaves every night. Hate spewed like fire from the angry voices of White men and rained down its fury through the overseer's whip. Every day, hate cracked the air and split the skin on the backs of slaves. It grew in puffs of cotton and hid among the tall stalks of sugar cane. Everywhere I went there hate was.

Slaves new to the Davis Plantation had stories about the hate they escaped. Somebody always had a story worse than the last. Wasn't long before they realized they hadn't gotten away. Folks learned quick the Davis Plantation was just as full of hate as everywhere else. No way to outrun it. No way to out-love it. No way to outlive it. Hate just is, and it's always gon' be.

When I was with Mama and it used to rain, she'd always say, "God crying."

Mama had a way of making every word sound like a song. I was scared of storms, so whenever it rained, she'd rock me in her arms and sing-talk to me. Some of my favorite memories are being with Mama during storms, her brown skin soft and warm like fresh bread wrapped around me.

"His tears gon' wash the land and make everything all right," she'd sing-talk. "Don't be afraid of God's tears and thunder. Don't worry now."

And Mama would always remind me, "God know what He doing."

Well, I kept waiting for God to make everything right.

With each storm, I prayed God would figure out a way to take away the hate. Wanted God to drown it in a big puddle. Or wash away all the evil people like He did with Noah and the flood. But after every rainfall, hate was still there. Hanging on like dew.

I used to wonder what was taking God's tears so long to do the job. Since Mama said God knew what He was doing and all. Truth be told, God's tears ain't got no power. Mama told me them words to make me feel safe. God ain't got the power to cleanse places where hate run deep. Even God ain't strong enough for that.

Seems like God's tears ain't do nothing but soak the hate deeper into the ground. Nourish the dirt so more hate can grow. Massa's hate covered us in thick dust that lingered on our skin. Hate sat in our hair, coating each strand and itching our scalps. And not just the slaves who were old and weary, those working the fields. Hate covered us all. Even the children.

It sure is something when folks learn about slave children. Folks don't want to believe there were children who suffered and died. It's easier to imagine children enjoy childhood, even slaves. Children are supposed to laugh and play in the sunshine. They should sleep under warm blankets at night.

It's easier for folks to think, 'Slave children might have suffered some, but not too much."

Perhaps this was true for some slave children. Not for me, though. I suffered more in my short life than I was happy. I died right there on Davis Plantation. And stayed there after my death. Even after the Massa packed up and moved away. And I was alone for many years.

One day I was playing in the cotton field. It's one of my

favorite places. That's where I used to work with Mama. I'd stand right by her side and help her pick white clouds of cotton. Sometimes she'd look at me, and we'd share our secret smile. If she winked, that meant the overseer wasn't nearby, so I could take a little break. And every so often, if Mama found a time when no one was looking, she'd reach down and kiss me on my cheek.

Awiti showed up right there in the middle of my memory. I saw her walking across the cotton field wearing a long white dress. First thing I thought was how pretty she was.

She walked up to me like she could see me and said, "My name is Awiti. What's your name, young man?"

"Amos."

And I went back to running through the puffs of unpicked cotton. I wished I could touch them again, feel their softness in my hands.

"What happened to you, Amos?"

"Oh, Missus Awiti," I warned, "you don't want to know what happened to me. It ain't nothing kind."

"Yes I do, Amos. Tell me. Please."

My death was a memory I tried not to think about often. I didn't really want to tell Awiti what happened to me, but she insisted. Said she had to know. So I told her how it all began. And how it ended.

One night, Massa came to Mama's cabin and said, "Come here, boy." He gestured for me to take his hand. "I need you to do something real special for me."

"Yes, Massa."

I was proud he picked me to do something special. I hugged Mama and walked straight to Massa. He was a tall man, even taller than my pappy who was sold away. Massa took me by the hand, and we walked to the big house. That was my first time inside the big house. I wanted to touch something, to see if things was real, but I didn't. I was never one to get into trouble.

We walked up the winding staircase to Massa's bedroom. It was a large room, with high ceilings and lots of windows with heavy, shiny, white curtains hanging to the floor. The Missus was in the bed. She was covered with lots of thick blankets and looked to be sleeping.

All the slaves said the Missus was set die soon. She was a pretty lady and always kind. But once she got sick, we didn't see her as often. And whenever we did see the Missus, she looked frail. Like if she fell down she would break into little pieces. I remember hoping she didn't die while I was in the room that night.

I stood by the side of the bed, and the Missus opened her eyes. She gave me a weak smile before closing her eyes and going back to sleep. Then I felt Massa's hands around my waist. He pulled my pants down to the floor. I stood there naked, feeling ashamed. I didn't feel right being in the Massa's bedroom without my pants on.

"Get in the bed, boy," Massa said. "Lie at the bottom."

I tried to do as Massa instructed. That was the first thing Mama taught me—always mind what Massa say to do. But the bed was large and wide, made of dark wood and four tall posts, one at each corner. It was high, and I couldn't climb in by myself. Massa reached down, picked me up, and put me in the bed with the Missus.

I lay across the bottom of the bed like Massa said. The white sheets were cool and soft. Goosebumps started to form on my naked body. There was that hot-cold feeling on my skin, but I didn't know what it meant back then.

Massa lifted the blankets from the Missus. Then he took her feet and placed them on my chest and stomach. The Missus' feet were cold. Massa made me stay there all night to keep them warm. He looked at me and smiled as I warmed the Missus' feet. That was why he needed me.

I warmed the Missus' feet until the day she died. That was a sad morning. The Missus was nice, and death always seemed wrong when it happened to nice people. After she died, I thought I would return to being with Mama at night. I was looking forward to sleeping with her again. But the same day they buried the Missus, Massa come to get me. Mama's eyes filled with tears.

"Be strong, baby," she told me.

That hot-cold feeling come over me right then. And it never went away until the day I died.

When we got to Massa's bedroom, he made me undress like before. And when I lay in the bed, he lay right beside me. Massa touched all over my naked body. He felt on the part that made me a boy until it became hard. I felt strange inside. And afraid. Every part of me was hot-cold. And I started to cry.

"Don't cry, Amos," Massa said. "Nothing is wrong. You belong to me."

After Massa touched on me, he made me lie at the foot of the bed like normal, and he put his big feet against my naked body. Massa slept, but I stayed awake all night.

I wanted to cry again, but I was afraid. I didn't want to wake Massa and have him start touching on me again. And the hot-cold feeling wouldn't let me sleep. Voice inside kept telling me to get up and run, but I couldn't move.

Massa touched on me for a few nights, and then, one night, he made me touch him. He took the parts that made him a man and put them in my mouth. I tried to fight him, but Massa slapped me across the face so hard I fell to the floor.

"Stop crying, boy," he yelled. "You mind what I say! You belong to me. Now you mind what I say!"

Then Massa did things to my body. Bad things that made my insides hurt. And every night, up until the day I died, Massa hurt my body with his own. At the time, I didn't think I was dying. Just thought I was suffering from having Massa's hate inside me. But I was—dying, that is.

The night I died, Massa seemed sad. He pulled out his bible and asked God to forgive him. Then Massa wrapped my body in his bloodied sheets and buried me on the part of the plantation the slaves were forbidden. He buried me along with his hate and his secrets, all of it covered with dirt in a shallow grave.

But someone was always watching. Old Jonny told Mama what he saw that night—Massa out walking late at night with a shovel and carrying something wrapped in a white sheet that looked to be my size.

I watched from above as Mama cried on the floor of her cabin all night. Some of her friends tried to comfort her, but she couldn't stop weeping. Seeing Mama cry was hard. I wanted her to know the pain was over, but there was no way for us to be together again.

It wasn't even two days after Massa killed me that he went to the slave quarters and took another boy from his mama's bed. The boy's name was Antony, and he was a tad younger than me. We used to play together before I died. Antony was nice boy.

I couldn't stop looking over the plantation. I didn't want Antony to suffer the way I had. So I pushed down. I went into the Massa's bedroom right as he was pulling down Antony's pants. And I showed myself.

Seemed like Massa didn't believe what he was seeing. He blinked several times. I stood real still because I wanted him to know it was me. Antony ran from the room, his pants gathered around his little ankles.

He yelled, "It's a haunt in the house!" His screams pierced the quiet stillness of the house.

The chambermaids came running, and I pushed myself up out of Massa's bedroom and faded into the night. Antony's pants were still around his ankles, his nakedness exposed. The chambermaids looked on the scene and said nothing. But their glaring eyes shamed Massa.

Massa didn't sleep that first night I showed myself. He read from his bible and drank from a glass bottle. Seemed like me showing myself would be enough to stop Massa, but it wasn't long before he went back to the slave quarters to get Antony from his mama's bed. His mama cried and tried to hold on to him. Word had quickly spread Antony was found running from Massa's bedroom with his pants pulled down.

"Don't take my baby," Antony's mama cried.

"Shut your mouth, wench. He ain't yours, or did you forget your place? The boy belongs to me."

Massa slapped Antony's mama right across her face, so hard she fell to the ground. Then he told her to hush unless she wanted the whip.

I was waiting for Massa when they returned to his bedroom. I made sure I looked real serious. The light from the moon shined on my bruises and showed the blood running down my legs. I wished I could speak.

I wanted to scream, "You let Antony alone!"

But all I could do was show myself.

Luckily, the second time I showed myself was enough to scare Massa for good. It wasn't long before he sold his plantation. He took his slaves and his secrets to some other part of South Carolina.

I was sad to see Mama leave. Before Massa left with his slaves, Mama came to find where I was buried. She cried as she sang-talked about how much she loved me.

Lots of folks came to the plantation back then, hoping to buy it. But I didn't want nobody living here with these bad memories. So any time someone came looking to purchase the land, I showed myself. I did other things to scare folks too. Made the floors creak or the cupboards rattle. Sometimes I'd rush past folks real fast so they'd feel a cool breeze. Soon word spread the Davis Plantation was haunted, and no one wanted to buy it. So it became mine.

Only a few times I felt bad about showing myself. A real fine couple came by. A young man and his wife. The woman was real pretty. Her hair was red and shiny. She reminded me of an apple.

"Would you look at these beautiful windows, Wilbert," she said. She sounded like a good Southern lady, one who entertained like the Missus did before she got sick and died.

"Yes, Charlotte, they are lovely," her husband replied. But he didn't sound like he meant it.

I rushed past her, a colorless blur.

"Oh my," Charlotte said, gathering her shawl around her. "There is one mighty draft in here."

"Go look around the kitchen, darling," he dismissed her.

She seemed used to him being mean and wandered off to explore the house without him.

I followed her from room to room, watching her admire this and that. She talked to herself about how fabulous the floors would be once they were restored. I wasn't planning to show myself, because she seemed real nice. But then she went into the Massa's bedroom. She started twirling around the room like it's the happiest place, singing about how she finally found the house she always wanted.

I couldn't let her live here. She was nice. So I showed myself. Felt bad about scaring her. But she needed to know.

And then there was the one family I wish had bought the plantation. The family with the boy named Pete. At first, Pete was scared when he saw me. Couldn't blame him, especially seeing my soiled clothing and bruised body. He was about my age the day I died.

I smiled at him. I wanted him to know I was friendly, didn't mean him no harm. And Pete smiled back. He reached out to touch me, real slow. When his hand went right through me, he jumped back. Don't know why that made me laugh. Pete started laughing too.

While his folks looked around the house, Pete and I talked about friendship. He didn't have a lot of friends, so I promised to be his friend. We had a grand time playing hide-and-seek all about the plantation. And Pete's folks almost bought the place.

"Well, your boy sure seems to love this place," the realtor said. "What do you think, young man? Should your father buy you and your mother this place?"

"Yes, sir," Pete said. "I quite like it."

"And what do you like about it so much?" the realtor asked with a smile.

"Well, for starters," Pete began, "I've already made a friend. There's a Colored boy in here, and we've had a grand time."

Pete couldn't stop talking about all the fun we had.

"Stop talking, Pete," I whispered. "You scaring your folks."

But it was too late. Pete's mama fainted right there in the foyer. The realtor and Pete's pappy had to carry her outside to get some fresh air.

"Ain't no way they buying the house now," I said.

"I reckon you're right." Pete seemed sad about it, even sadder than me.

"Well, Pete, it sure was nice to meet you."

"Come with me," Pete begged. "We can play in whatever house my folks buy."

I wanted to go. It sounded like fun, an adventure. Problem was, unlike me, Pete wouldn't always be a young boy. So we had to say goodbye. Pete was the last friend I had until Awiti came along.

"Are there any places that don't have hate?" I asked Awiti one day.

"No such place can be found for Black people," Awiti said.

"Not one place in this whole world?"

"Not one, Amos."

This made me sad.

"Well, can we make one?" I asked. "You know, a place where Black folks can be happy?"

"And how would we do that, Amos?"

"I think we just need a place to start over. Like in the bible when God washed away the hate with rain and a big ol' flood."

"Now that I can do," Awiti said with a smile.

"You can make rain?" I asked. "And floods?"

"Yes. And you can too."

That's what I wanted to do. I could hear Mama sing-talking in my ear, telling me to make everything all right. Since God's tears couldn't do it, maybe I could try.

"Teach me, Awiti."

16
LOST AND FOUND

Galveston Bay, TX (1900)

There was a time when the Ishak lived free. We respected Mother Earth. The land and game were plentiful. The Ishak knew to take only what we needed and to leave the land as we found it. This was before the White man arrived. The Ishak and the White man, we were like day and night. We could not dwell together.

They wanted to settle the land. And they set about to destroy all life that stood in their way. Land, trees, animals, and even people. It did not matter. Whatever stood in the White man's way of what he wanted, he destroyed.

Our Chief tried to reason with the White man's chief. But he learned White men had many chiefs. And so our Chief decided, before we lost everything to the White man's need to settle, we would leave. For a danger foreseen is half-avoided.

Although many of the Ishak wanted to stay, our Chief said, "I have prayed, and the ancestors have told me what is best for the Ishak. We are one people. And we will live as one people. Let us find a new land to call home before the White man destroys us just as he has destroyed Mother Earth."

We travelled to Galveston Bay. There, with many other tribes forced to flee their homes, we found peace. The Ishak knew to walk lightly in the spring when Mother Earth was pregnant. We were wise with our resources. We knew the frog should not drink up the pond in which he lives. But the White man did not know these things.

The Ishak promised to tell each other if we ever saw White men.

"If you see the White man here in Galveston Bay, do not try to stop him. Tell the others so we can be prepared. Wherever the White man is, destruction will follow."

It was often we encountered people with black and brown skin. Runaway slaves seeking to escape the White man's need to have others to do his work. We welcomed them, understanding their desire for freedom. But living amongst us was not their intent. Most passed through. All except Awiti.

When Awiti first arrived, I could see her for who she was. A burdened spirit trapped in an immortal body. Her past was an anchor around her neck.

"I am Teche," I told her. "And you are welcome here. I know what you are, and while I do not know what ails you, come be with the Ishak. Come find peace."

As a Healer, I made it my purpose to rebuild Awiti's spirit so she would walk upright again. It is important to not let yesterday use up too much of today. I believe that is why Awiti stayed.

I never question the Great One. It is not my place. But I do know no one was created to be alone. And so the Ishak welcomed Awiti.

"One has come to live among the Ishak. She is alone, and we know this is not the way of the Great One. Let us make it known Awiti is welcome here."

That night, as we celebrated and made sacrifices in her honor, Awiti did not speak. Even in the midst of love, she was encased in her sadness.

Awiti looked like the Ishak. Brown skin and thick dark hair, her dark eyes always pleading for the love being part of a family can bring.

After much prayer, I spoke with our Chief.

"I can heal Awiti." I said. "I can calm the sadness and anger that brews within her. Let her become one of us."

With the blessing of our Chief, Awiti became one of the Ishak.

We shared a bond of suffering—the loss of our lands and family at the hands of the White man. It was often we spoke of their unbelievable arrogance to not learn our names but to call us whatever they wished. Through her travels and witnessing the cruelty of so many, Awiti understood us. Her own story was so full of pain, it was no wonder her damaged spirit weighed her down.

"You know suffering, Teche," Awiti told me one day. "But you do not know suffering like I know suffering."

"It is not my job nor does it serve any purpose to compare our wounds, Awiti. Each of us has scars. Proof our wounds have begun to heal."

"My wounds will never heal, Teche."

"Yes," I assured her, "your wounds will heal, Awiti. You will never be the same, but you will be better than who you were each day before. That is the process of healing."

I served as Awiti's Healer. My concern was not for Awiti's

immortal body, but rather for her spirit. I know spirits who are not at peace can bring about great destruction.

Awiti possessed the power to resist the temptation to destroy. This would always be a constant struggle. The battle to choose good over evil. Both the living and the dead fought this same war.

It was often I had to remind Awiti, "Life is not separate from death. It only looks that way."

Awiti's spirit would never cross over, but if she could find peace, she could live fulfilled in her immortality. This was my prayer for Awiti.

I taught her to shape-shift. She would find great pleasure turning into various animals. Her favorite was a black bird. Awiti would soar the skies of Galveston Bay wild and free, her black wings bold against the blue sky.

"Look at me, Teche," Awiti exclaimed. "Look at me fly. I am free!"

These things calmed Awiti's life force. Belonging to the Ishak. Learning to fight the constant battle between good and evil. Being able to take a form other than her immortal body. These blessings silenced the spirit of the wind that once raged inside of her. And Awiti was at peace for many years.

At first, Awiti spent much time alone. I believe she reflected on her life. She dealt with the memories she needed to put to rest. She would hunt alone, fish alone, and pray alone. But Awiti knew she was not alone, for she was one of the Ishak.

This made the difference in her healing. Soon, Awiti's spirit was in a place to be open and receptive to receiving love. And this was a good thing. For the heavens did not create the spirit to be alone. It needed love for survival, to reach its fullness.

This is why the Ishak were happy when Awiti became fond of Flying Eagle. They would fly in the blue sky together in silence. Flying Eagle knew it would take time for her spirit to be completely open to love. Partially, yes. That was always easy. But loving completely after great suffering is more difficult.

"Teche," Awiti said in disbelief, "I cannot believe there is someone to love me for what I am."

Flying Eagle was patient. And in time, Awiti was never alone. They hunted together. Fished together. Prayed together. He knew Awiti was immortal, and thus, she would not be with him forever. But it did not matter. They looked forward to the time they had to share. Knowing her life was infinite and his death was certain made them cherish each day.

You see, true love sees no fault. No obstacles. Flying Eagle did not care Awiti could not have children, or that she would always stay youthful in appearance while he grew old. One day, he would die. And that too did not matter. For they are not dead who live in the hearts they leave behind.

Flying Eagle loved Awiti for who she was. And she loved him the same. Finally, the Ishak knew Awiti's spirit had found peace. But it did not last.

"The White man has come again," our Chief warned.

The Ishak were tired of running, and so our Chief decided this time we would defend the land and fight. We believe man has responsibility, not power. And the Ishak had a responsibility to Mother Earth and our children.

We fought the White man many times at Galveston Bay. They returned with more men and a deeper determination to settle the land. Many of the Ishak died. To save those of us who remained, our Chief decided to let the White man destroy the land. For once all the trees had been cut, all the water polluted, all the animals gone, only then would the White man understand he could not eat money.

Awiti did not want to leave the land.

"I will not leave, Teche. This is our home."

I am certain she was reminded of fleeing her village. Of never seeing her family and those she loved again. None could convince her to come with us to the reservation.

And Flying Eagle would not leave her side. Others also stayed to fight while the rest of us went to the White man's reservation. There we discovered yet another form of suffering the White man can bring.

Twenty-two of the Ishak survived. They were forced to join us on the White man's reservation. They told us the stories of battles won. And of course, because they were on the reservation with the rest of us, they had lost the greatest battle.

"And what of Flying Eagle?" I asked. "And Awiti?"

"Flying Eagle has passed on, Teche. He has passed into the afterlife to be with our Ancestors."

I was told Flying Eagle died on the land fighting alongside Awiti. They said when his body fell upon the ground, Awiti's scream filled the air. The sorrow in her cry had caused the Ishak to weep.

I knew Flying Eagle's death would reopen her wounds. The pain would reawaken the angry spirit that had found peace. And Awiti would once again be lost.

The Ishak said Awiti promised revenge for Flying Eagle's death. For the damage the White man did to Mother Earth. When I heard of this, my eyes closed, and I wept. I cried for the Ishak, for Awiti, and for the wrath she would one day bring.

So I am not surprised to hear of this destruction in

Galveston Bay. We have heard the storm killed eight thousand or more. The city flooded, and many lives were destroyed. Those of us who know the power of love and the persistence of a restless spirit know this great storm is the work of Awiti. And we know there will be many more.

17
STRANGE

Black River, Jamaica (1912)

I always been strange. Not strange in a good way neither, where folks drawn to me or find me interesting. More like strange in the way I feel.

No matter where I go or what I do, I feel strange. Like somebody right behind me, watching every move I make. I've looked plenty times, hoping to catch what's making me strange. But nothing's there.

I got a chance to look in a mirror one time. That's how come I know I don't look strange, just feel strange. My skin real black. But I had known that already 'cause I see some parts of me every day. What shocked me was everything black.

Black eyes. Black skin. Black hair. Black. And real pretty. Folks say the slaves with real black skin still pure. Say we special. So I guess I'm special. And strange.

Don't know much about my past, and even less about my future. All I know is I'm a slave with no kinfolk to claim me. Nobody I can point to and say, "We family." Like I just showed up one day.

Future seem as plain. Gon' work in these cane fields till I die. Used to hate the work, but now I find it peaceful. Something about doing the harvesting calms me.

Sometimes I imagine my life before I came here. Maybe I come from a life like the overseer. With a family, a big house surrounded by trees. No cane for me to cut through. Ha! That's a dream for sure.

I can tell folks feel bad for me. They feel sorry I'm different. It's no way for me to hide the strange. It's wrapped all around me.

Most of these slaves got kin. They get together at the end of the day and feel a part of something. Not me though. I'm not part of nothing.

I got one sometime friend. Slave girl named Gaye. She real nice. Got green eyes and long brown hair in two braids down her back. She can see the strange on me, but she don't seem to mind.

One time, Gaye tried to make me a part of her something. Didn't go so good. Her people said it's something called a "duppy" following me. So I had to leave Gaye's place and go be with my strange all by myself.

Storm hit soon after Gaye's folks made me leave. It was a real bad storm, with lots of wind and rain. Gaye's folks tell everybody it's my fault. Got something to do with my strange.

Lots of folks mad at me now. Wasn't my fault though. Not like I asked the storm to come. Whole thing added to my strange.

After the storm, whenever I saw Gaye in the fields, she didn't speak. Even when I tried to wave to her in secret. Day after day, she passed right by me. Seem like a long time, and soon, I gave up.

I got lost chopping cane. Found peace being alone with my strange. Every now and again, I'd catch Gaye looking at me. Staring at me with them sad green eyes. Until yesterday.

Was swinging my machete, making the cane fall, and here come Gaye. Came right up on me and said, "Come with me quick! Now!"

I dropped everything and went running, following after Gaye. We was hidden amongst the tall stalks of cane in no time.

"Sorry my folks won't let me talk to you," Gaye said. "I feel real bad about it, 'cause I likes you."

This made me smile. Gaye still liked me, strange and all.

"Feel bad you all you got," she continued.

"Me too," I wanted to say. "Except I'm not alone, remember? Got my strange with me everywhere I go. And that duppy your folks was talking about."

But I don't say nothing. Just keep listening.

"I asked my folks," Gaye whispered. "Asked them why folks leave you alone the way they do."

Can't believe Gaye did all that asking for me. Guess she my friend after all.

"You know what my folks say?"

Of course I don't know. Can't do nothing but shake my head from side to side.

"They say you come here on a slave ship, one with lots of trouble."

The sad green eyes look to see if I'm making a connection. I don't know what Gaye talking about.

"Well, my folks say only two folks left know what happened on that ship. One is the duppy who follow you, and…" Gaye paused.

"And who?" My voice much louder than I intended it to be.

"Hush now," Gaye scolded me, her green eyes looking fearful. "You gon' get us caught!"

What she meant was, I was gon' get *her* caught.

"Sorry. So, who else?" I ask, my voice much softer.

"Well," Gaye was still hesitant. "They say Old Miss Simi know 'cause she was on it."

Gaye sat still, letting this fact sink in.

Old Miss Simi's blind. She so scary even the overseer let her alone. She sit and suck on sugar cane all day. And at night nobody know what she do. She real black like me. Her true name is Simisola. But somewhere along the way folks started calling her Simi, and it stuck. No matter what folks call her. She don't answer most times.

No way I'm talking to Old Miss Simi. She got something worse than strange wrapped around her. I start to object, but Gaye don't give me a chance to speak.

"Thought you'd want to know," Gaye said. "Take care of yourself now."

Then she run off.

I can't stop thinking about Old Miss Simi. Keep wondering what she know. Maybe she knew my kin. Or maybe she know why strange follow me around like we friends.

Next time I see Old Miss Simi, she looking crazy like always. Chewing on sugar cane with her rotted teeth, looking nowhere and everywhere all at once. I can't bring myself to do it. Last thing I need in my life is more strange and crazy.

"She gon' come 'round, Uzo," Old Miss Simi said, her blue-gray eyes staring at me. "Wait and give her time."

"My name Andrea, ma'am," I say, trying my best to be respectful.

"Know your name, child. I wasn't talking to you."

Old Miss Simi standing there, and I feel like now's my chance. If I don't do it now, I might never get up the nerve.

"Miss Simi?" I make certain to leave out Old. "Do you know what happened to my mama?" I ask. "Do you know why I don't got no kin?"

Old Miss Simi start smiling. Not necessarily at me, 'cause she looking around. Finally, she says, "Sometimes what folks fear the most exactly what come to pass. Focusing so hard on what they don't want, what they afraid gon' happen. That's exactly what they get."

"What now?" I ask.

I'm not trying to sass, but she ain't making no sense. Old Miss Simi crazy for sure.

"I hear you, and I ain't crazy," she said, looking at me straight in the eyes like she can see me. "I'm saying the thing your mama didn't want was exactly what she got."

"And what's that?" I ask.

"Losing you."

Old Miss Simi look past me. Right over my shoulder. I turn to see if someone is behind me, but no one there.

"I'm gon' tell her, Uzo."

Don't know who Old Miss Simi talking to. Strange starts to feel heavy, like it's sitting on me.

"Listen, child," Old Miss Simi began. "Your mama wasn't much older than you when they stole us. Took us aboard the *Zong*. Ship was big, but not big enough to hold us all. You wasn't taking up much room, though. You was in your mama's belly. And your mama's only concern was you.

"She talk to you all the time. All of us come to love you. We pray for you. You moving all around in her belly, running out of space. You ready to get out.

"'Stay in my belly now,' she'd say.

"And I believe you tried. But it was time. When the pains came, your mama start to panic. Any mama would have acted like she did. Folks was dying all around us.

"There was no food. No water. Seem like the White men finally figured out it was too many slaves on the *Zong*. And well, your mama, fearing she would lose you, panicked more. Brought more pains, and then, here you come.

"Come rushing out from between her legs. She didn't make a sound, 'cause she didn't want the White men to know you was born. And you didn't make a sound neither. Like you knew you needed to be quiet.

"Your mama was real weak. She trying to hold on for you. Then one of them White men took his knife and cut the cord that made the two of you one. Your mama died. Just like that.

"They threw her body in the water, but she stayed. Whole bunch of the dead stayed on the *Zong*. All us stayed together till we reach this land.

"Some still walk the cane fields from time to time. And your mama? Well, she never left. Never left your side. She right there with you day and night.

"So you got a mama who love you. Make sure no harm come to you.

"She here right now," Old Miss Simi said. "Can you feel her love, Andrea?"

The strange is all over me now. Pressing down on me, squeezing me tight. Like a big rock sitting on my chest.

"You feel that?" Old Miss Simi asks again.

"Yes, ma'am."

I can hardly breathe. The strange about to kill me.

"All that love made the storm come. Don't like the way folks treat you."

I'm trying to make sense of it all, but the strange on me so heavy, I can't think. Can't move.

"Let her go now," Old Miss Simi said. "Don't love on her so hard. It's too much! Look at her 'bout to fall over from all your love!"

Old Miss Simi start laughing. The strange keeps pressing on me. I can't hold it up, so I fall to my knees.

"C'mon now," Old Miss Simi whispered. "We all love her. Turn her loose, Abioye. Mojisola, you too. Awiti, let her go now. Let her mama have some time wit' her. Go on, Uzo, take hold uh ya' baby girl."

The strange turns me loose, the weight lifts off my chest. I still feel the strange, but it ain't as heavy. Just there. Warm.

"Got one question 'fore I leave ya'," Miss Simi says to me. "Why you call ya' mama strange?" she asks. "Her name Uzoamaka, Uzo for short. Go on and love your baby, Uzo."

18

HATE

Okeechobee, FL (1928)

White folks see Florida as a sunny place. Beautiful beaches and perfect weather. Well, for Black folk? For us Negroes? We never seen it that way. It was hell on Earth. A place most of us wanted to escape.

We heard things were better up North. Many Negroes tried to get there. Problem was you had to pass through more of the South to get to the North.

We lived in fear every day, wondering if a lynch mob was coming for us. If a White girl who wanted attention claimed we whistled or looked her way. It wasn't safe to be a Negro in Florida. But it especially wasn't safe to be a Negro man.

All my life I lived real careful. I said "yes ma'am" and "no ma'am." "Yes sir" and "no sir." I was home before it got dark. Stayed on the right side of the tracks. I let White men, women, and children call me "boy" even though I was a man. It wasn't enough.

Seems like we saw or heard about a killing or a lynching every day. Somebody was always losing a husband, father, brother, son, or friend. Wasn't just men. Negro women was lynched just the same. Sometimes, folks we knew disappeared. If they didn't tell someone they were leaving town and didn't return within three days' time, well, it was best to start mourning like they already dead.

It was my turn come September 23, 1919. I took a known shortcut. Dixie Road was a direct route to the Negro side of town. It was mostly used by Negroes, a quick way home from work. I heard a vehicle coming down the road and turned to see a red pick-up truck coming my way. I stepped into the grass so it could pass. Instead, it slowed and stopped right beside me.

I knew I was in a bad situation—two White men in the front with the driver, and three in the rear. I could tell they were looking for trouble. And they had found it. I was walking on Dixie Road alone. No one else around except the seven of us.

They hopped out the truck, and I kept walking. Everything in me wanted to run, but I couldn't. If I started to run, that would mean I had done something wrong. They would justify their actions by saying, "Well, he started running…"

"Stop walking, nigger," one of the men said. "I know you see us."

So I stopped walking. Kept my head low, my eyes low. No eye contact if I wanted to survive.

"That's a nice shirt you got there, boy," another man said. "You stole it."

"No, sir. It's mine."

Even though he was younger than I, smaller, I knew to call him "sir."

"It ain't yours, nigger, 'cause I want it!"

His breath reeked of liquor.

He grabbed at my shirt as his friends laughed. Buttons flew off and landed in the dirt. The short man held up my ripped shirt for his friends to see.

It was my favorite shirt. Blue plaid. Tina purchased it for me when I first started to court her. It was a birthday present. The shirt was special. But none of that mattered now.

"Told you we'd find us a dumb nigger out here walking. Looks like we gon' have us some fun, boys!"

The air was static. Even the birds were quiet. Everything stood still waiting to see what the White men planned to do to me.

It started with a push. Then they shoved me back and forth between them, spitting and kicking. Their fists rained down on me in a bitter fury. I tried to protect myself as they beat me like I'd wronged them.

Of course, I hadn't. Never seen them before. The only thing I had done wrong was be a Negro man walking alone on a shortcut road through town.

Those White men beat me near death. I heard my bones crack. Felt loose teeth as they rattled around in my mouth. Pain ripped through my body. But they were not done with me yet.

"Tie him up, John," the smallest of them shouted. "Tie that nigger up!"

I lay on the dirt road balled up from the pain. My right eye was swollen shut. But with my left eye, I saw the man called John walk over to the back of the pickup truck. He pulled out a long, thick rope and a can of gasoline. That was when I knew my life would end.

John tied a noose in the rope. There were lots of tall trees along the dirt road, and they selected the closest one. They put the noose around my neck and hoisted me up. I dangled above the ground. My feet scraped the dirt, enough so the noose tightened but did not hang me. They laughed as my feet shuffled trying to get a foothold.

"Look at that nigger dance!"

John tossed gasoline all over me while the others hopped around dancing a jig.

One of them sang, "We gon' roast a nigger" over and over in a childlike taunting tune as the gasoline burned my opened wounds.

I'm not sure which one lit the match, but they all watched me go up in flames. Like lighting a bonfire. They were unaffected as they burned me alive. Once I caught fire, they pulled the rope. My feet kicked in the air. Skin was scorching hot. I knew this was it. I was dying.

I smelled my flesh burning. Felt the noose tighten around my neck. Watched the White men dance around my burning body.

In quick snapshots I saw my life. My mother's face. How would she feel when she saw my burned body? When she learned her only son had been lynched? How sad would Tina be when she learned I was wearing the blue plaid shirt on the day I died?

I recalled little things too: laughing with friends, Tina's long legs, the beauty of a setting sun. I recalled being born. Running as a child. The first time I lay with a woman. They were fast memories. And then, my body died.

I looked down on the White men hitting my body with sticks. I felt nothing. Smoke rose in a fury above the tree as my body swayed in the wind.

The men bent down and pick up burned pieces of my flesh. They blew on my skin to cool it down before putting pieces of me in their pockets. They snapped off my fingers and lowered my body to the ground so they could take my charred ears. Souvenirs. Bragging rights to show their friends.

Once they collected what they wanted, they made certain my charred body was visible to anyone who walked the short-cut. A warning to other Negroes passing through about being in the wrong place at the wrong time.

I watched them get into their red pickup truck. They laughed and congratulated each other. As if they had won a game rather than beaten, burned, and hanged an innocent man. I do not know what became of my body, because I left it there hanging on the tree.

I followed them. Chased their red pickup truck as it stirred up clouds of dust. My spirit was so angry. So full of hate for the men who ended my life for sport. Winds began to blow, and a large tree fell across the dirt road.

The truck slammed into the tree at a high speed. Bodies flew from the back of the pickup truck. Those in the front seat went through the windshield.

They died not far from where they lynched me. I didn't have time to confront their spirits, as they passed over quickly. Regardless, I looked upon the scene with joy. It was the first time I felt powerful. Strong and invincible. Hate. That's what I felt.

Crimes against Negroes seemed to intensify. Ocee, Perry, Rosewood. So many Negroes were dying. Lynchings by mobs, attended by Whites eager for pieces of burned Negro memorabilia.

I travelled throughout inflicting my wrath. I blew over

trees. Caused damage to homes and businesses. I made creeks rise and people drown. Destruction came in whatever way I could bring it.

By the time 1928 came around, I had such hatred, I wanted more than fallen trees and creek drownings. I wanted to send my wrath down on Florida in a major way.

Seems like as soon as I had the thought, I heard a voice say, "I can help you."

It was the voice of woman, soft. Reminded me of Tina.

It was common for spirits to speak to each other. But to offer help? This was something new.

"How can you help me?"

I looked down and saw a Negro woman. Honey-brown skin and long dark hair. Beautiful. And as dead as she was alive.

"I understand your pain. I understand your hate."

She told me her story. She had suffered more than I could ever imagine. She had suffered for centuries.

"I will show you how to bring about pain," Awiti promised. "Most Negroes will never be free until they die. Don't you agree?"

I know I didn't feel free until the day I died, looking down on the White men as they took pleasure in killing me. And not until I avenged my death and the deaths of so many others with my wrath. That was the feeling death could bring. Freedom from worrying day to day about being a Negro man in the wrong place at the wrong time. Their hate could no longer hurt me.

"Yes, I agree."

"So why don't we do them all due justice?"

"How?"

I was ready.

Together we created a magnificent storm. Sent a force of wind and rain so great, the surge breached the dike surrounding Lake Okeechobee and flooded the area for miles. Many people died as Awiti and I looked on with pride. It was beautiful.

Hate. That was the eye of the storm. But it was not enough. We weren't done yet. And I knew I would never be done.

19
EL ISLENO

Key West, Florida (1935)

You gots to be careful when you looking for someone who don't want to be found. They hiding for a reason. And what you think that reason is might be different from the *real* reason. I'd be lying if I said I wasn't scared. But still. Ain't nothing gon' stop me from finding Miss Angela. Not even being afraid of what I might find.

I done travelled all this way, and I know one thing for sure. Polly best notta sent me the wrong way. If she did, I'm gon' let her have it. Now, I trust Polly. She one of the few I can call a friend. But like everybody else in this world, friend or not, Polly known to lie from time to time.

I'm supposed to go down this dirt road right here till I see a small wooden piece of a house with a black door. Ain't gon' be much else around.

"Ella, look for the chicken bones."

That's what Polly told me.

And there go chicken bones, hanging by strings, so I guess this got to be the right place. If I go 'round back, there's supposed to be a garden. And in that garden, it's gon' be a brown woman, tending to her business.

Well I'll be. There she is.

"Hello, ma'am."

I introduce myself 'cause I want her to know I been raised right. But she grunt and wave her hands in the air to shoo me away.

"I said, *hello, ma'am.*"

I'm not being disrespectful, but to the point. Firm, as Mama used to say.

Need this woman to know I mean business. After I done came all this way? She ain't 'bout to ignore me. Not today.

"*Si*, I hear you."

But she don't look up. She stay bent over, her big white dress hanging off her. That dress got to belong to somebody else. Ain't no way she pay money for a dress look like that. The hem all a mess from brushing up against the ground. I can't even see if she got shoes on. Probably don't.

"My name Ella," I say. "What's yours?"

I want to know her name 'cause if she say the wrong name, I'm gon' head back over to Petronia Street and give Polly a piece of my mind.

"Angela."

She still don't look up. Keep picking through whatever growing in her garden, with a basket sitting on her hip. She steady pulling from the ground and putting whatever she grab in her basket.

"Are you *the* Miss Angela?" I ask. "The Miss Angela someone like me might come looking for?"

"Probably."

"Well, all right now!"

I don't even try to hide my excitement. I done found Miss Angela.

She don't seem keen on me visiting. Probably 'cause she don't want to be found. I don't even care. If she wanted to hide, she shoulda never let Polly know where she stay.

"So much I want to talk to you about, Miss Angela!"

"Well, talk then."

Now that I'm closer, I can see she pulling at weeds and picking herbs and roots from the ground. Wonder if they for that magic I heard Miss Angela like to use on people. That voodoo.

"Well, let me see now…"

I didn't actually think about the first question I'd ask.

"Um, well, I guess, to make certain I gots the right Miss Angela, is you part Cuban?"

Polly said she wasn't sure if Miss Angela was part Cuban or not, but she definitely mixed up with something. And even though I can't understand a word she saying, Miss Angela sure 'nuff cuss me out in Spanish talk. She loud and real angry. I know she ain't saying nothing nice.

"All right, well. Guess that answers that question."

Now that I'm looking at her, I can see she mixed with something. Her skin golden brown, and her hair is dark, kinda straight. I want to kick myself. That's a waste of a good question. I gots to think before I talk.

"What do you *want*?"

Miss Angela's basket is getting full. Them chicken bones hanging all around her house start swaying in the breeze. Never thought I'd say this, but chicken bones make nice music in the wind. I like the way they sound.

"Want to talk. You see, I'm collecting history."

"History, you say?"

Miss Angela seem somewhat interested. Polly told me she would be. She finally look my way,

"Yes. History. About Key West."

"And I'm proud to be doing it," I want to add.

But I don't want to sound pleased with myself.

Everybody agrees somebody needs to collect stories about Key West, but don't nobody else seem up to the task. Polly say it's real easy for history to get lost. And once it's gone, ain't no way to ever find it again.

"The history of Brown folks, that is."

I make sure I don't say Black folks. I'm collecting history 'bout anybody in Key West that ain't White. For some reason, this makes her smile. Miss Angela done smiled her first smile at me.

"Oh, *Señorita*, I got lots of history!"

Miss Angela smiling big now. Her teeth white and shiny. She sure is pretty. I can see why Polly say Mr. Manuel fell in love the first time he laid eyes on her.

"I know you do."

I'm so close, I can see about everything that makes her who she is. Dark eyes and full lips. Her golden-brown skin. She short too. Well, shorter than me, and that means she downright tiny. But she got a nice shape. Full of curves men like. Negro men and White men.

Polly told me before Mr. Manuel came 'long, Miss Angela ain't have a problem lying with no man, no matter what color he was. Long as his money was green.

"'Cause of your history. That's why everybody tell me to come see you. Especially Polly. Polly told me…"

But Miss Angela don't even give me a chance to tell her what Polly said.

"*Si*, Polly. She crazy, that one."

"Ain't she now!" I got to agree.

Polly known to say some of the wildest things. Like the time she told me there was a White man who liked to make his shoes from the skin of the blackest Negro he could find. Said Negro folks' skin never wrinkled and he could wear his shoes for years and years. Polly always telling stories like that. She said Negro shoes is a real thing, but I don't believe her.

"Anyhow, Polly the one told me to come see you. That you can tell me a whole lot 'bout Key West. She say that…"

And all of sudden, I ain't quite sure how to finish what I was 'bout to say. What Polly told me was sure 'nuff something. I have to be careful how it come out.

"I know what Polly told you."

Miss Angela sit her basket on the ground. She raise her head and look up to the sky, the sun shining on her face.

"Well then?"

Ain't no nice way to ask her 'bout it. So I best just go on and ask, "Is it true?"

Miss Angela look me right in the face.

"*Si*. It's true."

Well I'll be damned. Don't know what I'd do if something like that ever happened to someone I love. I mean, everybody gon' die one day, but to know someone you love died like Mr. Manuel? Left this earth like *that*? Ain't no way your heart ever gon' be right again. It's gots to stay broken forever.

For some reason, I'm hoping Miss Angela gon' tell me the sayings 'bout her and Mr. Manuel isn't true. That it's a story. Something impossible to happen in real life. Like the White man who liked to wear shoes made from Negroes.

"You too hopeful 'bout life," is what Mama always told me. "Stop expecting the best from folks. Expect the worst and let folks surprise you. Most times they won't."

"Can you tell me what happen?" I ask. "You know, in your own words?"

I try to sound fancy, like a real historian gathering facts. All I have is bits and pieces 'bout Miss Angela and Mr. Manuel. And even the parts Polly told me is hard to believe. No matter how I try, I can't believe some of the cruel things folks think up to do to one another.

Miss Angela sitting in the grass, her too big white dress laying all around her. Look like she sitting on a cloud. Soft breeze blowing through her hair. Her face still up to the sky. Her eyes closed now. Chicken bones blowing in the wind, making music. Wish I could stay in this moment right here forever.

"My Manuel."

Miss Angela voice is soft, like she whispering to him. I don't say nothing. I can tell Miss Angela in a place only she know 'bout. Somewhere special for her and Mr. Manuel.

One thing I know for sure—Mr. Manuel loved himself some Miss Angela. That's the one part of the story everybody agree on. And I can tell by the look on Miss Angela face when she say his name. She look and sound like somebody who was once loved.

Miss Angela don't seem ready to talk yet, but I don't mind. I'm gon' let her stay in that place with Mr. Manuel till she ready. I suspect it take some time to tell a stranger how the man you love was taken from you. How the life you had plans for was snatched right out your arms.

"Manuel love me."

Miss Angela don't move. I'm not quite sure she even talking to me. I be as still as I can and listen.

"Even when everyone told him he was wrong to love someone like me, he love me. Love me extra 'cause he knew I need it."

Miss Angela fall real slow-like into the grass. She stretch out in her garden. Arms open wide like she 'bout to give someone a hug.

"Still can't believe I was so lucky in this life. Can you believe a man like Manuel love me?"

I can tell she not expecting me to answer. I listen.

"Out of all the women in Key West, he coulda had any fine woman he want. But he love me. Me!"

Miss Angela start laughing and rolling 'round. Grass in her hair. Green stains on her dress. Her basket tip over, and instead of being mad 'cause everything fall out, she laugh even more.

Polly told me Mr. Manuel was quite something. He was all Cuban, not mixed like Miss Angela. Real handsome and something tough. And strong.

Far as I know, any man who come back alive from any war was strong. They say Mr. Manuel took care of poor folks too, no mind they race. Folks of all kind called him *El Isleno*. That's the only Spanish I know. Learned it from Polly. It mean, "The Islander."

"That shole is mighty special Mr. Manuel chose you, Miss Angela."

I want her to remember I'm here.

"Yes, I suppose. Special. And stupid."

Miss Angela stop laughing and sit up. She got a look on her face. That kind of look that say, "Stay back, 'cause I don't know what I might do."

Then she says, "Perhaps, if he didn't love me, he'd still be alive."

Miss Angela start putting herbs and roots back in her basket. She moving fast, the way people that's angry do things. I look at them chicken bones on strings, dancing in the wind. They don't sound as nice.

"I told him, you know. It was enough for him to love me in secret. But for him, it was not enough."

She say something in that Spanish talk as she raise her hand to the sky, her fist shaking. Only word I can make out is Manuel. Guess she fussing at him.

"He knew better, Ella. No man with White skin can love a Negro woman."

"Oh, they can love us in private, *si*. Give us money, buy us nice things. We can smoke and drink rum while we lay together. But every White man knows you cannot let your Negro live with you.

"That's what Manuel did, though. Took me off the streets. Told me never again would I need to lie with a man for money. Only for love. You only supposed to lie with a man for love. Did you know that, Ella?"

"No, Miss Angela. Can't say I outright knew that."

I suspect it's a good time to be honest with her, since she's being honest with me.

"I never lay with a man before."

"You *never* lay with a man?" Miss Angela start laughing again. "Oh, you poor thing!"

"Well, I never had the chance to," I say, trying to defend myself. "But I s'pect if I did, I'd lay with a Negro. And of course I'd love him. Don't think I could outright lie with a White man, though. Not even for love. They skin kinda make me think of raw chicken."

This make Miss Angela laugh, tears running down her face.

"Oh, Ella! You funny! Manuel would have liked you."

"I bet I woulda liked him too. Everybody say he was nice."

"Who is *everybody*?" Miss Angela shouts at me. "They don't know Manuel. They don't know *him*! Stories is what they know. I *know* him! I *feel* him!"

She hitting her chest, looking at me like she 'bout to put some voodoo on me. I know what she mean, though.

That's how I felt when Mama died. Folks crying and hugging on me. Talking about what a good woman Mama was. That it was a shame she was leaving me on this earth while she went on to heaven.

They didn't *know* her, though. Just knew Mama made the best fried fish. That she was a good church-going woman. She never talked bad 'bout Daddy even though he gambled away almost every penny Mama made. And that was before he took off to Jacksonville with some young hussy.

"Your mama gon' watch over you from heaven." That's what folks told me.

Guess Mama got to heaven and was having such a good time with the Lord, she forgot. Still, I was the one to know Mama. I know she loved me. Don't even blame her for getting to heaven and forgetting 'bout me. I blame the Lord.

For taking Mama from me. And everybody ain't stuck with the pain. Just me.

"I know what you mean 'bout everybody, Miss Angela. Guess I was trying to say Mr. Manuel had what folks say is a good reputation. That's all."

But Miss Angela can't let the fact I said everybody go.

"*Everybody* wasn't there when the Klan came through our door. Pulling Manuel right from my arms. *Everybody* didn't see him get covered in tar and feathers. So *everybody* know nothing!"

She right. Wasn't nobody else there that night. This Miss Angela and Mr. Manuel story.

"My Manuel. He fought the Klan. Hiding behind those white hoods. Cowards!

"He ripped some of their hoods, you know. We saw their faces. Not *everybody*. *We* saw them. Me and Manuel."

Look on her face let me know she right back in that moment. Watching the Klan tar her man. Damn.

"But the Klan don't know me. Don't know what I can do. "Black magic" what some folks call it. But voodoo is not magic. It's like…"

Miss Angela cock her head to the side while she choose her words.

"Voodoo is like the one you call Lord."

"Like Jesus?" I ask. I can't hide my surprise. Never heard of Jesus and voodoo in the same sentence before.

"Yes! Like Jesus! Power and love. Love and power so strong, you can do anything. But only if you believe."

Mama told me voodoo was evil. To stay away from it. Something 'bout light and dark can't dwell together. What

Mama know? Got to heaven and got blinded by Jesus and His light.

"So you did your voodoo. Then what happen?"

"It was Christmas time, you know. Who do something like that on Christmas?"

It's hard for me to look at Miss Angela.

"Don't know," I say. "It sound awful. Sound like something only the Klan would do."

"Christmas Eve. The night they came. They were angry. Manuel had taken a Negro whore off the street and into his house. To love me. That's why they came, you know. Because of me."

Polly had told me that part. She say the Klan love Negro women more than they own. That's why they always hiding behind them white sheets. They the ones afraid. They know if they take off them hoods, every Negro woman they love on gon' recognize 'em right away.

"Well, perhaps it wasn't *really* your fault, Miss Angela. I reckon…"

"*Cállate!*" Miss Angela shouted at me. "You don't know what you talking about. I'm telling you. They came for Manuel because of me!"

"All right, Miss Angela. I reckon they must have, like you saying." I ain't 'bout to argue with no voodoo woman.

"Manuel want to make them pay. Want the cowards to fight him like a man. So…"

Miss Angela looking at the sky again. I look up too, trying to see what she seeing. Nothing there but blue sky and white clouds. The heavens, as some folks call it. Wonder if Mama looking down on me. Wonder if she mad I'm making friends with a voodoo woman.

"Then what happen?" I ask.

"So Manuel went to find the Klan."

Miss Angela say this like it's nothing. Like Mr Manuel set out on Front Street to find the beach.

"Wait, wait, wait," I say. Need to make sure I got my facts straight. "You tellin' me, you and Mr. Manuel at home getting ready for Christmas? The Klan come and tar and feather Mr. Manuel? He happen to see some of the Klan who tar him? And then he set out to find 'em?"

Miss Angela nod at every word I say.

"Well, did he?" I ask. "Did he find the Klan?"

"Yes."

"And what he do once he found 'em?"

"He kill him."

Damn. It's true. Everything Polly done told me is true.

"Did Polly tell you the rest of the story?" Miss Angela asks me. "Since she seem to know so much? Talk so much?"

I can tell Miss Angela hurt. All these folks 'round Key West talking 'bout her and Mr. Manuel. Telling her story.

"No, Miss Angela," I lie. "Polly the one told me to come see you."

"Lies! But it's okay. I know Polly is your friend. Friends lie for one another, you know?"

"Yes, Miss Angela."

Since everything Polly told me been true, guess the rest of the story is too. The Klan finding out about the death of one they own. Sheriff putting Mr. Manuel in jail on Christmas Eve, claiming to protect Mr. Manuel from the Klan. Marines come too, trying to keep the peace 'cause White folks call from all 'round demanding to have a piece of Mr. Manuel for killing one of they own.

But late at night, the Sheriff send everybody home. Say he got things under control. But he really sent everybody away so he could let the Klan can come in and beat on Mr. Manuel. Next morning, Christmas Day, Mr. Manuel hanging from a tree. Dead.

"I don't want to talk about it."

Miss Angela turn away from me. Her shoulders moving up and down like she crying. I feel bad. But she don't seem like the type of woman who want you to hug on her. I can tell she work on her problems alone.

"I understand, Miss Angela."

"Do you?"

"No, Miss Angela."

I was trying to be nice. No way I understand.

"I make them pay, you know. Anyone who touch my Manuel? Who hurt him? I make them pay."

"How?" I ask. "With your voodoo that work like Jesus?"

Miss Angela laugh. "Yeah, something like that."

"All by yourself?"

"Sometimes. But sometimes, others help me."

"Like who?" I ask. "Folks like me?"

Wonder how many folks it is like me. Can't move on 'cause they Mama forgot to watch over 'em once she got to heaven. I'm afraid I might see Mama in heaven. That's why I won't go. I'd end up fighting with Mama and Jesus so bad, I'd sure 'nuff get sent straight to hell.

Living was so hard! It seemed the best thing for me to do was end it than to go on another day. Wasn't even hard for me to put that knife on my wrists. Slit 'em open like I was guttin' a fish. Don't even remember the pain. Just remember being free. I'd like to meet some folks like that. Folks like me. Can't have Polly be my only friend forever.

"Come," Miss Angela says.

She look at me and she smile. Miss Angela done smiled at me again! This right here the best day of my life since Mama died.

"Ella. I want you to meet Awiti. Me and Awiti got plans for Key West. For Labor Day. Big, big plans."

20
CITY OF ROSES

Quai de la Fosse, France (1946)

I used to love Quai de la Fosse in the summer. My sister and I would walk about the streets, arm in arm, laughing and talking about some wonderful memory. We were simply happy to be together.

We were the living image of a postcard, a picture of beauty, youth, family, and love. Long dark hair blowing in the wind, and our lips, always rouge, wore smiles. Our biggest worry was to make certain that our heels did not get stuck in the cobblestone streets.

Emilie was happy then, the fiancé of one of Nantes' most desirable bachelors. I was still too young to wed, but not too young to plan for that fateful day. I dreamed I would meet a brave soldier who survived the war. My love would nurture his tortured soul and erase the memories of battle. We would have children and grow old together. And we would visit my sister on Quai de la Fosse every summer.

These were my dreams before my sister became ill.

Emilie is not well. We have all tried to deny this for too

long. We wanted to believe she was mourning the loss of her children that their deaths had pushed her into a momentary place of sadness from which she would recover. But this is far worse.

A sickness has entered her mind, and I fear I will have to institutionalize her. There is no other choice.

To find Emilie wandering the streets, it pains me. Whenever I touch her arm to guide her home, she is seeing me for the first time. I am a stranger. I bring her back to *Maison Montaudoin*, and she wants to listen to Edith Piaf all day.

Before the tragedy, we saw Edith Piaf perform live in Paris, and Emilie, like so many others, fell in love with her voice. Edith made us forget the war and think of love, if only for a moment. The war was all around us. We all knew someone who had suffered loss.

"*La Vie En Rose*," Emilie says with a smile. "*La Vie En Rose, n'est-cette pas une belle chanson, tout comme ma Rose...*"

"Isn't it such a beautiful song? Like my Rose?"

I already knew she would ask this question.

"*Oui, c'est magnifique*," I always say, for it is a beautiful song.

But Emilie's demanding repetition of it and the same questions she asks about Rose, well, I am starting to loathe the recording. But this is the only conversation we have, and so, I endure it.

"Yes," I say to her.

"Rose was beautiful."

Then Emilie begins to cry out for the daughter she will never see again.

I blame Michael. Five children were too many for any woman to bear, even one of wealth and prestige. But he wanted many children to carry on the Montaudoin legacy. Of course, once Emilie had them all, she could not manage them.

I watched my beautiful sister, so full of promise, go from enjoying the simple pleasures of life to what is surely hell on Earth. Her dark hair, once shiny, luxurious, and the envy of many, now dull and limp, unwashed and unkempt. When I look into her blue eyes, they are empty. Nothing is there.

Emilie is gone.

It was Michael who suggested she hire help. We were from a modest family, and Emilie wished to keep the house herself. But keeping a *maison* was different from keeping a small *maisonnette*.

And with the birth of her children so frequent, she was soon overwhelmed with not just the upkeep of the young, but their home. Still, she took great joy in trying to care for the home and children herself.

"They bring me life," Emilie would say of her children. "I did not know love until I became a mother."

They were petite versions of her and Michael. There was Michael Jr., whom we called Little Mister. He was a mirror image of his father, with dark brown hair and serious brown eyes. Why, to have Michael look upon his heir was to watch a man look upon the thing he loved most.

I believe it was the birth of Little Mister, a boy child to secure the family name and legacy that started Michael's desire for a large family. His wish for miniature versions of himself to admire.

Sarah soon followed with her fiery spirit and a smile that would melt the hardest heart. She had her mother's blue eyes and dark brown curls that made her look angelic even in her most devious moments of childhood. She was feisty, yes, but a joy. We all speculated on the amazing woman she would become.

The twins, Alexandre and Antoine, came next and were as mischievous as twin boys could be. They favored their mother. Their dark hair and smiling blue eyes made it difficult for Emilie to discipline them.

Then there was Rose, a sweet cherub of a baby. She was the type of infant that made a childless woman yearn for one of her own.

Yes, Little Mister was Michael's favorite, and Rose was Emilie's true love. The rest of the children were also loved. They filled in the gaps between the oldest and youngest and entertained each other as middle children do.

They would run through the *maison*, their feet pounding the marble floor, leaving minor scratches, as the white marble was not intended for such roughhousing.

Emilie, unmoved, all the while rocking Rose in her arms, would say, "Let them be children."

Their childhood was nothing like ours. We ran through medieval streets of *Rochefort-en-Terre* while our mother and father grew vegetables and sold them at the market. We had great freedom, and we roamed about exploring the beauty of our country.

Perhaps that was why Emilie let them be, wild children running about their meadow made of white marble, glass, and expensive things. It was the best she could give them as a normal childhood.

It drove Michael into a fury, for they were not normal children. They were aristocrats. Their surname alone opened doors throughout France. He felt they behaved as animals, but he was unable to control and discipline them.

He was always on travel, his shipping company heavily involved in supplying goods for the war. He came home bearing gifts only to leave again. And so he was a father they knew by name, not by presence.

"You must get help," Michael told Emilie after arriving home from one of his trips to find the *maison* in disarray. "We have more money than half of the families in France, and yet, you are the wife who wishes to tend to her children and keep to the house as if we are poor."

Michael had spoken, and it was final. Emilie started her search for hired help the next day.

After interviewing many, Emilie chose a French African woman named Awiti Akoth. Michael was pleased Emilie had acquired a nanny and housekeeper. And Emilie, after heeding the advice of other rich women about the importance of hiring help the man of the house would find undesirable, felt comfortable and certain in her choice. Her only criteria had been that the woman not be blonde and attractive.

Awiti cooked and cleaned well. She was different, something new and exciting, so the children loved her. All but Rose.

The baby would cry a screaming rage whenever Awiti tried to tend to her. Spoiled from being held daily by her mother, no doubt. So Awiti tended to all the children except Rose and kept to the house.

Awiti took great care to keep Michael's office clean. She spent much time there dusting and cleaning. I am sure she looked at the photos of the old men, who years ago had brought many of her people to France.

Slavery is a messy, embarrassing piece of our history, one not often discussed—except by Michael, whose name and wealth reflected the legacy of one of the most prosperous families in the Nantes' slave trade. This must have been odd for Awiti, but she cleaned Michael's office nonetheless.

The twins were the first to fall ill, the fever ravishing their bodies until they succumbed to the heat within them and died. Such a terrible funeral it was, two small, polished silver caskets holding the bodies of once rambunctious boys.

A few months earlier, they had broken an expensive vase, and Emilie had been furious. The vase, an import from one of Michael's many travels, meant nothing now. How she would allow them to break a dozen vases if she could hold them again.

The *maison* was quiet without the twins, for they had been the liveliest of the children. The other children mourned in their own way, playing with the twins' toys and hiding in nooks and crannies where they once played games. It was an effort to be close to the siblings they would never see again.

Sarah fell ill next, her body already frail from her insistence to eat only cheese and fruit. The fever took hold of her tiny body within a matter of days. The sickness coupled with the heartbreak of losing her younger brothers made Sarah weak, and she succumbed to the fever more quickly than the twins.

Never was there a sadder time than to watch Emilie and Michael bury another child within such a short time after losing the twins. Well-wishers filled *Maison* Montaudoin. And Michael, unable to deal with the tragedy affecting his family, threw himself into his work.

Emilie held Rose nonstop, unwilling to put her down for even a moment. She clung to the child she loved the most.

Little Mister hid within his heartbreak and developed a silence, his laughter taken by childhood tragedy. He rarely spoke, and this was fine for the adults, for no one knew how to answer his questions about sadness and death.

Awiti continued to help tend the house and looked after Little Mister. When he fell ill, it was too much for all to bear.

Michael stayed by his bedside throughout the ravaging fever. He wiped the sweat from Little Mister's body and changed the bed linens as soon as they soaked. He begged Little Mister to survive. And Little Mister held on for much longer than any of the younger children, but soon, he could fight no more.

Emilie was a waif. Her figure dwindled in size with each child's death, and at the time of Little Mister's burial, she was but skin and bones. The black dress that had hugged her curves during the twins' funeral hung as an oversized drape over her tiny frame.

Michael wept at the funeral. While he had been stoic and a pillar of strength at all the others, being strong for Emilie, he could not contain his pain and loss any longer.

There was nothing more heart-wrenching than the sound of a man weeping. Emilie held Rose close, her body too weak to cry for her firstborn.

"I have run out of tears," she told me.

Although troublesome and a handful, the handsome boy had been her first experience with motherhood, and they had learned together. Emilie and Little Mister had shared a special bond that was only overshadowed by the bond he had with his father.

I stayed with them for a while after the death of Little Mister. The large *maison* was quiet. Michael and Emilie passed like ghosts, invisible to each other.

Emilie took to having Rose in the bed with her, as Michael

slept in his office, exhausting himself with work and scotch. Emilie would stare at Rose while she slept. She watched Rose's little body rise and fall as she took tiny breaths

I watched the entire scene in sadness as my sister's once joyful, chaotic life had turned to one of eerie silence and predictability.

Awiti cleaned the house after each death. She tried to wipe out the sickness and memories. She washed the fevered bed lines and small clothing. She cleaned and hid the tiny cups used to offer the children water and medicine to break the fever.

Michael and Emilie hoped the clean environment would erase the proof of their tragedy, but it left the house medicinal and sterile. The memories of the children still lingered.

The day Rose became weak and started to show familiar signs of fever, Emilie became a shell of the sister I once knew. Certain of what was imminent, she refused to let anyone near Rose, not even the doctors. She allowed Rose to be comforted only by her mother's arms. And that is where Rose died.

Her casket was so small, none could bear to look at it for longer than a few moments. The church echoed with sniffles and the sounds of women weeping softly. Michael somehow found the strength to carry the silver casket in his arms, the single pallbearer to his last child.

Emilie sat lifeless and still. She clasped her hands together in her lap, so tight that her knuckles turned white. Within a few months' time, the life she had grown to cherish was gone.

Emilie and Michael came home to the large, empty *maison*, the marble floors so cold and the space so vast without the busyness of the children. They had made the *maison* a home. Awiti's services were no longer needed, and so, she left.

Michael could not bear with Emilie's emptiness. She was not someone to talk with or cling to. They could not mourn and rebuild their lives together.

Emilie was simply there. A body in their empty house. She was a constant reminder that he was once a father and she was once a mother.

Like most men in times of sorrow, Michael dedicated himself to his work, an excuse to be away rather than confront the pain. He left Emilie home alone to deal with the memories. Especially once they found the note.

It was written by Awiti. Each word written perfectly, each phrase written with the intent to hurt them. She was happy the little Montaudoins were gone forever. It was her revenge. For her people. For all of the Africans Michael's forefathers had packed into boats and sold into slavery.

The words were written in red ink to remind them of the blood of her people... and of their children. Michael took the letter directly to the authorities, but Awiti could not be found.

I try to visit Emilie as often as I can. When I cannot find her at home, I find her wandering the streets in her bathrobe—the one she was wearing when Rose died in her arms.

The neighbors offer sincere condolences, for none can imagine having to endure such hardship. I appreciate their apologies and prayers, but none can truly help us.

Whenever I find Emilie in the streets, I take her home to *Maison* Montaudoin. I bathe her and wash her hair with her favorite shampoo. I brush until it shines—one hundred strokes.

Then I feed Emilie the soup that I prepared a day or two before in case she wished to eat in my absence. It always remains untouched.

Soup is the easiest to slip into her mouth while she sits in the parlor with her eyes glazed over and blank, her legs folded beneath her in the rocking chair, our grandmother's red knit throw over her shoulders. It was there she often rocked Rose to sleep.

Then Emilie asks me to play Edith Piaf. I reluctantly turn on the record, for it makes her smile, if only for a moment.

"*La Vie En Rose est une très belle chanson, tout comme ma Rose*," Emilie says with a smile.

It is such a beautiful song, just like her Rose.

And then, the mourning begins.

21

I AM NOT CRAZY

New York, NY (1957)

The Professor of Africa. That's what they used to call me.
I was so renowned in academia, scholars would come
from all over the world to hear me speak. My areas of
interest were colonialism and imperialism. The historical and
lasting implications of the trans–Atlantic slave trade.

I have published many books. And I believe my royalties
are in an account I can access when I become well again. That
is, when *they* say I am well. Because the thing is, I *am* well.
Except I am here.

Confined to this room where everything is white. Even
the clothing they force me to wear. They have diagnosed me
with schizophrenia. Said I have gone mad. But I am not mad,
nor do I have a mental illness. In fact, I am quite lucid.

The problem is no one believes me. My department does
not understand how one day I went from intellectual brilliance
to being unable to recall the simplest material. Ill-equipped to
teach the most basic of lessons. All of the information I spent
my life studying just vanished.

I tried to explain to them what happened. I awoke one morning and my scholarship was gone. And so was Awiti.

Whenever I speak of Awiti, the doctors take lots of notes. Later, a nurse comes with a combination of meds that cause my mind to fog, and I sleep for days. Like my department, the staff here refuses to believe Awiti is real.

But I know she is real. I have held her. Caressed her skin and made love to her. I have heard her voice whisper in my ear saying she loves me.

I was giving a talk in Louisiana when I met her. I cannot remember at what university or the topic of my lecture. But I remember her.

Her dark hair hung almost to her waist. Brown, flawless skin, her face flushed and rosy from rushing in as she searched for a seat. Her dark eyes offering a silent apology for her tardiness. Then she smiled. And for the first time in my lengthy teaching career, I found myself attracted to a student.

The University warns professors during faculty orientation about the dangers of teacher-student relationships. I had many beautiful students in my classes over the years. They offered themselves in exchange for high grades. Others were genuinely attracted to me. But I never indulged.

I told myself they were still children. Fresh and new into their adulthood. The thought of them as childlike was always enough to deter me. But Awiti was different.

After the lecture, she approached me.

"That was a wonderful presentation," she said. "Very enlightening discussion on what slavery did and continues to do this world."

"Thank you very much…" I held out my hand.

"Awiti. My name is Awiti, Professor. I would love to take one of your courses."

"But I do not teach here. I teach in New York. At NYU."

"Then I will transfer and become a student at NYU."

At the time, I thought she was merely flattering me, and we stood there, flirting and playful.

But guess what? She did.

When I saw Awiti enter my lecture hall the next semester, I could not believe my eyes. I am certain I stumbled through my discourse. And while the other students eagerly took notes, Awiti stared at me as if mesmerized. I guess you could say we were instantly captivated with each other.

Awiti often arrived early and flustered me. I tried not to look at her, but it was impossible. The hypnotizing dark eyes stared at me from the front row.

I often called on her randomly to answer questions, difficult questions, for I became paranoid my attraction to her was obvious. She was always prepared, her responses intelligent and well-thought-out. This only intensified my attraction.

When Awiti came to my office for her mandatory midterm evaluation, it was almost too much for me to handle. I stayed seated the entire time out of fear that if I stood up she would see the bulge in my pants. Enclosed in the small office with no windows, no circulating air, the narrow faculty desk between us, I could hardly focus on the evaluation.

"Keep up the good work," I muttered. "You're doing great."

I wanted the fifteen minutes to end, and yet, I did not. I wished for time to move slowly. I prayed for the minutes to drag on so I could be close to her.

She smelled so lovely, like sandalwood and jasmine. Her

fragrance filled the small space and lingered when she left. I had to excuse myself before my next appointment. Shit. I was in trouble.

During our next office visit, Awiti smiled at me. It was a smile that told a man everything he needed to know. She found me attractive. She wanted me. And in case I was being hopeful in reading her smile, when Awiti stood to leave, she reached over and slipped her phone number into my hand as confirmation. When her soft hands touched mine, it felt electric. I could still feel her touch long after she left.

I stared at the number for hours before I picked up the phone to call her. Awiti lived nearby, within walking distance to the university. She asked me to join her for the evening. It was more of a demand than a question. And I could not resist.

When Awiti answered the door, I knew then I had crossed the threshold I promised myself I would never cross. She was wearing a thin cotton dress, her dark nipples pronounced through the white fabric.

Her hair was loose and fell over her shoulders, down her back. A soft jazz record played in the background. John Coltrane, if I remember correctly.

Candles were lit, and their light emphasized the few possessions a student on a modest budget would be proud of: a record player with an impressive vinyl collection, stacks of books organized alphabetically, an oversized map of Africa, and fresh flowers from the street vendor.

The minimalism of the studio was not lost on me. The room contained the necessities—a desk and chair that doubled as a dining room table, and a futon that functioned for both seating and sleeping.

"Have you heard of the game *uku-hlobonga*?" I asked.

I had recently written a book review on the sensationalism of E.A. Ritter's *Shaka Zulu*. While the novel had made for a highly entertaining read, I found it to be more fiction than fact. Yet another European's fantastic idealism of Mother Africa.

Yet, one aspect of the story was undisputed—Shaka was the illegitimate son of Senzangakona, a young chieftain of the Zulu tribe. His father had played the tempting game of *ukuhlobonga* with a woman who was not his wife.

The beautiful art of extended foreplay was common. Young lovers released their sexual tension by teasing each other's bodies to the point of orgasm without actual penetration. Although, Senzangakona found himself in a quite precarious situation, as I am sure most men did while playing this game. Unable to resist, he succumbed to the temptation, and Shaka was conceived.

"No."

Awiti had never heard of the game. And without even knowing the details and instructions, she was ready to engage. Rather than ask for the rules, she whispered,

"I want to play. Teach me how to play."

Her lips brushed against my ear. The room seemed to dim as the candles flickered, shadows dancing on the walls. I did not want to have intercourse with Awiti. But I did want touch.

Awiti leaned in closer to me, sensing the game involved intimacy. My mouth seemed paralyzed by the wetness of her lips. I was unable to return her kiss, unable to speak. I sat in the sweetness of Awiti's kiss.

I felt myself begin to harden. I slowly unbuttoned her dress, making certain to exaggerate each release, revealing more and more of her brown flesh.

We were naked and on the futon moments later. She was an inexperienced lover, but that only made me more passionate and attentive to her needs. As an older man, rushing into the act of sex was no longer of importance to me. I knew the female body needed attention and stimulation more than it needed a quick orgasm.

I kissed every inch of her skin. I felt like I was kissing honey, her skin so golden brown and fragrant. Her small breasts fit perfectly in my mouth. I kissed and sucked them until her nipples were hard and pronounced. Then I tasted her, the wetness sweet in my mouth.

She moaned and squirmed, her thin thighs pressed against the sides of my head. I held her around the waist so she could not escape the flickering of my tongue. I wanted to make certain if she had other lovers before me, I would be the best. And I wanted to set the bar for any lovers who might follow.

We explored each other's bodies into the early morning. We could not get enough of each other. After we released the built-up sexual tension between us, we talked. For hours. Until the sun came through her tiny window, bright and intense.

It shined a guilty light upon me, reminding me I was a professor who had spent the night making love and having intense conversation with his student. I had a faculty meeting in two hours.

Awiti joined me in the shower. We made love again, her dark hair soaking wet. The warm water flowing over the honey-brown skin. It did not take long for me to climax.

I arrived at the faculty meeting in the same clothes I had on the day before, my hair still damp. I heard nothing the faculty chair said. My mind kept replaying the last several hours of my life. And like that, she had me.

Awiti loved me. She shared many things with me. We talked about her immortality. She shared with me her ability to control the winds and rains. But she talked most often about the pain of her losing the family she would never see again. That her country would never be the same.

And there was so much she did not know about her past. So much she felt she needed to know.

"Can you help me?"

Even if I had wanted to, I could not help her. I could only speculate. Genealogy was not my thing. And even if it were, I had such limited information to work with.

A Luo name. Memories of a beautiful village that sat high above the road. Mountains with flowers. I was working with nothing. And this was further complicated by what Awiti wanted to believe.

She wanted to believe her family had gone to one of the slave ports on the coast of West Africa. And from there, to Nantes. Then on to Saint Domingue to harvest sugar. And if they had not died in the War of Independence, they were sold to plantations in Florida, South Carolina, Georgia, or Louisiana. And Louisiana seemed to be the place that called her the most.

Her family died as slaves, and that was if they did not die during the journey and hardships they endured crossing the Atlantic. This was the story Awiti had created for herself. It had sustained her for centuries.

But it was likely that—a story. Patchwork pieces of her history and facts she'd learned throughout time. A way for her to justify her searching. A legitimate reason for her revengeful hurricanes and storms. Awiti had found them, and in her own way, avenged their deaths.

I tried to tell her one evening, "Even though you have visited these places, slave ports on the coast of West Africa. Followed slave traders' vessels across the Atlantic. Caused storms and hurricanes in retaliation. It does not change anything."

I thought it best to be honest, for that is what you are when you love someone. You are honest, even if it hurts.

I showed Awiti a map of ancient Africa and highlighted the vast distance between ancient Luo and Oyo. If she were of Luo ancestry, it was quite unbelievable she made it to Oyo. This information made her weep softly, and I tried to comfort her.

"The family you lost the day your father told you to run… it's true that you will never see them again. You will never find them, for they have long since passed on. But you have gained an entire village.

"Black people are your descendants, and they are all over the world. There are White people and other ethnicities who denounce slavery. Those who are devoted to helping Black people heal from their past and obtain equal rights. They are your family now. I am your family now."

Awiti continued to weep. My love could not console her. Although I had been honest with her, Awiti would not rest. She continued to ask me questions about imperialism and slavery. The Africa before the Portuguese attacked her village.

She demanded we research books and maps. I loved her, so I shared with her all the resources I had. But it became all-consuming for her, and thus, for me. While I understood her pain, I longed for the carefree relationship we once had.

I expressed such, for that is what lovers are supposed to do— share their true feelings, and Awiti became enraged.

How dare I be selfish with my knowledge? How could I love her? How could I know facts about her country and not share them with her? She was furious with me. And forceful winds began to blow as a storm appeared amidst a bright sunny day.

One night, Awiti said to me, "I love you, Professor. And I am sorry."

"Sorry for what?" I asked.

"For everything."

When I awoke the next morning, Awiti was gone.

I showered, got dressed, and went to the university. I prepared for class as usual. And when I went to begin my lecture, all was blank. I had no knowledge of my research or the history I'd spent my entire career mastering.

At first my department believed the demands of being a top-rated professor, the research and publications, had been too much for me to manage. They placed me on sabbatical. When my sabbatical ended and I was still unable to meet the academic demands, the University placed me on administrative leave.

When I went before the board to petition for reinstatement, I decided to be honest. I told them I had fallen in love with a student named Awiti Akoth. And that she had taken my knowledge.

Awiti had the ability to acquire the gifts of others. She had told me so.

"Look into the academic records," I said. "There aren't that many transfer students. Find her and she will explain everything."

The board said they looked into the matter, but there was no one at either university with that name registered as a student. I do not believe them.

I tried to tell them. Hurricane Audrey. Did they not see the damage done in Texas and Louisiana? It was Awiti. I tried to warn them. There will be more raging storms, more death. Because Awiti will forever be angry.

I will never forget the faces of the board members. Expressions of pity and sadness. Disgust. I remember snatches of conversations about mental illness, schizophrenia and how these things affected the most brilliant. And then, the men with the white coats came.

I have lost track of the amount of time I have spent in this room. I used to have visitors. Colleagues and students who remembered who I once was. But now, no one comes.

I am alone in the room with nothing but the memories of Awiti. My life that once was.

I know Awiti is real. She took my livelihood, but the memories I have of us, they sustain me. I lost everything for loving her. But it was worth it.

Sometimes I yell hoping someone will hear me. I try to tell them Awiti is real. I want her to return to me because I still love her. I need her to tell my department they made a mistake. She can return my knowledge, and I can teach again. Perhaps, we can even marry.

Are you listening to me? Is anyone listening to me?

I am not crazy! Awiti is real!

"Professor," a voice says softly.

"Yes?"

"It is time for your medication."

22
FIGHT

Waveland, Mississippi (1969)

If there is one good thing that comes from having to evacuate for Hurricane Camille, it's getting to spend time with my favorite uncle. Soon as the news announced this hurricane was going to be one of the worst of its kind to ever hit Mississippi, Daddy made a decision. We had to go.

Daddy called Uncle Mike, his youngest brother, and said, "We need a place to stay to escape this storm."

And before I knew it, Mississippi was far behind us. We were headed up the highway toward Washington.

Normally during hurricane season we hunkered down and boarded up the windows. Mama purchased lots of water and non-perishables. And Daddy made us all huddle together in the living room, surrounded by candles and flashlights.

One time during a bad storm, the winds started making the house sway. Daddy made us all climb into the bathtub. My older sister Telly, Mama, Daddy, and I sitting like we were in a canoe. I still don't understand how the bathtub was supposed to save us if the roof caved in.

But there will be no bathtub survival tactics for Hurricane Camille. The weatherman said Camille's winds are going to be so strong, the storm might level all of Mississippi.

Before we got on the road, Daddy made me, Mama, and Telly gather our most important papers, some clothes, and a few of our favorite things. Daddy didn't even board up the windows. We just left. Don't think I've ever seen my folks move so fast.

Daddy had tried to be patient with Mama, but she seemed to want to pack everything—pictures, little vases, pots, and pans. Finally, he couldn't take it anymore, and he snapped at her.

"We got to get moving, woman," he yelled. "Ain't got the time nor the space for you to be taking all that mess!"

Daddy hardly ever talked like that to Mama. And he sure made her some type of mad. She went slamming and throwing things around, packing up her things in a rush. Now we're all crammed into Daddy's Chevy riding to Uncle Mike's house in silence.

I know it's wrong to wish you had a different daddy, but sometimes I can't help it. I wish Uncle Mike was my daddy. He's the best, so smart and fun. He's the first one in our whole family to go to college. And not just regular college neither. He went all the way and earned himself a PhD. He works at Howard University, which is where I want to go to college one day.

No matter how busy he is, seems like Uncle Mike always has time for me. He makes sure to take me one week every summer, just the two of us. And we always do something exciting. Last summer, he took me to Annapolis in Maryland and showed me the place where the real Kunta Kinte came on a slave ship to America.

Everywhere we go always has some educational value, a piece of history. Uncle Mike is serious about Black people and their education. He calls himself one of the talented tenth.

"It's my life's purpose to enhance the Negro race, to make certain that the world is a different place for the future. I want to make sure the future is different for you, Greg."

We had this conversation two summers before, on my twelfth birthday. We were walking near the Anacostia River when he sat me down and had a serious talk with me.

"I like spending time with you, Greg," Uncle Mike said. We were eating ice cream in our favorite park. That day had been perfect.

"I know, Uncle Mike. Me too." He had no way of knowing how much.

"I invest in you not because you are my nephew, but because you're a young boy who will one day be a man."

Uncle Mike always reminded me of that. I wouldn't always be a boy. One day, I'd grow up and I'd be a man. And when I became a man, I'd have a chance to change the world.

"Yes, Uncle Mike. I know that. I sure do appreciate it."

"A great man once said, 'It is easier to build strong children than it is to repair broken men,'" Uncle Mike said wisely.

I think it was a nice way of saying, "I know your daddy ain't 'bout much, so I'm going to help you."

"You know, Greg, only one in ten Black men are poised to become leaders of the Negro race. And that Black man, the one of the ten? Well, he is an exceptional man. He is among the best. And the best must guide the worst of our people. The Negro race will only be saved by exceptional men. Will you be one of those men, Greg?"

There was nothing I wanted more. I wanted to be like Uncle Mike.

"Absolutely, Uncle Mike. I will be an exceptional man. I promise."

That night he gave me his copy of *The Negro Problem* to read. It was a bit mature for my age, but it lit a fire in me. I had a desire to be more than another little Negro boy from Mississippi. I read and reread every page, especially the passages Uncle Mike had underlined. It made me proud he felt I was worthy of reading it.

When we finally turn on the street leading to Uncle Mike's house, I can't wait to get inside. Telly is fast asleep, snoring, and Mama and Daddy still aren't speaking to each other. I feel like jumping out of the car as soon as we turn into the driveway.

We pull up to the large, red brick house with green grass and flowers planted in the front garden. All the houses on Uncle Mike's street look nice like that. And the houses are big too. Nothing like our little house in Mississippi. As Mama always says, "Negroes sure know how to live the further you go North."

Uncle Mike and Aunt Kay are standing outside waiting for us to arrive. They make for a most attractive couple. Their kids are sure going to be lucky one day. I know they will make fine parents. And I start wishing Uncle Mike was my daddy again.

"Hey there, Greg," Aunt Kay says. She looks genuinely happy to see us.

Aunt Kay is beyond pretty. She looks like one of those women on the cover of Mama's magazines. She has light brown skin and long, light brown hair. And the nicest green eyes. Uncle Mike met her in college. That's another reason I want to go to college. I want to find me a wife like Aunt Kay.

A couple of their neighbors are out, other wealthy Negro families who live in Southeast Washington. The community sits high on a hill, and from almost every angle, you can look down and see all of Washington, even the Capitol. During the summer, Aunt Kay loves to sit outside on their back porch and watch the sunset.

All the men start talking about the hurricane that's getting ready to hit the South, so Mama, Telly, Aunt Kay, and I head inside. The two ladies share a look, a stare between wives they think kids don't notice. It's a look that says,

"He makes me so mad, but I love him."

Mama and Daddy often fight in silence, but they always make up by the next morning.

I go to put my things in the room where I know I'll be sleeping. I call it my room, not out loud, of course. But it is nice to pretend it's my room. Nothing like my room in Mississippi. I throw my bags on the bed and go to my favorite room in the house: Uncle Mike's office.

His office is filled with lots of things—memorabilia from his college pledging days (I've promised him I will be an Alpha man one day), maps, his teaching notes, and books. Uncle Mike has a lot of books.

Each wall in his office contains a built-in bookcase filled with bound copies of texts that explain the history of the Negro race. I love spending time in Uncle Mike's office looking at all the books and the framed drawings and portraits of Negro leaders.

I walk around to admire a new drawing that's on the wall. It's a portrait of Negro man, standing bare-chested with his fists raised in a boxing stance. And he looks to be paired up to fight a White boxer. Several other men are gathered with them in the ring while dozens of White faces look on, preparing to watch the fight. I lean in closer to read the small writing underneath the drawing.

"Like my new piece, Greg?"

Uncle Mike steps up behind me and puts his hands on my shoulders.

"I acquired it a few weeks ago. It's not the original, unfortunately, but it's a fine copy. It's something, isn't it?"

"Who is that Negro man, Uncle Mike?" I ask.

"The man that's set to fight that White man? Well, that there is the famous Thomas Molineaux. The Moor, he was often called. He was once a slave, right up the way, from Virginia."

I've never heard of him, but that doesn't surprise me. Uncle Mike always has information on Black folks I've never heard of.

"There's a story behind him. Want to hear about it?" Uncle Mike asks.

We sit down on the couch in his office. Of course I want to hear about it. He knows that.

"Tom Molineaux was once a slave. His master, seeing how large and strong Tom and his brother were, forced them into boxing—pugilism, it was called back then. Tom and his brother were forced to fight other slaves to entertain their masters and earn money for them. Tom's father was a fighter too, but among the three men, Tom was the best.

"So Tom went around from plantation to plantation, from state to state, forced to fight for his master, and he won every fight. He earned his master large sums of money, and believe it or not, one day, his master granted him his freedom. Tom knew there was not much for him in the South, so he took his earnings and moved to England to become a professional boxer.

"England had more tolerance for Negroes than the United States, but racism still existed. They did not want to see one of their White prized fighters beaten by a Negro.

"So when Tom set out to fight one of the White boxers, and it looked like Tom was going to win the fight, the crowd intervened. They caused Tom to lose the fight. His career was never the same thereafter, and he died, penniless and starving while still a young man."

"That's a horrible story."

"Well, the story doesn't end there," Uncle Mike continues.

"You see, lots of Negro slaves were forced to fight each other, for entertainment and sport. Tom was lucky to receive some of his fight proceeds. That was rare. Bill Richmond, Hannibal Straw, John Finnley. They were some of the more famous Negro slave fighters.

"But think of all the hundreds of thousands of Negro slaves who were mediocre boxers, forced to fight their own brothers. What do you think happened when they died? Do you think they died peaceful?"

"Well no, of course not. How could they?" I respond. "They didn't live peaceful lives, so how could they die peaceful?"

"Exactly, Greg. Exactly."

Uncle Mike gets up from the couch and walks over to the portrait of Tom Molineaux.

"There's a saying among the old folks, about the spirits of slaves like Tom and all the others who died at the hands of slavery. That their spirits are not peaceful. That they will never be at peace."

Uncle Mike walks back to the couch and crouches down in front of me.

"They say their spirits are embodied in the winds of hurricanes, storms that form off the coast of West Africa, travel the route of slave ships through the Middle Passage, and exact their wrath on the South. Where Negro slaves suffered the most."

He's looking at me in the face, and I start to feel cold, tiny bumps forming on my skin.

"Do you believe that, Greg?"

I think about it a bit. "Yes, Uncle Mike, I believe that."

"Do you believe Hurricane Camille could embody the restless spirits of slaves? That they've banded together, their anger at slavery and the plight of the Black man stirring in its epicenter? The eye of the storm?"

"I guess it could be those slaves, Uncle Mike. I guess they're still fighting."

23
NOT DIVIDED

Mobile, Alabama (1979)

Looking at these storm clouds brings back fond memories for me. She hasn't forgotten about me. Even after all these years.

"Hey, Mama."

My dear, sweet daughter. My only child. Lord knows any other child would have put me in an old folks' home. But not my Elizabeth. Not my Lizzy.

She and her husband Paul took me in. Even though I know it isn't true, Lizzy says I live with them as family, not as a burden.

"Paul is almost done packing up the truck. Then he's gonna board up all of the windows, and then we'll be on our way, okay?"

Lizzy speaks to me gently, like I used to speak to her when she was young, telling her something important. I love her. Still though, she's interrupting my memories.

Whenever I feel the winds of the hurricanes or the tornadoes rush through this state, I know Awiti is returning to me. That's my time.

I wish Lizzy would go away, leave me to my thoughts. I stare out the window, making eye contact with nothing. That's what old folks do when we want to be left alone.

Lizzy walks over and kisses me on the cheek before walking out of the room. She's the one thing I did right in this world. Aside from that, my marriage to John wasn't worth nothing.

Well, that's not entirely true. He did buy me Awiti for my eighteenth birthday. Best birthday of my life.

Awiti and I were more like sisters. Partners in crime, that's what we were. Sure, I treated her like she was hired help when folks were around, bossing her about. But when it was the two of us together, when no one else was around, Awiti and I were the best of friends.

She was beautiful and wild, something different in my predictable life. Awiti saved me from those years I was forced to be a Southern belle.

John was wealthy, which is why Mama made me marry him. Life was hard in the South once slavery was abolished. The Yankee troops destroyed plantations, ruined the crops and livelihood. There were some businessmen, like John, who escaped the war unscathed. They managed to remain wealthy and successful despite what was happening all around them.

And they were the kind of men who had their pick of the most beautiful young girls in the South. Fathers and mothers married away their young daughters to whichever man had the best bank account, the most prominent name.

It wasn't that John wasn't a nice man. He was plenty nice. And even though he was twenty-two years my senior, he was still rather handsome. He had gorgeous, sandy-brown curls, which thankfully, Lizzy inherited. His eyes reminded me of the blue waters of the Coosa River. And he never treated me poorly, unlike some of the other unfortunate girls who were married off.

It was just I wasn't quite ready to be married. I was only sixteen when Mama came and told me she had found me a most eligible suitor.

"His name is John Buchanan," Mama said as she laced up my corset. "He is quite handsome, but more importantly, he is extremely wealthy."

The word "wealthy" rolled off her tongue with a Southern aristocracy, dripping with desperation.

We had at one time been wealthy, and now we were poor, a word Mama did not like to say often. Of course, no one knew how poor we were. But our surname had surely lost its value.

"This is our chance to return to the life we had before the war. If John falls in love with you, your marriage will help us reclaim our place in high society," she said to me.

"Our place" meant the future of our family was riding on me. It was a heavy burden for a teenage girl, and a task at which I could not fail.

"Yes, Mama," I responded.

She turned me around so we could see my reflection in the mirror. I was quite beautiful.

My dark hair hung in perfect spirals, and my skin was like fine china, clear and unblemished. In those days, I had the figure that caused men to turn to watch me pass and trip over themselves if they weren't careful. Mama admired her greatest work.

"Now, he may try to touch on you, because as you know, not all Southern men are gentlemen," Mama warned me.

I had heard the stories of young girls who were tainted,

ineligible to be top contenders because some Southern gentleman had forced himself upon them.

"You are to let him down gently, like a lady. Do not slap away his hand or kick violently. You are to be demure, yet firm. If he wants you, he's going to have to marry you."

Her voice was matter-of-fact as she pulled at my dress. I imagined my Grandma Ann having the same conversation with her as a young girl. I prayed it was not a speech I would have to repeat to my own daughter one day.

John met me that night and courted me for several weeks thereafter before asking for my hand in marriage. I was pleased for my family, not so much for myself.

It was a grand wedding, attended by anybody who was anybody. Mama beamed and floated on my wedding day. Her life's purpose had been fulfilled.

I began to live a life many Southern women could only dream of, yet still, I was unhappy. But that all changed the day John came home with Awiti.

"Happy Birthday, darling," John said to me, smiling.

He pushed the Colored girl in front of him, grinning with excitement.

I was his young wife, and he wanted to make me happy. What better way than to gift me with my own Colored girl, even more impressive since slavery was abolished.

She was to brush my hair, clean my garments, hold an umbrella while I walked to protect my porcelain skin from the Alabama sun. This gift of a domestic servant was intended to please me. John knew nothing about pleasing a woman.

All the while, John was jovial as he introduced my present, Awiti. I could not stop staring at her. She was beyond lovely, tall, and stately. Her skin reminded me of toffee candies, and I was tempted to reach out and stroke her, to see if she was sticky.

Her hair was dark and fell over her shoulders, and she looked at me with shy, dark eyes. She seemed not much older than I, both of us trapped in lives that were predestined for us. It was so unfortunate, unfair that we had no say in the matter.

The next morning, when John left for business, Awiti and I stared at each other. I had never had a servant, although I knew how to treat one, as Mama had often treated me as such. Still, I had nothing for Awiti to do, and so I sat on my bed while she stood by the door waiting for my orders.

Then, I smiled at her, and she returned my smile. And that was the beginning of our friendship.

Awiti was the perfect guise. No one ever suspected her of being anything other than my servant. But during John's long absences for business, we helped each other survive as we learned to navigate the world of young adulthood. Always sharing secrets and making mischief. Until that one fateful day.

We found ourselves in the middle of the cotton fields. Of course, there were no slaves to pick cotton—field hands and machinery did the work that was once the responsibility of Awiti's people.

The puffs of white surrounded us like soft clouds. Long blades of grass were a thick green flooring beneath our bare feet. We chased each other around, laughing and hiding, enjoying the youth that had been stolen from us.

On the farmost corner of John's property was a lake. It served no purpose other than for admiration, something to look over when the sun set. Still, it was nice to dip one's feet into the cool waters on a warm summer's day.

"Let's go for a swim, Kate," Awiti said.

She looked at the water longingly. Awiti loved to swim.

"Oh, I cannot. I have no swimsuit," I responded. Then I reminded Awiti pointedly, "*We* have no swimsuits."

"No matter. We don't need them."

Awiti looked at me and smiled as she began to undress. We had seen each other naked before, plenty of times, but there was something different about this day.

I found myself excited, longing for something I couldn't explain as Awiti stood there naked before me. Her skin seemed to glow in the Alabama sunshine, and the tingling between my legs intensified.

"Well, come on now," Awiti said, beckoning me.

She stepped into the lake, and I watched her body disappear beneath the water, inch by inch, as she went in deeper. And I began to undress.

We were both in the water, up to our necks, our faces only inches apart. I had never been with a woman before that day. Hell, the only person I had ever been with my whole life was John.

But if I was honest with myself, I had always found women's bodies beautiful. My eyes were drawn to the shape of their lips, the size of their breasts. It didn't matter, though, because women were off limits.

Even if someone knew my thoughts, I could be punished. Or perhaps even institutionalized. Loving another woman was unnatural, and thus, of course, illegal. An abomination in the eyes of God.

But there was no one there to judge me that day, no one in the cotton fields to tell my secret. Just me and Awiti.

"I know you love me, and I love you, Kate," Awiti said before touching her lips to mine.

Her lips were so soft, and the skin on her face like fine silk. There was no harsh facial stubble, no scratches like John's beard, just soft. Everything was soft.

I reached for her breasts under the water, and we moved closer, retreating toward the shore until her breasts were above the water. Her nipples tempted me, like small mounds of chocolate, and before I knew it, they were in my mouth.

I kissed and sucked until Awiti's nipples became erect and soft moans escaped her lips.

She began to touch me beneath the water, her fingers pushing and stroking between my legs. She pleasured me until I cried out from the joy, the shaking of my body. Never had I felt such a longing. Never had I been so in love.

That moment became all-defining for us. We were all we had in a cruel, dark Southern world filled with hatred and bigotry. But our love could only sustain us for so long.

Although we both wanted to believe it could, love wasn't enough to keep us alive and nourish us forever. I was White and adored; Awiti was Colored, and because of that, she was hated. Besides love, there was only so much we could do for each other.

Awiti told me one night, "I have to leave this place, Kate."

We were lying in the bed John and I shared whenever he was home from his travels. It never felt quite right when he was in it.

"But what will I do without you?" I pleaded. "I need you!"

I was crying, hysterical, for this had become the topic of every conversation—her leaving, and me crying, begging her to stay.

"There is a life for you here, Kate, even if it is a pretend life. It's a good life. What's here for me?" she asked.

The dark eyes looked sad. We had discussed every

possibility—running away together, going to Canada. But we knew there were few places, if any, that would be accepting once they learned of our true relationship.

"I refuse to hide forever, Kate. But I will never leave you, I'll always be near. Our love is like the force of the hurricane—strong, unforgiving, wild, and damaging. When you feel those winds, you'll know it's me. Nothing can stop me from loving you, Kate."

I understand why Awiti left me. For who could endure a lifetime of hate? Even for love, it was too much to ask of anyone.

Of course, if she had to go, I didn't want her to leave empty-handed. She had saved me all these years, pretending to be my hired help, but all the while loving me, teaching me to have a voice and believe in myself. There was only one thing I could think to do.

I knew where John kept his money. Yes, he had some in the bank like all wealthy men, but not all of it. He kept a very generous amount in the home safe. And so the night before Awiti left, I took it all. Emptied the safe and gave my love enough money and jewels to afford her a lovely life.

Awiti was long gone by the time John discovered the theft. I acted just as shocked as he did. I echoed his angry sentiments that someone had robbed us blind without us even knowing. I was so meek back then.

Today I would tell him, "I gave your money to my Black lover. Wanted her to live a good life. Or squander it all gambling and drinking moonshine. Whatever she wanted. I was only fair. You know, since her family earned most of your money for you."

I could see John passing right out! He would have never heard the end. He would have surely had a heart attack at the words "Black lover." Or better yet, when I said I gave his money away.

Don't know why these thoughts make me laugh, but I do. Loudly.

"You all right, Mama?"

"Yes, Lizzy. I'm all right." I'm better than all right.

Throughout my life, like she promised, there are times Awiti reminds me she is there, always loving me.

One time, after Lizzy was born, John and I travelled to New York. I became a better wife after Awiti left, more resigned to my role. I was sitting on a park bench, with Lizzy in my lap, and a lady came and sat next to me.

Her face was shielded by a scarf, and her entire body covered with clothing. But her hand—I would recognize that brown, toffee skin anywhere.

She placed a book on the park bench, and then she got up and walked away. *The Well of Emotions.*

I still have that book, dog-eared to my favorite part, the words that got the author in a whole lot of trouble back then:

"And they were not divided that night."

That's me and Awiti.

"Mama," Lizzy calls out. "Looks like this Hurricane Frederic is going to be one heck of a storm."

I know it is my love. She is coming to make them pay. Make them suffer. I never blamed her for it, for the damage she caused. I understand what it is to be hurt and angry. To hate a world that refuses to love you.

"Yes, Awiti. Come wash over me."

24
BLACK BIRD

Palm Beach, FL (1981)

Grandfather was evil. And not like, "he was a just a mean old man" evil. Like, he was super evil. And he was the worst kind of evil because he was rich. I think the only reason my dad didn't turn out like him was because he left the South for college, went up North, and never looked back.

When I was younger, Dad never talked about his childhood much except to say he was glad it was over. He clung to his father-in-law like he was the father he never had.

In fact, we spent every vacation and holiday we could with Mom's crazy, liberal, amazing family. Every holiday except Christmas.

For Christmas, we had to go to Florida to spend it with my grandfather.

"To secure our future," Dad would say.

Once I got older, and I could understand life a little more, Dad and I really talked about things, including his childhood. The stuff I found out about my family didn't make me proud.

Liberal White guilt, Tammy called it. And well, I love her

and believe everything she says because she's so freaking smart. So I guess you can say I have a case of the liberal White guilt.

From a young age I knew Grandfather was racist. He was a deep-seated Southern boy, blue-blood true racist. He talked about Black people as if they were rabid dogs—diseased, dirty, wild, dangerous, and deranged. And he believed the world would be a better place if they, like rabid dogs, were put to death.

Oh, and of course he didn't call them "Black people." That would be too humane. They were "the others," "those people," or his favorite, "niggers."

Last Christmas, Dad told me there was a room in Grandfather's mansion that was full of stuff from when my grandfather was a young man. Grandfather called it his History of the South room. Dad said it was Grandfather's jack-off room.

According to Dad, Grandfather went in there to jerk off and get high off of all the violent things he did in his youth. I decided it would be best if I didn't go in there. I was tempted, but I'll be honest, I was afraid of what I might find in that room aside from Grandfather's cum stains.

I told Tammy about the History of the South room over spring break, and she wanted to know what was in there. She was always curious about stuff like that. So this year, I promised I wouldn't be a bitch about it. I would check it out.

Whenever we crossed the bridge to get to Palm Beach, my grandfather always said the same thing.

"Thank God for the bridge. That's the only thing that separates us from them. You know niggers don't like water. Hell, they can't even swim!"

He said it in his annoying Southern drawl that made him sound like a Confederate soldier. Dad rolled his eyes; Mom picked imaginary lint off her skirt. I looked out the window at the beautiful blue intercoastal that just that quickly, my grandfather made ugly.

We arrived at Grandfather's mansion as scheduled, his driver made certain of that. The Florida sun reflected off the pink stucco with white trim. His house always made me think of ice cream. Lots of rich and famous families lived nearby. We even ran into Donald Trump one Christmas. I think that was the only time my mother truly enjoyed herself, because whenever she could, she worked her brief run-in with "The Donald" into conversations.

I can't say I have ever enjoyed myself. Usually I tried to spend as much time as possible at the beach or driving around with Dad in one of Grandfather's antique cars. Christmas holiday seemed to be the longest week of the year.

This Christmas would be like all the others, except I planned to check out Grandfather's jack-off room. I decided I would check it out after Christmas Eve dinner while everyone ate desserts and the children sang Christmas carols. I just wanted to take a peek. I told Tammy about the History of the South room over spring break, and she wanted to know what was in there.

Grandfather always had his huge pine Christmas trees decorated by a professional. This year's theme was cats and dogs. The trees were decorated with hideous, expensive ornaments of various breeds and way too much trimming. I wanted to knock it down, watch all those glass ornaments of cats and dogs break into a million pieces. Man, I really hate here.

On Christmas Eve, all of my family gathered in the large dining room for our annual feast. There was enough food to feed an army. The older I got and more exposure I had of the world, I became aware of such lavishness. It made me sick. We would never be able to eat it all.

The caterer had prepared an excessive number of sides, which guests were to pair with fish, turkey, chicken, duck, and if that wasn't enough, turducken. We sat around the table, laughing and talking as we paid our dues so that when Grandfather died, he would leave us a portion of his big fortune for being "family." Everyone was eating dessert when I excused myself. No one even noticed I left.

I walked down the main hall and headed toward Grandfather's History of the South room. For some reason, I was nervous. I felt like I was sneaking around a place I shouldn't be, instead of walking around my grandfather's house. It was eerily quiet on the south wing of the house. Everyone was still in the dining room faking like they were having a good time.

The door to the History of the South room was slightly cracked. I carefully pushed it open, real slowly. Next thing I knew, I had stepped into a museum honoring the antebellum South. The room was full of everything one would expect a racist to have, except, well, you would never expect to actually see it.

There were thick ropes with nooses that had dried blood on them. Several Confederate flags adorned the walls. Klan head coverings sat atop mannequin heads, and a full Klan suit was memorialized in a glass frame. One of the walls contained shelving that held little glass jars filled with God-knows-what.

The remaining spaces on the walls were covered with newspaper clippings and historic headlines. There was even a framed newspaper highlighting the day Martin Luther King, Jr. was assassinated. I felt sick. But I was all the way in now. It was time for me to see who my grandfather really was.

A blue photo album sat on top of a wooden desk. Although I could only imagine the horrors I would find inside, I opened the cover. On the first page was a newspaper clipping from the St. Louis Argus.

"Outspoken Negro killed," I read aloud.

I knew I should close the book, to stop reading. But I couldn't.

"Palm Beach, Florida. June 13. The body of Henry Simmons, Negro, riddled with bullets, was found today hanging to a tree on Palm Beach Island. Simmons was a native of the Bahama Islands. He is said to have been an industrious and conscientious worker at a local ice cream plant, but he also made enemies because he was outspoken on the treatment of American Negroes by Southern Whites."

"I see you found my brag book."

It was my grandfather's Confederate soldier voice.

I had been so absorbed in the horror I was reading that I hadn't even heard him enter the room. And when I turned around to face him, I knew what my dad meant.

I had never seen such happiness on my grandfather's face. His wrinkles seemed to fade. He had stepped back in time a few years by just walking into the room. This was definitely his jack-off room.

"Don't be shy now. Look around. This is who we are."

He walked around the room proudly.

"Everything in that book you holding, I did it. Every picture you see, I took it because I was there. Or one of my friends was there. That was the time when White men ruled the world. None of this equality and segregating they got going on now. You know what I mean?"

I wanted to run from the room. He thought I was like him.

That we were the same because we were family. A good ol' racist grandfather and grandson bonding moment. But we weren't. I was nothing like him.

"You know what's in these jars? These real nigger parts from lynchings. Come see now!"

His voice was excited, his cheeks flushed. Grandfather grabbed me by the arm and steered me toward the wall that was covered with jars.

As we moved closer, I could see what was inside the jars—ears, fingers, toes, and my God, there even was a penis! The parts sat in a clear solution that only intensified the view of the charred black skin. I felt my stomach lurch. I was going to vomit.

Upon hearing me gag, Grandfather admonished me.

"Now don't be weak like your daddy! That boy always been weak about niggers. I took him with me to a lynching when he was a boy, and he cried for days. Shamed me, he did."

Grandfather sounded angry. The memory of his weak White son at a lynching still infuriated him.

"All these nigger parts you see here, they got what was coming. All of them did something wrong, and they had to pay for they crime. Justice. That's how things was done back then," Grandfather said.

"When things were that way, when White was right? We didn't have all these problems we have today. All these niggers running around committing crimes, and nothing being done to them."

He spit on the hardwood floor, disgusted. I wondered if his housekeeper would know that was spit when she came to clean.

"I'm not weak, Grandfather. I just…"

I tried to defend myself, but I didn't know what to say. I was in my Grandfather's jack-off room. He had killed Black people, kept their body parts, and was proud of it. What was I supposed to say to that?

"I just...didn't know you had all this stuff in here," I finally said.

"Yup! And it's yours once I pass if you want it," he replied.

His Southern drawl was laced with pride. He looked at me eagerly.

He wanted me to want it. *Needed* me to want it. Every piece of his racist soul leaned forward, eager for my response. His blue eyes stared into mine, and I knew this would be a defining moment in our relationship. I thought of Dad reminding me that Christmas holidays were to secure our inheritance.

"Of course...of course, I want it. It's cool," I said.

I instantly felt sick. I had sold my soul to my blue-eyed Confederate-soldier-voiced Grandfather in his jack-off room. What was wrong with me?

"That's my boy! Now c'mon back to the party. The little ones are about to start singing," he said with a smile.

Grandfather walked out of his History of the South room like he walked out of the garage after we had a discussion about one of his antique cars. The dead body parts and racist memorabilia were just another part of his collection. He believed he had really given me something.

I had sold my morals and values to my evil Grandfather in hopes of gaining my inheritance. I ran to the bathroom and vomited.

When Tammy called me later in the evening to say our good nights, she could hear it in my voice. I was not myself.

"Is everything okay?" she asked.

"Yeah. You know my dad's side of the family stresses me out. We'll talk about it when I get back."

I changed the subject and asked about her Christmas Eve activities I was sure were quite different from mine.

How could I tell my sweet, liberal Tammy that one day we would inherit my grandfather's jack-off room, complete with Klan hoods and the burned body parts of Black people from crimes he committed but was never charged for? Yeah, that was a conversation that must be had in person, if ever.

On Christmas morning, my stocking was stuffed with envelopes, cards full of money every college student needed. I usually walked away with several grand. But this year, the money didn't make me happy.

As was custom, I also received my ugly sweater to wear next Christmas. It was bright green and covered with red Christmas ornaments and silver tinsel. It was revolting. At the end of the obsessive amount of gift opening, one present remained under the tree.

"Looks like Santa left you something extra," Grandfather said.

He looked at me with proud eyes.

I reached for the small box covered in Santa-printed wrapping paper, a White Santa, of course. I was afraid to open it. Surely Grandfather wouldn't give me a racist memento that would scare the children. But I had seen his jack-off room, so I could not be certain.

"Go on now. Open it," he said excitedly.

I started to unwrap it carefully, for I expected a charred black body part to fall out at any moment. Those jars filled with the parts of lynched Black people haunted my dreams last night. I didn't sleep well at all.

The wrapping came off easily and revealed a white box. I lifted the lid of the box, and inside, underneath white tissue paper, was a wooden box.

I was reminded of those annoying dolls where each doll held a smaller doll inside. I might pass out from anticipation before I opened the actual gift. My heart pounded.

The wooden box looked antique. All eyes were on me as I opened the box and slowly pulled out my gift. It was a gun, an antique gun with a beautiful bone handle and long silver barrel.

The men, excited, leaned forward for a closer look.

The women all smiled. Their smiles said, "Men and their toys."

Had I not gone into the History of the South room last night, well, I might have been excited. It was old and in pristine condition, probably worth a fortune. But now I couldn't help but wonder how many Black people had been killed with this very gun. My hands started to shake.

"Thanks, Grandfather. It's beautiful," I said.

"Beautiful and practical. You never know when some nigger might come breaking in your home. Especially once you have yourself a fine, young, blue-eyed, blonde-haired wife like your mom here," he said with a wink.

Mom started to pick at imaginary lint. Dad excused himself and went to the restroom.

I thought of Tammy. She was as far from blue-eyed and blonde haired as any woman could be. I saw my mom smirk. She was surely thinking of Thanksgiving dinner.

Tammy had come over with her hair in braids and her dark brown skin glowing from our recent trip to the Bahamas. We had returned to the states with tans, full of smiles and stories we shared at Thanksgiving. My parents loved Tammy.

"Better marry her after your grandfather dies," my dad had said with a chuckle when he first met Tammy. "If not, you won't see a red cent of your inheritance. And if you do it before then, please make sure I'm around so I can have the pleasure of watching that man die from a heart attack."

Dad and I had laughed, even though it wasn't really funny.

Now that I had seen Grandfather's History of the South room, I didn't want any part of his dirty, racist money. I returned the gun to the box and decided to go for a walk. I needed fresh air and space to think. The rest of the family went to put on their bathing suits for our traditional Christmas morning swim in Grandfather's swimming pool.

I crossed the street and sat on the ledge that separated the sidewalk from the beach. I loved the ocean breeze, the smell of salt water in the air. Normally I would hop over and go for a walk along the sand, but the recent revelations had drained me. I just wanted to sit.

A little black bird flew down and landed on the ledge right beside me. It sat so close that I could see the detail on its dark feathers. It had a tiny dark beak and small dark eyes that looked at me as it cocked its head to the side.

It was so close, I was tempted to reach over and touch its beautiful dark plumage. The bird looked at me and then turned its head to look out to the blue water and clear skies.

"Burn that room," I heard the voice of a woman say softly.

I looked around to see who was speaking, but no one was there. The beach was empty. Just me and the bird. I needed to sleep. Clearly, I needed to sleep. I was starting to hear voices.

"Go burn that room," the voice said again.

Was the bird talking to me? Shit!

I shifted my body slightly, uncomfortable at hearing

random voices talking, and the bird flew away. I watched it fly out over the ocean and into the skies until it was just a dark speck against the blue.

Then I got up from the ledge and walked toward Grandfather's house. I could hear the family laughing and talking, the children enjoying themselves as they splashed around the pool.

I opened the front door and headed to the kitchen where I knew Grandfather kept his lighter, right next to the humidor. I took the lighter and walked down the main hall toward the History of the South room.

"What are you doing?" my mind was screaming.

But I could not stop. I continued with quick, silent steps. Something was leading me, determined.

I pushed the door open, and the room appeared just as evil as it had last night. I grabbed my grandfather's brag book off the desk. I turned to the newspaper clipping of poor Henry Simmons, and I set fire to it.

The book caught fire quickly, and the heat burned my hand. I dropped the book on the floor. The area rug caught fire, and the flames slowly started to spread, dancing along the expensive tapestry.

The glass jars filled with charred black body parts started to break open from the heat. They spilled onto the floor and fueled the fire. The fire was spreading quickly, and the room filled with smoke. The smoke detector started to wail an angry warning.

I ran outside to the pool.

"Fire," I yelled. "Fire!"

PALM BEACH POST

Monday, December 28, 1981

OBITUARIES

Christopher Michael Williams, age 76, of Palm Beach, Florida passed away on December 27. He suffered a heart attack after an unfortunate fire damaged substantial portions of his home on Christmas morning. Christopher was a long-time resident of Palm Beach and key figure in Palm Beach County politics before he retired. He was predeceased by his wife, the lovely Mary Ann Williams. He will be lovingly remembered by his family, including his son, Christopher Michael Williams, Jr. and only grandson, Johnathan Williams; his brothers, George Williams and Theodore Williams, and their wives; his sister Suzanne Williams Smith; and several nieces and nephews. The family will hold a private burial. Those who wish may send a memorial gift to the American Heart Association.

25
WRITE IT DOWN

Louisville, Kentucky (1987)

66 I hate it when this happens, Mama!"

"I know, honey," Mama says. "I know."

She's trying to comfort me, but her words ain't comfort. Don't help me one bit. All those words do is remind me she don't understand. Remind me that she don't know. Nobody knows. And if they do know, they damn sure don't tell anybody.

It's the one secret I wish had kept to myself. Been happening since as long as I can remember. Then one day, like any child might of done, I told Mama what I was seeing and hearing from time to time. Worst thing I ever done.

"Let me go get my bible."

I knew she was gon' grab her bible. "Ain't gon' help, Mama."

"Don't know that, child. God stronger than anything. And it's written that ain't no such things as evil spirits. No inbetween. You live. Then you die."

"But Mama…"

"Ain't no 'but'. It's life on Earth. Then death. And heaven or hell. And I'm trying to keep you from the latter."

Mama starts flipping through her bible, the pages held together by tape and the pressure of her hand on the spine. I can see her favorite passages underlined and circled. All on account of me, I'm sure. Ain't a single one of them scriptures gon' help me. But no matter what I say, Mama won't believe me.

Like that time I told her Awiti showed me her face. I was standing, looking in the mirror and getting ready for school. I knew she was near 'cause I could feel her, that cold breeze right up on my back. I closed my eyes, and when I opened them, there she was.

She didn't look much older than me. Her skin was light, and her face real pretty. Long curls every Black girl dreams of.

But it was those sad, dark eyes. I couldn't stop thinking about those sad eyes, even after she left. That's why I told Mama I saw her. Boy, she beat me something awful that day. Whipped me so bad trying to "get them demons out" of me, I ended up with a busted lip and two swollen eyes.

Mama didn't even say sorry. Just yelled at the air and said, "Don't ever come back 'round here, ya' hear?"

But of course, Awiti came back. Many times. And that's why Mama stays flipping through her bible.

"Here's the passage," she says excitedly. Little beads of sweat running down her forehead. I can see her roots starting to curl up. When this is all over, she gon' blame me for sweating out her press.

"Hebrews 9:27. 'Man is destined to die once, and after that, to face judgment.'" She yells the words into the air and then turns to face me. "Now you repeat them words."

"'Man is destined to die once, and after that, to face judgment,'" I say.

"And what's the scripture?"

"Hebrews 9, verse 27."

"So you see," Mama says matter-of-factly as she closes her bible and places it on her lap, "ain't no such thing as no spirits. That face you see and them voices you hear, that's a demon."

I say nothing. I've learned it's best to say nothing. 'Cause whatever I say trying to defend what I've seen and heard just gets me into more trouble. Best for me to just nod and agree, repeat whatever scripture she says, and let her pray.

"I think I'm gon' call on the Pastor."

"No, Mama," I beg. "Don't do that. Please!"

Last time she called on the Pastor to help me, he told her he needed to be alone with me. "Just me, her, and the demon," is what he said. When Mama left, he placed his hands on either side of my head while he prayed for me. Then I felt his hand under my dress. His other hand was inside his pants moving in a hurry. His fingers poking and pushing at me till he fell over in huff. Said the demons made him do it and not to tell anyone. And I knew it was best not to.

"Please, Mama," I begged.

"You hear that demon fighting in you, not wanting to get out?" Mama's excited now. Grabbing her coat and putting on her shoes. "It don't want me to get the Pastor. That demon ain't no match for Jesus!"

I'm trying to think of what I can do to make her stay. Anything to keep her from going to get the Pastor.

"No, Mama!" I cry out. "Don't leave me!"

As best as I can, I start to cry. The tears ain't real, but I've gotten real good at it. Fake crying so Mama will take pity and love on me.

Mama stops. She looks at me, and I can tell she sees her little girl. Her only daughter. Not the child who hears and sees demons.

"Well, all right. Calm down now. I can wait until tomorrow before talking to the Pastor."

"Thank you, Mama." I go to hug her, but she flinches. I'm sure she's thinking of the demons.

She grabs a notepad and a pencil and says, "Write down what the voices sayin'."

"All right, Mama." And I start to write exactly what I hear,

Spiritual world ain't what people think it is. They think it's a separate place. Apart from the world they live in. But it's very much the same. Existing on the same plane. Like layers on a cake. We right here with the world of the living. Right on top of one another.

In fact, we more here with the living than they are with themselves. The spirits, we feel each other. See each other. Acknowledge each other. The living don't do that.

There are many open channels for us to speak to those who are alive. Many ways for us to let you know we are here. And every so often, we find the one. Our one. And we can't leave them. It's an unspoken arrangement. When we find that one who can feel us, see us. That one who can hear us. We just can't leave.

That's who you are to me, Tina. You are my one. I know

it frightens you. But I mean no harm. Makes me feel bad, actually, when I wake you from your sleep. When you cry out for your mama 'cause you feel that heavy weight sitting on your chest. It's just hard for me not to be near you.

Don't want to hurt you. That's for sure. But because you're an open channel, I have to talk to you. Did I scare you when I showed my face tonight? When you looked up in the ceiling and saw me? I was smiling! Wanted you to know I'm not gon' hurt you. Did you see me smiling at you?

I know you don't like it much, but I actually like when your mama tells you to get the pen and paper. To write down my words. I get to speak through you. And you write so well. So beautifully. You capture every word I say.

Did you know I was not much older than you the day I died? My first death, that is. That was the day they came to my village. I think that's why you can feel me. I think if you were a girl in my village, we would have been friends.

They came and took it all. Everything I loved scattered that day, and we've never been reunited. And that day, as my family and my people went in different directions, I died. Even though I was still very much alive.

It was the love for my family that kept me moving forward. If I could just make it to that tree, I would say, maybe they will be there. If I just cross over this river, they might be on the other side waiting for me. These are things I told myself to keep me putting one foot in front of the other. To keep moving forward to find them.

But what I found was trouble. You know how your mama tells you, "trouble has a way of finding you"? That's me too. Trouble always seems to have a way to find Awiti.

That day, trouble was named Oranyan. He tricked me, Tina. He tricked me with love. Don't worry, though. I'm gonna stay by your side. I won't ever let a man trick you. Never.

Sorry to wake you. Just wanted to talk. To let you know I'm here. You got to stop being afraid. You got to stop calling for your mama when you hear me. Can't tell her you saw me. They won't never understand what we have, Tina.

These next words just for your mama. I'm not gonna hurt Tina. We friends. I'm Tina's friend. You can call me by name. All you got to say is, Hey Awiti. That's how friends do.

And write this down for your mama too. I know the preacher told you to have Tina write out the words I say to her. When the voices speak. I promise you this, if you give this paper to the preacher. If you show him these words, Tina good as dead. They gon' say she evil. That the devil got a hold of her. And nothing you ever gon' be able to do or say to make that change. You know who the devil got hold of? Your preacher. Ask him how it felt under Tina's dress. See what the good preacher has to say then!

Best thing for you to do is read these words Tina wrote. Read them as many times as you need to understand. That is to say, you need to know these here worlds of the living and dead. We all here together. And I found me a friend in Tina. Me and your daughter is friends. Got something to say to me, just call on me. Just say, "Awiti, I'd like to have some words with you."

"You almost done writing, Tina?" Mama asks. She's standing far away from me as she can.

"Yes, ma'am," I say. "I'm done. I'm gon' let you read these words, Mama. And when you done, we gon' rip up this here paper and throw it away."

"What you say?"

"You heard me, Mama."

"What's come over you, Tina?" Mama asks. "You scaring me!" She starts to cry and pray, holding her bible. She got it aimed at me like it's a gun.

"Don't be scared," I say. "We friends." My voice sounds different. Deeper.

"Why you looking like that?"

"Like what?" I ask. I can't see myself.

"Don't sound like you," Mama says. "And you don't look like you."

That's 'cause I ain't me. I can feel Awiti in my skin.

Breathing through my lungs. And when I speak, it's her voice. Not my own.

"Tina?" Mama asks, unsure.

"Tina's all right. You talking to me now."

And right then, Mama fell out. Strangest place for me to be in, watching my mama laid out on the ground. She fell, real slow, like in a movie. Wonder what she saw. Did she see Awiti? No matter. I'll deal with her when she comes to.

I pull my blanket off the bed and place it over Mama. Take my pillow and put it under her head. She don't move, but she's breathing, so I know she's all right. I'll let her rest awhile. Reckon she's gon' need a bit of sleep to read what I wrote. I reckon things gon' change 'round here.

26
QUESTIONS

Fredericksburg, VA (1990)

Loren loved and hated visiting her grandmother at Bay Ridge Senior Residences. She was fortunate to have time with her MeeMaw, but still, there were depressing moments. They spent most Sunday afternoons reminiscing about Loren's childhood days and arguing over Scrabble. Every so often, Loren would play her violin in the main hall for entertainment.

At least MeeMaw wasn't suffering from a terminal illness or dementia. She was simply dying from old age, an occasion not afforded to many. Still, Loren missed going to her MeeMaw's house. Bay Ridge never quite felt like home.

The two had been close ever since Loren was young. Her mother and father worked long hours in their dental practice. So it was always MeeMaw who picked her up from school and took her to all of her activities. MeeMaw nursed her broken heart over ice cream and chocolate chip cookies and attended every single one of Loren's lacrosse games.

When Loren quit playing lacrosse in high school due to

her demanding academics and focus on music, MeeMaw confessed she hated the game. In fact, she had spent most of the time sipping vodka from her water bottle. The memory of their conversation made Loren smile.

During Loren's high school years, they were often mistaken for mother and daughter. The two were similar in appearance, right down to their blue eyes. Over the years, Loren watched her MeeMaw's hair change from strawberry blonde to gray to silvery-white.

MeeMaw was once an avid runner. They used to run in local 5k and 10k races, everyone cheering on the grandmother-granddaughter duo. But then MeeMaw's bones began to fracture and break easily. Now, she was confined to a wheelchair, standing occasionally with the assistance of a walker.

Thankfully, MeeMaw still had her wits about her. Loren could not imagine the day her grandmother would become incoherent. She sighed and entered MeeMaw's personal code to access the building.

It was a lovely facility as far as senior residences were concerned. The grounds were well-manicured and orderly. Loren had accompanied her MeeMaw during her senior home search. Nothing had seemed quite good enough.

Bay Ridge was the only residence that met most of the requirements. MeeMaw had enjoyed horticulture, so whatever senior residence she entered needed to have a garden. She wasn't old and senile, so MeeMaw needed a community with others like her—intelligent, wealthy people she could relate to. Seniors who were growing old, encouraged to leave their homes by family members concerned about their welfare and safety.

As Loren walked through Bay Ridge's main entrance, she

was happy to see Amos, the security guard. He was always so friendly. He went out of his way to bring happiness to a place often filled with sadness, grief

"How you doing today, Miss Loren?" Amos asked as he smiled. He tipped an imaginary hat.

Amos was an older African American man. He had salt-and-pepper hair and a jovial figure that reminded Loren of Santa Claus. It was hard not to return his smile.

"I'm doing great, Mr. Amos. Here to see my MeeMaw."

"Ah, she's doing good today. Saw her in the cafeteria this morning, causing trouble as usual."

Amos gave Loren a wink. It always amused Loren when the elderly said full words that could be effortlessly abbreviated. Like "cafeteria." It was so much easier to say "cafe."

"Good to know, Mr. Amos."

Loren took the elevator to the fourth floor and stepped out onto her grandmother's wing. The walls were painted a pale blue. The air smelled of old people—peppermints, Bengay, and mothballs. The smell used to bother Loren when MeeMaw first moved into the building. Her MeeMaw's home had always smelled of baked cookies.

When she was sixteen, Loren laughed hysterically when MeeMaw gave a confession. She showed Loren the Yankee Candle she lighted before guests arrived. The candle had a fresh-out-of-the-oven baked sugar cookie fragrance. But now the peppermint-mothball smell was comforting, familiar. Loren walked to room 408 and knocked on the door.

"Come in, Loren," her MeeMaw's voice called out.

It was 2:00 p.m. on a Sunday afternoon. MeeMaw knew it was Loren, as always.

"Can you leave the door open, darling? I want air circulating in the room."

It was possible MeeMaw wanted fresh air, but it was equally possible she was showing off. Her beautiful granddaughter—the tall, blonde college student who played violin—was visiting her today.

Visitors were a sort of bragging right among the elderly. So few received regular visits from family. Having a visitor, especially a child or grandchild, meant you were still loved by somebody.

Loren held open MeeMaw's door with the brown rubber doorstop. It used to be at MeeMaw's house, holding open the backdoor while Loren ran in and out during the summer. It was worn and tattered from all of the abuse doorstops seemed to manage over the years.

Loren sighed as she sat down in one of MeeMaw's blue wing-backed chairs. She sighed a lot whenever she visited MeeMaw.

Loud laughing echoed from the unit across the hall. Loren could see a large number of Black people gathered around an older Black woman. The old woman must be the new resident since Sister Nancy passed.

Loren missed Sister Nancy. She had often come over to have tea with Loren and MeeMaw. She had been a quiet, sweet Christian woman who prayed for Loren during final exams. Loren knew Bay Ridge was a business, but it seemed unfair another resident was already in Sister Nancy's apartment.

The Black people were loud, much too loud. Didn't they know they were in a senior community? Older people were trying to enjoy their final moments before they moved into a more depressing assisted living facility. Or even worse, passed away.

And Sunday was a major visiting day. It always amazed Loren how loud and inconsiderate Black people could be. She noticed it all the time, especially outside the dining hall on campus. Black students congregated in large groups. They laughed loudly and made inappropriate comments, cursing and such. At restaurants, in movie theaters, in parks—Black people always seemed loud.

"I'm going to close the door, MeeMaw. The new family in Sister Nancy's place is so loud."

Loren sighed as she got up from the chair and walked toward the door. And then, under her breath, she muttered,

"Niggers."

Loren wasn't racist. One of her close sorority sisters, Kim, was African American. They had pledged Lamda Delta Nu their freshman year. Kim had been Loren's first real inside peek into the lives of Black people.

Kim was one of the few of Loren's sorority sisters who were Black (there were only two, actually). Her complexion was perfect. She always had the perfect tan ("So unfair," Loren had lamented). Kim permed her dark brown hair so it was straight. That had been a funny conversation—Kim explaining to Loren when Black people permed their hair it was to make it straight, not curly.

But Kim wasn't like most of the Black people Loren encountered. She had graduated from a top-rated private high school, where she excelled on the swim team. Kim was a classically-trained violinist, like Loren. Her father was a doctor, and her mother a stay-at-home wife. It was Kim who had explained to Loren the difference between niggers and Black people.

"Listen, this is going to sound strange, Loren, but Black people hate niggers too.

"Being a nigger is a state of mind, not a racial classification. It means you are ignorant, uneducated, and want less for yourself. Niggers are loud and embarrassing. I am not a nigger. And so the word doesn't bother me, because it does not define me or anyone I know.

"I am Black. And if I must choose a racial classification, African American. Although, that is technically an incorrect classification because I am American. Born and raised in America. But I am definitely not a nigger."

It had been an enlightening conversation. Loren asked Kim question after question about Black people, niggers, and most importantly, why most Black people didn't seem to want more for themselves.

Loren spoke to her boyfriend at the time about the conversion. She had been fascinated to learn there was a difference within the racial classification of Black people.

"Whatever," John had said with a laugh. "They're all niggers!"

"Did I hear you call somebody a nigger, young lady?" MeeMaw asked.

MeeMaw was liberal and tolerant. Loren was certain MeeMaw hated the N-word. Loren's cheeks flushed from embarrassment knowing MeeMaw had heard her.

"Yes, MeeMaw," Loren sighed. "I did. Sorry. I wasn't trying to be racist or anything. It's just the Black people over there are so loud. I mean, why do they have to be so loud all the time?" Loren exclaimed.

"Do you think you're better than them, you know, because you're not loud?" MeeMaw readjusted herself in her chair.

"No. I mean, I know everyone's created equal in God's eyes," Loren began.

Her parents had drilled this into her from a young age. It was the right thing for White people to say. Even if they knew it wasn't true.

"I'm not talking about God's eyes," MeeMaw interrupted.

She was always quick-witted. Old age hadn't taken that from her.

"I'm talking about *your* eyes."

Loren looked at her MeeMaw, uncertain of how to respond.

"It's a fair question, Loren. Do you, as a White person, think you are better than them, Black people? I mean, most White people do."

This was why Loren loved MeeMaw. She was candid and fair when passing judgment. She didn't expect you to be a saint.

"Well, to be honest, yes, sometimes I do," Loren said. "I know I'm like, technically not better than them. But I do feel that way sometimes."

White privilege, Kim called it. According to Kim, Loren was lucky to be White. She was given the benefit of the doubt all the time.

"Well, you're not," MeeMaw laughed.

It was a mocking laugh, gentle. A way of scolding Loren that MeeMaw had mastered over the years. Her mother had never mastered it.

"I'm going to tell you a story. A story your great-grand-mother told me. This is a story from slavery time."

Loren loved whenever MeeMaw told her stories. There was always a lesson, but she made it fun and interesting. Loren settled in the chair and pulled one of MeeMaw's knit throws around her shoulders.

"Once upon a time," MeeMaw said. She looked at Loren and smiled.

"MeeMaw!" Loren laughed. "I'm twenty years old!"

Whenever MeeMaw began one of her stories, whether truth or fiction, she started with the words "once upon a time." The fact she still did this made Loren laugh.

When Loren got married one day and had her own children, she wanted to tell stories like MeeMaw. Loren curled into the chair and pulled the knit throw closer around her. She listened as MeeMaw began.

"So, as I was saying, once upon a time, there were two slave girls. They were purchased by the same master at the same auction. That's how they came to know each other. They became fast friends.

"They were the same age, the same height, and they both knew how to read even though it was forbidden. And they were both beautiful. They had no family, for they were sold apart from them when they were young. And so, the two slave girls came to have each other.

"Despite all of their similarities, there was one major difference between them. One of the slave girls was a Negro, fairer than most slaves, but still clearly a Negro. She had brown skin and long dark hair and the blackest eyes you've ever seen.

"The other slave girl could pass for White. She had long blonde hair and bright blue eyes. Freckles appeared on her face during the summertime. But she wasn't White. She was a slave. And both slave girls dreamed of being free.

"One day, the Negro-looking slave told the White-looking slave she had an idea. The White slave looked so White, she should run off and be free. The Negro slave would hate to see her go, but at least one of them would live a life of freedom. And when the White slave grew to become a woman, she could buy her friend and free her from a life of slavery.

"It was a dangerous plan. But the more they talked about it, the more it seemed like a foolproof idea. If the White slave got caught, she could say she was White. That she had never been a slave. So one day, the White slave girl ran off. And she never saw her Negro slave best friend again.

"The White slave made it safely to another state. She began adjusting to pretending to be White. It broke her heart to see how White people treated slaves and the things they said about Negroes. But she had to pretend to be White so her secret would never be discovered. She took up a job as a seamstress and began to live her life being free.

"Little did she know, her master began a search. She was his property. He had purchased her fair and square. He even had his proof of purchase.

"Word came to the town she was in that a master was looking for his slave who looked White. She became afraid. She ran to the authorities and asked for protection. She remembered the plan her Negro slave friend had concocted, and she began to tell her story.

"She told the authorities she was never meant to be a slave. That she had been stolen from her parents who were as White and Christian as everyone else in the town. She cried tears that made the White people have sympathy for her.

"How horrid this poor little White girl had lived a single day in slavery. But her master was insistent. She was not White.

"The matter became so hotly contested, it went before the highest court in the land. The judge called in experts and local citizens. They heard testimony from anyone who wished to be a witness to attest to the slave girl being White.

"'Look at how blonde her hair is,' one man stated.

"'And her hair is so straight, nary a curl,' another woman testified.

"'"Her skin is white and pure as snow,'" one witness argued.

"'The freckles on her face are more plentiful than my own,'" another offered.

"More and more people gave their sworn testimony. The slave girl must be White. You could tell by looking at her. So the slave girl was deemed White. And she was allowed to live a life of freedom. And she never did return to purchase her best friend."

"That's awful, MeeMaw," Loren exclaimed. "Why didn't she return to get her friend? She wouldn't have been free if it wasn't for her friend."

"That's true. No one but the White slave knows the real reason why. But they say her Negro best friend was so heart-broken, that every time it storms, those are her tears."

"So what happened to the White slave?" Loren asked. "You know, once the court ruled that she was White?"

"It is quite interesting," MeeMaw began.

"Although she hated the idea of it, she married the Whitest man she could find. She bore him several White children. She told only one of her daughters the secret and to keep the matter discreet. Each generation was allowed to tell only one child so the story wouldn't be forgotten and they could remember their good fortune.

"They looked White. They would pass for White. But there, forever in their ancestry and blood, was the lineage of a Negro slave girl who had lied to earn her freedom.

"I believe the White slave girl's name was Alexina Morrison. You should look up the case when you get the time. Might find out something about yourself."

MeeMaw smiled and closed her eyes. Loren didn't need to do any research. She already knew. If there was one thing her mother was adamant about, it was keeping her maiden name.

"One does not simply give up every part of themselves when they become married," she would explain at dinner parties, after one too many glasses of wine. "My name *means* something, and I'll be damned if I throw it away to become someone's Missus."

Her father would cower.

She often reminded Loren, "Your name isn't Loren Alexina Morrison for nothing. Your grandmother named you. It's a name to be proud of."

27

BOX OF TRUTH

St. John the Baptist Parish, LA (1992)

Hurricane Andrew had not been kind to our neighborhood. Trees littered the ground, branches and leaves strewn about like confetti after a party. Peoples' lives lay about in wet piles—papers, articles of clothing, and old shoes. Seemed like all the storm entered every house on the street, went inside and tossed everything outside, like a scorned lover discarding of memories. Every house but ours.

"You got my box?" Granny asked. She sat upright in her wheelchair, the female matriarch of our family.

"Yes, ma'am," I replied.

Of course I had it. It was all we had.

"Put it in my hands. Let me feel it."

Granny had to feel it because she sure couldn't see it. Her once brown eyes that watched over me when I was a boy were now blue-grey and blind. It didn't matter she couldn't see, though. Granny knew everything that was in the box just by touching it, or holding an article up to her nose so she could smell it. I put the large brown box in her hands, and she smiled.

"Yes, there's my box."

The box had been in our family for generations. It was always the matriarch's job to put items inside that tell the story of our family—newspaper clippings, letters, and such. Dated back for generations, started by a lady named Celestine Lindor.

"What's the streets looking like?" Granny asked. But she answered herself before any of us could respond. "I already know. Things looking bad. Real bad, ain't it." It wasn't a question.

"Bad" didn't seem like the right word. Things looked bleak, troublesome, and desolate. Horrible. Hurricane Andrew devastated the parish, torn down our street, and ripped apart the homes and lives of everyone who resided there. Well, everyone but us.

Granny's house was untouched. Not a scratch or broken window. We had all decided to gather in her home for the storm because one, we couldn't all get out of town together, and two, if we were going to die, we wanted to die together as a family.

"There go Miss Mary's dog!" Abby yelled. The mutt walked down the street looking as dazed as everyone else, combing through the items. His owner was nowhere in sight. "I'm fixin' to get him." And before anyone could stop her, Abby was out the door.

For such a young girl, Abby seemed unmoved by the damage of the hurricane. She had sat patiently while the winds howled and shook the house, rattling the wooden boards that covered the windows. We could hear articles that hadn't been secured flying up against the outside of the house. Sounded like an army of people knocking, begging to come in and out of the storm.

The lights had flickered, and then, we lost power and lit candles. And even in the darkness, Abby had sat with her legs crossed, looking and listening. And now she had run outside, a few hours after the destruction, barefoot and unafraid, chasing after an old mutt. Kids.

The adults—we were affected. Granny's house had withstood the storm, but judging by the looks of things outside, there wasn't much likelihood the rest of us would be as lucky. Not that we had much, but what we had was ours. I wondered what was left.

"We one of the few standing, ain't we," Granny said.

As usual, she didn't need her eyes to see. She could hear the destruction, feel the sadness in the air. As more of our neighbors came outside, cries began to fill the eerie quiet that exists after such a storm.

"I know why we was saved. It's this box here," Granny said. "They didn't want nothing to happen to it." She stroked the wooden box lovingly.

Toni began to grunt, Michael rolled his eyes, and his wife stood by his side looking annoyed. I knew what they were thinking.

Crazy old lady.

I said nothing. I was used to her references and admiration of *them*. "They" meant the dead. And that usually was the buzz word to leave Granny alone.

Everyone found a reason to conveniently leave the living room. Toni went into the kitchen to grab a bite to eat. And suddenly, Michael had to go to the bathroom, and his wife went to check on the children. In a matter of seconds, it was me and Granny. And the box.

"Never understand your generation. Don't know nothing 'cause they don't want to know nothing. That why I'm gon' leave the box to you when it's time."

Seemed like the burden of the box was already mine. She'd been telling me that for years.

"This place got slave blood on its hands. Them slaves ain't never gon' forget what folks done to 'em. They gon' keep sending they hurricanes. They angry, and they gots a right to be."

All the while, Granny stroked the brown box resting on her lap.

When I was young and she used to say stuff like that, it scared me. Granny went blind years ago, and she said when she did, she could see things better than when she had her sight. She said being in the darkness helped her to see. That's around the time she started to tell me haunts were real.

"People say folks is crazy for believing in the haunts, but they real," Granny had told me. "I've seen them and heard them. Those folks who practice voodoo? They know. Slaves died right here on this land. You think they gone? Where they got to go? They still right here."

Granddaddy was alive at the time, both of them raising me. Whenever the topic of haunts came up, they argued about it like there was a way for the other to see their point of view. It never happened. They argued for years, and Granddaddy died not believing in haunts.

"When you feel that wind whipping or feel like someone watching and you looks 'round but ain't nobody there? That's them. They always watching. That's what Awiti told me."

Granny was always saying Awiti told her something. No

one in the family had ever met this Awiti except for Granny. Aunt Dot said Granny never met anyone named Awiti. It was some voice in her old head she claimed made all these profound statements.

"She thinks things sound more believable if she say Awiti told her," Aunt Dot had always said.

Aside from talking about haunts, Granny had been telling us all about the box since I can remember. It's filled with history about our whole family. She was willing to share the stories with whomever wanted to listen, but nobody could have anything that was inside. Not even if they offered us lots of money.

One time, I went to a festival at an A.M.E. church in New Orleans. It was Black History Month, and one of the universities had put an ad in the paper asking locals to come share their history. Sounded like the perfect time to share what was in the box. But Granny didn't want to go.

"They always trying to give us something less than and try and make it seem great," Granny said. "February's the shortest month of the year, and they acting like they gave us December or something. I'm Black all year long, so can't nobody make me celebrate being Black for one short month out the year."

Then Granny laughed and snorted, which meant that was the end of the discussion. So I went to the festival alone.

I met lots of nice folks at that festival. Lots of locals shared stories that sounded much like our family's stories. But I had the most stories, and I had all the papers and facts to prove what I was saying was true.

Of course, I didn't have the box with me. No way would Granny let me take it without her. But I'd heard the stories so many times, listened to Granny read the letters and news stories, well, I surprised myself at how much I knew. It felt good to tell folks about my history and my family's box full of truth.

There were some big-time professors from up North at that festival. And they loved my stories and took pictures with me like I was famous. Had a big picture of me, right on the front of our local paper. Granny made me cut out the entire article and put in the box. She was proud of me.

"Still glad I didn't go," she had said.

A few months later, some of those professors from the festival came back down here and said they wanted to see the box. Claimed they wanted to publish all the history that was inside.

"It's an amazing collection," one of the professors said. "It's something the world needs to see. It's history!"

They said if I shared the box with them, I might even become famous.

First, they told me and Granny they wanted the box for free and that they were going to borrow it for the publication and bring it back. Yeah, right.

Then, when Granny said no, they offered her money. Lots of money, until I finally had to tell those White men there was no price they could put on the box. No way was Granny ever going to let go of that box.

"If I turn it loose, what's gon' protect us?" Granny asked.

I could see the professors getting angry, their faces turning red. Wasn't long before Granny showed them the door.

Didn't stop them trying again, though. Next time, they came with a Black professor, or a Black man pretending to be a professor—I couldn't be quite sure. He tried to talk to Granny like they were old friends. Please. She knew those games. Sent that Black professor running right out of our parish.

The box was all we had, and I was with Granny. I wouldn't let anybody take it away. Not even for money. That's what was wrong with folks these days. They seemed to think everybody's soul had a price. Not mine. Well, not for our family's box.

As long as we had things from that time, from slavery time, the hurricanes would keep coming and passing us by. I believed in the spirits.

One time, I went to New Orleans and saw voodoo people do magic. The voodoo people saw things we couldn't see and heard things we couldn't hear. People say they're connected to both the spiritual world and the physical world, and I believe it.

I asked a voodoo lady about what Granny says. Asked her if the slave spirits were coming back to the bayou because they were mad.

"They ain't got to come back," she said. "They right here. Ain't never left."

I've always found it strange, though. If the White folks caused all the trouble with slavery and the spirits were mad at them, why didn't the haunts go somewhere where there were only White folks, like in the mountains or something? Why didn't they send a hurricane that just wiped out White folks?

Granny told me it didn't work that way.

"That's not where the spirits' hearts at," she told me. "Them spirits ain't going to no mountains. They go where they hearts at. Where they peoples' blood was shed.

"It ain't about White folks or Black folks. It's about the hurt. That's why they hurt whoever there. Black, White, it don't matter. Them spirits tied to the land. To the blood. It's about the past. They keep returning to the past.

"That's what Awiti told me."

28
MY NAME IS BARBURY

Freeport, Bahamas (2001)

I once had a mother who loved me. Master Vanderhart sold her away when I was young, so I have no memory of her. Had a father too. But he was killed before I was born, and so, I have no memory of him either. All I have are pieces of what the slaves at the Vanderhart Plantation recalled.

I remember when I first understood my name.

"C'mon, Barbury," Tessy said. "It's time you learned to do some things."

Tessy took me by the hand and led me to the cotton fields. I remember thinking, "My name is Barbury. What a strange name."

At thirteen years of age, I went aboard the *George Washington*. I listened to every word being said around me, even though sometimes I didn't know what they meant. I learned the ship's master was James Curry. And the shipper was named E.W. Copeland. My owner was Master J.C. Vanderhart. But I had known that already.

There were many unfamiliar faces on the *George

Washington. And a few familiar faces from my plantation. And of course, there was me. Barbury. All of us headed to a new place in South Carolina.

I met another slave on the ship with a strange name. His name was Polidore. I thought his name sounded even stranger than mine. But of course I didn't say so.

Polidore was real smart. He knew lots of things because he worked in the main house at his last plantation. He and the other slaves would snoop around when they were supposed to be doing work. Polidore said he once saw a large map of the world. And that the world was made of water, more water than land. He saw land in the water that looked far away from slavery.

"I'm going to the Bahamas one day," Polidore told me.

"Me too." Even though I had no idea where it was.

We were headed to Charleston. It sounded like a place that would not be kind. But then again, no place was kind to slaves. When we got off the ship, some of the slaves went to their owners waiting at the dock. The others, like me and Polidore, went to be auctioned.

It was my first and last auction. Aside from my death and the horrible thing that led to me dying, the auction was the worst experience of my life.

I was taken to a room with other slaves where our bodies were washed. Then they wiped us all over with an oil of sorts so our bodies shined. Afterwards, Master Vanderhart made me stand on a block raised off the ground so everybody could see me.

I was so scared with all those White men circling around. The greasy substance made my skin slick. I did not like the feeling of their hands sliding across my body. They opened my mouth real wide, looked in my ears and eyes. They grabbed my breasts. Made me spread my legs apart and touched me down there too. That made me cry.

One White man saw me crying when they opened my legs and asked, "How much for that doe?"

The White man and Master Vanderhart negotiated a price. And like that, the White man owned me. He purchased a few other slaves, but not Polidore. Then he packed us into the back of his wagon. Our bodies filled the space along with the other goods he had acquired—four wooden chairs, a small wooden table, tea leaves, and a small bag of ribbons.

When we arrived at his plantation, it was a sight to see. It was much larger than Master Vanderhart's plantation. It had a big house with large columns, and the driveway was lined with tall green trees. The breeze blew softly through the trees, and the leaves swayed like they were dancing.

There were lots of small cabins in the back. I knew that's where I would live. We got off the wagon, and an old Negro man led us to the slave quarters. Lots of slaves were there tending to their tasks. A group of slave women came over to clean us up.

"What's ya' name?" a woman asked.

She was old. Her hands as wrinkled as her brown face. Her eyes stayed on her task of cleaning the greasy substance off my body. She dipped a rag in a bucket of water and wiped my skin in rough circular motions.

"Name's Barbury, ma'am," I answered.

The greasy water ran down my legs. It made me itch, but I said nothing.

"My name's Hany," she told me. "Been here since I was young. And let me tell ya', ya' ain't in no nice place. Know it's a pretty place, but it ain't nice. Slaves here gets whipped for the simplest things. So you mind and do what ya' told. I help when I can, but I ain't taking no whippings for ya'."

"Yes, ma'am," I said.

"And you's a pretty girl," Hany said, shaking her head from side to side. "They gon' come for ya'. Massa or one uh his sons. Perhaps all of 'em. They gon' come for ya'. I hates to be the one to tell ya'."

She kept shaking her head from side to side.

"What you mean, ma'am?" I asked.

Hany fell silent. She grabbed my face with both of her hands, real gentle as I suppose my mother would have. Her hands were rough and calloused. She looked me right in the eyes.

"One of them White men gon' come to where you sleep. He gon' take ya' clothes off. Then he gon' take off his clothes. Then he gon' touch on ya'. Here and here."

She touched my barely formed breasts. And then she patted me softly between my legs.

"And then, he gon' take the part of him that makes him a man. He gon' put it in the parts that make you a woman," Hany continued. "It's gon' be bad. It's gon' hurt. But ya' mind what he say and it'll be over quick."

She looked at me with sad eyes and said, "I sorry, baby."

And for some reason, I started to cry.

Hany dipped the rag in the bucket of water and rubbed my skin while I cried. For a few moments, Hany allowed me to be a young girl. Her face softened, and the scrubbing became not so harsh. And then, the moment was over. Hany hardened.

"Now you hush that fuss, girl. Them tears don't do nothing but make you weak. You got to be strong now."

I tried to stop crying.

"This ya' life now. Not sure where you come from where ya' massa ain't touch on ya', but that's what happens here.

"You start to bleed yet?" Hany asked.

"No, ma'am."

One of the slaves at the Vanderhart Plantation had told me I would start bleeding soon. Said she would show me what to do when it was time. But then I was sold away.

"Well soon as you do, soon as you starts to bleed, you gon' have a baby. This how ya' life is gon' be, okay," Hany said matter-of-factly.

"Yes, ma'am."

Hany was right. Like she said, the sun had not set before the White man who bought me came opening my cabin door. He looked at me how I guess someone real hungry might look at a meal—eager and ready to devour it.

He grabbed my dress and started to pull it off. And I fought him something bad. I kicked, bit, and scratched at him. Seem like a long time we was wrestling in the small cabin.

My voice didn't even seem like me. I sounded like an animal as I defended myself. As I struggled about the cabin floor, I saw a rusty nail. I grabbed it, and with all my strength, I jabbed the nail into his right eye. He screamed, and folks came running. All I remember is folks coming inside the cabin and pulling me off him.

When I came to, I was naked and strapped to a whipping post. The White man who had tried to take off my dress was standing nearby looking wild. There was a patch over the eye I put the nail in. The other eye looked at me real mean. Other White men were there. They wanted to watch him make me pay.

Slaves were gathered around. I could tell they were there because they had to be, not because they wanted to be. Hany looked sad. She knew what was coming. I had never had a whipping, but I had seen it before. I knew it was gonna be bad.

The White man walked over and slapped me. Hard. He kicked me and spit on me. I couldn't do nothing, not even protect my body, because I was bound to the wooden stake.

"Let me show you niggers what happens to slaves who don't mind. She gettin' a hundred lashes," the White man yelled.

There was a collective gasp from the slaves. Hany dropped her head.

I heard a male voice whisper, "No, Massa. She young. She gon' die."

"Damn right she gon' die! That'll teach her 'bout puttin' her hands on a White man. Y'all watch. Watch what happens when you don't mind!"

He grabbed a whip by its braided handle. As he walked over to me, he dragged the whip across the dirt slowly. The whip was like a thin black snake preparing to strike.

I heard the whip in the air. It whirled and whistled until it came down with a crack onto my back. My skin split open, and I cried out from the pain. The lashes kept coming while the man I'd stabbed in the eye said horrible things about me.

I counted as each lash hit my body. Each one stung and burned more than the last. My back was wet and warm from my blood. When the sixteenth lash landed, my spirit let go. My body separated from life, and I entered death.

Wasn't quite sure what happened. I was looking down on the scene of my whipping. The slaves huddled together as they looked at my crumpled body in the dirt. Hany cried, covering her face with her hands.

The White man continued to bring the lash down on my bleeding, broken brown body. He whipped me with all his strength until he reached one hundred lashes. His shirt was soaked with sweat from the exertion. But I felt nothing.

The spiritual realm is different from the physical realm. From the moment of my death, I had peace. When my body and spirit parted, I saw a light, bright and beckoning. But I didn't follow it. The light faded into a circle that grew smaller and smaller until it disappeared.

I was free. I could go anywhere, except, I didn't know of anywhere to go. I didn't want to go back to my old plantation. And I definitely didn't want to stay in Charleston.

I thought about my conversation with Polidore. The Bahamas. He'd made it sound real nice. An island in the middle of a world made mostly of water.

So I willed myself to the Bahamas. For years I waited for Polidore to come. But he never did. Finally I came to accept Polidore created memories in some other place. Polidore had forgotten about the Bahamas. And surely, he had forgotten about me.

But Polidore was right. The Bahamas was a nice place. Many spirits came from all over the world. They told me about different places. Some spirits stayed awhile and then moved on to someplace else. But not me. I have never left the Bahamas. It's my home. And it's where I met one of my closest friends.

Awiti was not much older than I when the strange men came to her village. Sad as my story was, hers was worse. Awiti was surprised I didn't want to return to Charleston to make the White man suffer for my pain and death. She offered to go and handle the matter for me. But I didn't need that. Had everything I wanted right in the Bahamas.

"I got peace, Awiti. And that's all I need."

But Awiti wasn't like me. She didn't have peace, and I don't think she ever will. And she stayed doing things to make others suffer. Always sending storms and hurricanes, trying to make folks pay for slavery. Every time she would get those thoughts, I'd try to stop her.

"Stay with me, Awiti," I'd say. "Don't go doing bad things."

Sometimes she would listen. But most times she didn't.

On the morning of August 23, 2005, the winds started to blow in such a way, I knew it was Awiti. She was on her way to make somebody pay. Getting ready to rain down her wrath on some memory she couldn't let go.

29
SORRY

Ninth Ward, New Orleans, LA (2005)

Nobody wants to listen to the old Obeah woman. These days, all folks want is for people to do tricks and such. Want to watch folks float in the air and disappear like that man on TV does. That ain't nothing. That ain't no real magic. Tricks of the eye, sleight of the hand. Anybody can do that kind of mischief. I do the real voodoo. I speak to the dead.

Always had a way with the spirits. Ever since I was young, the spirits and I been connected in a special way. I ain't have many friends, 'cause kids wasn't allowed to play with me. They mamas told them to stay away. Afraid some of my voodoo powers might rub off.

The kids did as they was told. But they made sure when they crossed me to call me all sorts of names—Hoodoo Voodoo, Devil's Child, Crazy Crawfish, and Evil Eyes was just a few. Names I'm sure they learned from they mamas. Funny, though. First time any one of they mamas needed some special potion to trap a man, keep they man, or needed to talk to someone who passed on, first house they came to was ours.

It was my grandmama's house. Everybody call her Mama Obeah. She more like my mama than grandmama. When I was young, my real mama would stop by from time to time, stumbling in drunk and smelling like all the things the streets is made of, especially sadness. Believe it or not, sadness has a smell. Sadness smell like my mama.

When Mama hugged me, I could smell that sadness, liquor, the bayou. She'd hug me so hard, sometimes both of us would fall to the floor. Mama Obeah would help me up, then she'd pick up her daughter and clean her before she'd lay her down in the bed.

All we heard for the next day or so was Mama throwing up, crying out, and yellin' 'bout how life ain't fair. Once she felt better, Mama would swear us up and down she was gon' get herself right, that things would be different. And then she'd be right back in them streets again.

Finally, when I was around eight years old, my mama left me with Mama Obeah for good and said she leaving to find a new life. Once she got settled, she said she was gon' send for me and get me out the bayou too. Told us she was tired of them haunts speaking to her.

"They been driving me crazy all my life," she yelled at Mama Obeah.

Mama Obeah didn't say nothing. She let Mama ramble on in her drunken rage. Mama was convinced that if she left the bayou, she'd leave the spirits here too.

When my mama passed out, exhausted from all her yelling, Mama Obeah picked her up like always and took her into the back room. Mama Obeah let her sleep away the pain. The next morning, my mama was gone. I never saw her again.

"Ain't no way you can fight hearing the spirits," Mama

Obeah always said. "They always gon' be there, so you might as well make 'em ya' friend and not ya' enemy. Remember, what we got is a gift. Spirits chose us to listen to 'em, and that's mighty important."

Unlike Mama, the gift never bothered me. I kind of liked hearing the spirits around me. I never felt alone.

Like Mama Obeah said the day Mama left, "The gift is all we got, and God ain't give it to just any ol' body."

Mama Obeah the one who taught me to be proud the spirits speak to me. All the women in our family got the gift, all the way from when our folks came over from Africa. She say we came from one of the tribes that was known to have powerful medicine women. And they passed the gift on to us. It's in our blood.

"We blessed to be chosen," Mama Obeah would say while she stirred up some requested magic potion.

Sounded like we was lucky to me too. But Mama had thought otherwise. Mama Obeah said the voices of the spirits drove Mama to the bottle, and the bottle drove my mama to the grave. I didn't know my mama well enough to miss her all that much. Just remember that smell of sadness.

Everything I know I learned from Mama Obeah. Folks came to see her from all 'round the bayou. Mama Obeah was real tuned in to the spirits. It was often folks left our house crying happy tears 'cause they got some answer they was waiting on.

Mama Obeah knew potions to stop men from cheating on they women, make somebody repay a debt they owed, all kinds of remedies. Folks was so grateful to Mama Obeah for helping them.

Sometimes the folks she helped paid Mama Obeah with

money. But most of the time, folks didn't have the money to pay, so they gave her food or did work 'round the house. She was fine, s'long as they paid her somehow or promised to in the future. Mama Obeah never turned nobody away who came calling for her help, whether they had a way to pay her or not.

"The spirits speak to you because you got the gift, not because they want you to earn a living. Don't never turn anybody away who need you—people or spirits," Mama Obeah would say.

Soon as I was old enough, folks started to ask me to help them too. Mama Obeah told folks I was best at talking to the spirits, so people asked me to talk to their children who died. That's how they came to call me Baby Obeah. I didn't mind much. Made me feel important to help folks, like Mama Obeah. Most times, after a family spoke to a child who passed and said they last goodbyes, the children would find peace and cross over.

"It's not the babies who have a hard time crossing over, it's the adults. The ones who can't seem to get over that they been wronged," Mama Obeah would say. "They can't let go of the pain and the folks who wronged them."

As I got older, Mama Obeah taught me lots of ways to deal with the living and the dead. Soon more folks was coming to see me than they was seeing Mama Obeah.

"That's how it supposed to be," she said in a proud voice. "Now I can sit back and let you do all the work."

We both laughed when Mama Obeah said that, 'cause everybody knows she never could sit still.

Although the living people love to come see me for help, the spirits love me more. The spirits love to talk to me, ask me questions about the past, or some of 'em like to talk about themselves. They likes to reminisce about who they once were and who they woulda been if they was still living.

Spirits stayed 'round Mama Obeah's house, especially if we been friends for a long time. I can always feel when they there, so I never feel alone.

When Awiti first came to see me, a sadness filled Mama Obeah's house like never before. The air felt heavy and thick. And that was the smell of sadness. Mama Obeah felt it too, because she kept moaning in her sleep. That's how I knew. Most time you felt a spirit before they spoke to you.

"Who here?" I asked.

"Awiti. How are you?" she asked.

I responded quickly because don't nothing make a spirit more upset than knowing you heard them and you act like you didn't. That's what Mama had tried to do. It only made them spirits mad; made they voices more loud and forceful. Spirits don't like to be ignored.

"Hi now. I'm good," I responded. "What you need?"

Because they all needed something. They all had something to tell you or something they needed you to tell them. No spirit ever came calling to say hi 'less they knew you.

"What's your name?" Awiti asked.

Of course, Awiti already knew my name. She knew about me or she wouldn't have come. That's how it worked. The spirits know who got the gift.

"Name's Baby Obeah.

"Baby Obeah," she said. "I like that name."

Then Awiti was quiet. I knew she was taking it all in. Mama Obeah tossed and turned in her bed.

"What you need, Awiti?" I asked again.

I don't mind spirits lingering 'round s'long as they speak and let me know what's on they mind. We ain't friends yet, so she ain't got the right to hang around like some of the spirits I know.

"Oh, Baby Obeah, I don't want much. I want you to hear my story. I want you to help me find peace," Awiti said.

They all wanted you to listen to their story. Wanted you to hear how they was wronged so you would agree with them and say, "Yeah, that wasn't right what was done to you."

Some spirits used their stories to justify the evil things they did.

That first meeting of ours was in 2000, and Awiti stayed 'round me for a whole year. Took some time before she showed her face. Not much older than I was when Mama lost her last battle with the bottle. But I knew Awiti wasn't never gon' find peace.

First, she'd made a bad deal. If someone come along asking you to be immortal because they tired, they telling you a lie. Immortal one of the best things to be, and if somebody don't want it no more, well, they ain't telling you the whole story.

Seemed like the man who did the Exchange tricked Awiti. He didn't tell her the whole truth about the deal she was making. Immortals supposed to stick together, because unless you spend your life with someone like you, someone who can understand you, life is a curse.

Man who switched with Awiti was wrong. Selfish to do that to a young girl. He was trying to get out of his own mess. And he tricked her with life's greatest trap, love. Awiti was trapped in that space in-between, and that's a hard place to be.

She wanted me to make her mortal so she could die, but I can't. Then she wanted me to make her spirit cross over. I can't do that. I ain't got that type of power. Awiti was gon' have to keep living. That was gon' be hard to do forever.

I told Awiti to stop the suffering. She had to stop hurting folks because she got wronged. All of us been wronged one way or the other, by our choices or life dealing us a bad hand.

"What you gon' do? Keep getting together with them other angry spirits and stir up trouble? Every time you have a bad memory, you gon' keep hurting folks?" I asked her one day.

I was glad to have her to talk to. Mama Obeah didn't talk much anymore. She'd lie in the bed and do things only when she had to—talk when she had to and move when she had to. Otherwise, Mama Obeah was still and quiet.

Awiti said nothing, but I knew she was listening. Whoever her folks was trained her real good, because she minded her elders.

I always told her, "I know you older than me, but I'm older than you!"

This always made her laugh. Even though she was immortal, Awiti was still very much a child.

"You gots to let go, Awiti. You got to find you some place you can be where you ain't got no ties. Some place your spirit can rest and be easy," I told her.

"I don't know a place like that," she said. "Everywhere I go, trouble follows."

"So what? You trying to tell me you done visited the whole world? I know you ain't. I know it's places you ain't been or places you passed through quick," I scolded her.

She was being difficult.

"I wouldn't mind you staying with us, but you know, Louisiana, 'especially New Orleans, is a place of pain for you. And then what you gon' do when Mama Obeah and I die?" I asked. "Then you'll be looking for a new place to be. You gots to think things all the way through, Awiti."

She was quiet again.

"You need to go far from this place to find some peace," I told her. "Too much hurt here. The peoples you hurt, the hurt you lived, and the hurt you caused. You gots to stay away from Louisiana."

"Once, I passed through an island called the Bahamas. I followed another spirit there," she said.

She was trying.

"Let me look it up in my book," I said.

I pulled out my book with maps of the world. The Bahamas seemed nice. Not a lot of people, and far away from most of the places Awiti couldn't seem to stay away from. I was worried because Haiti was close enough, Florida too. But Awiti was certain she could be strong.

"Haiti doesn't call me as often as Louisiana," she reasoned. "Florida either."

"So go to the Bahamas," I said. "You ever need me again, I'll be right here."

And then, Awiti was gone.

I ain't hear from Awiti for a few years. I thought she had found the peace she was looking for. That's why I'm surprised she's speaking to me again, this time from afar.

"I'm angry, Baby Obeah," Awiti says. "I'm angry again. Why did they do those things to my people? Make them suffer? Enslave them, beat them? Why did they put their heads on poles all around the levee? It ain't right!"

Mama Obeah starts moaning and tossing in her bed.

I know what this means. Awiti thinking about Louisiana. The pain is calling her again; the memories that haunted her have returned. She's still trying to avenge all those slaves' heads on the poles that lined the streets and was posted on the levee. Can't imagine these are easy things to let go of, but she has to try.

"Awiti, you have to let it go. You was wronged. Those you loved was wronged. Innocent people was wronged, but you have to let go."

"I need you to leave, Baby Obeah," Awiti says softly. "I need you and anyone you love to leave, because I'm coming back."

"No, Awiti," I say.

I try to use the best mama-like voice I can. I want Awiti to hear me speak to her with love. But I know it's gon' be hard to stop her. Once a spirit put they force in motion, it's already too late.

"Awiti, why you coming? You gon' kill more of ya' own kind than anybody. We the ones down here now, suffering. You want to make it even harder for us?"

I hope she will consider this and change her mind. Maybe the storm will be mild if she isn't so angry.

"I can end that. I can help people get to the afterlife. A place of peace. No more suffering."

All spirits think this is the best way to do things. They think that by killing folks, they helping them to get to the afterlife faster. They think they helping to stop the pain. In Awiti's childlike mind, she don't understand she ain't ending suffering. She bringing more.

"You can't end all the suffering this way, Awiti. Besides, it ain't your place. Who you to decide whose suffering gets to end and whose don't?"

We go on this way for some time, bickering back and forth. Mama Obeah gets up out the bed. She moves slow as she starts to pack up her important things.

"You wasting time, Baby," Mama Obeah says. "You need to get to packing because Awiti coming, and it's gon' be bad."

Mama Obeah moves now only when she has to, so I know things is serious. I call out to Awiti, but she don't answer. I start packing, little things here and there because we never had much. I turn on the TV. The forecast say a hurricane brewing off the coast of the Bahamas.

"Damn, Awiti."

I try to tell as many folks as I can to come with me and Mama Obeah. We can fit a few extra folk into our old station wagon. Folks need to get to higher ground. But folks here never run from no storms. They stay and fight them.

The only people leaving got the gift like me and Mama Obeah. They done heard Awiti is on her way again; most of them done already packed up they cars and on they way. I'm the only one don't want to believe Awiti is coming.

I call out to her one more time. No answer. She's coming.

Mama Obeah and I finish packing up the things we love the most. We say goodbye to our home because deep down we know we ain't never gon' see it again. Even though she wrong for coming, I feel sorry for Awiti. I truly do.

30

IN THE END

They say the pain from heartache and suffering eventually passes. That new moments of happiness replace tormented memories. Dark stories that were once told as an explanation for the sadness become cautionary tales, perhaps even shared with candor and laughter. The heartache becomes a lesson disclosed to others about overcoming adversity. Proof that time heals all wounds.

I can say with certainty such reconciliation is not true for everyone, and most certainly not for me. I have never resolved what was taken from me. There have never been moments more beautiful than those from my youth. I cherish the remembrances of my family and village. But I believe time has made matters worse. Time afforded me more opportunity to ponder as anger and resentment hover over my memories like flies. And there is no way to swat away the bitterness.

They say that when you are truly loved, even in death, you still exist. You live in the hearts of those you leave behind. And that is what my heart encompasses. It is filled with images from my past. I dream of the faces and voices of those I love. Some speak to me with happy memories, while others beckon for restitution, pleading with me to make things fair. To make the world pay for what was done to them. When the latter occurs, I often call on Flying Eagle.

I cry out to him,, "I wish you were here with me. I need you." For aside from Father, he was the only man who truly loved me. And just like Father, Flying Eagle was taken from me. He has crossed over, so he does not answer.

I only hear words from our past as Flying Eagle says, "Find peace, Awiti. Promise me."

"I promise." And I do find peace occasionally, but it is always temporary.

And that is the difficulty. The peace is never longstanding. It is only enough to sustain me for a short time. And before I know it, the heartache returns. Although I tried many times, I have never found peace that eradicates suffering. The type of peace that brings stillness and calm. Does there even exist such peace to overpower the hate?

As Amos once told me, "Even God's tears can't do that."

Yes, even children know the lasting effects of misery. Sometimes it stays with you forever.

And I am never alone in my sorrow. Many have been wronged, for suffering is a part of the Great One's design for humanity. Good and evil remain in a constant battle to ensure a proper balance in a world filled with uncertainty and free will. Ill-fated circumstances plague some and not others. Evil strikes at random. There is no way to protect one's self from suffering. The mere act of being born makes you vulnerable to heartache.

They say this is what happened in the beginning when I was simply a girl in my village. Random acts of evil descended upon Africa and cursed our people. We became slaves, and even when our chains were removed, our minds remained in bondage. The world continued to look down upon us and treat our descendants as though they should still be enslaved. Yes, hate can be diminished with each generation, but it will always remain. No way to outrun it. No way to out-love it. Hate just is, and it's always going to be.

The strange men took what was most valuable to our village, to any man, really—our freedom. I can still see the fear in Mother's dark eyes as she looked at her children. Surely she knew she would never see us again. I can hear the voices of the women and children outside our home, screaming as they watched the strange men descend upon our village. I can still hear Father saying,

"Run."

Whenever I think of that fateful day, I cry. Rain falls from the skies, and storm clouds gather. Some in the spiritual realm try to comfort me, but I am often inconsolable when I think of what was and could have been. Rainstorms for Father and Mother. Storm winds stir for Amondi and her smile none could rival. Hurricanes rage against the prayers for what I wished and hoped for.

Jaramogi, Owino, and Onyango—I never saw them grow to become men. Father never made the sun go home again. And we never sat beneath the baobab tree waiting for him to help it to rise. There were no village feasts under the stars. And I never learned to sing like Mother. A man from my village never took me as his wife and smiled as I danced. My belly will never be swollen with Love.

My tears remind of the day Oranyan found me. I was so naïve and afraid. His arms and charm were there to rescue me. Was he waiting for someone like me? Hoping to bargain with someone who still believed in hope and love? Praying to find a foolish girl who believed such things could conquer all injustices?

"Do you truly love me enough to give me the one thing I desire most?" Oranyan asked.

"Yes."

And it was my love for Oranyan that enslaved me in a different type of bondage. I sold myself with the promise of immortality. With the hope of giving myself an eternity to find my family. Yes, the choice was mine, but to this day I do not think it fair. For even with all of my sacrifice, I never saw them again.

Many have suffered, for the evils of slavery extended far beyond Africa. Our small village by the mountainside was but the beginning of many years of suffering for people with black and brown skin. So many have died at the hands of slavery and other injustices, it is impossible to count them all. And while many have passed on after their deaths, an infinite number of the dead remain among the living.

And when we find each other, we share our pain. Our memories rustle the air, and there begins a breeze filled with resentment. Gaining momentum off the coast of West Africa, we move across the Atlantic. Our sadness lingers in the air like the salt from the sea. A light white coating that stings like saltwater on broken flesh. We gather the suffering and anger, swirling and brewing, screaming and raging. And soon we are no more in control of the storm as we were our destinies.

As we move across the Atlantic, we gather the energy of those thrown into the sea. The storm goes to the sources of our pain, for our suffering and misery are entangled in the winds. We are the eye of the storm, striking the descendants of Black

Faces and White Faces. We force them to reap the pain their forefathers sowed. In the moment, our stormy restitution is just and invigorating. But in the end, it is not enough.

No matter the destruction that ensues, I have learned no amount of vengeance can replace what I lost. There is no reparation great enough to substitute what was stolen. Is there truly a cost for an altered destiny? There is nothing that can overturn the curse of a nation that was once blessed.

Fragments of my past haunt me daily. A man with eyes like Father. The woman with skin like Mother. Flesh so dark I want to wrap myself in the black arms and remember. Laughter of children reminds me of my siblings. The memories remain at war with peace.

For eternity you will feel me in the wind. Whenever your skin turns cold, you will know I am near. I am one of the many dealt an unfortunate life. Awiti Akoth. A child born of misfortune as the rains fell on her village. One who should have been thrown away, for she was a girl sure to bring trouble. How I have lived up to Father's naming of me.

"Remember what makes us special, Awiti," Father reminded me all those years ago. "When your heart desires, you can control the rain."

They say I will find peace when I am ready. I have tried for centuries, but I know this peace will never come. I am certain. And as much as this pains me, it is my truth.

A NOTE FROM THE AUTHOR

"There was a time when you were not a slave, remember that.
You walked alone, full of laughter, you bathed bare-bellied. You
say you have lost all recollection of it, remember... You say there
are no words to describe this time, you say it does not exist. But
remember. Make an effort to remember. Or, failing that, invent."

— Monique Wittig

The above quote is one of my favorites. Monique's words truly embody how I felt when writing *The Truth About Awiti*.

There was a time when slavery did not exist. Many recollections of that time have been lost, history forever remaining in the uncollected stories of those who passed on. But I had enough information to remember. I had enough evidence to invent.

I enjoyed researching the factual events that appear in *The Truth About Awiti*. Many of the occurrences are so rich on their own, it was often difficult to fictionalize.

As a native of West Palm Beach, Florida, I was exposed to hurricanes and their damage from a young age. Our family actually had to evacuate for Hurricane Andrew, and I will never forget hearing the roaring winds. The gusts sounded like wailing and screaming. It is providence that these experiences, along with my educational background and love for fiction, have evolved into a historical fantasy novel.

I must admit there were times I was surprised to learn many of the deadliest hurricanes occurred where some of the most horrific crimes against Black people transpired. For example, in 2001 when Hurricane Andrew hit the same parish where dozens of slaves were killed during the 1811 German Coast Uprising. Or discovering that the Black River Hurricane devastated the exact region where the *Zong* Massacre occurred in November 1781.

Other connections were sensational in their own right, such as the Labor Day Hurricane of 1935. The deadly hurricane occurred only a few years after a Cuban man was murdered for his open love affair with a mulatto woman—a voodoo priestess who vowed to avenge his death. These are facts authors of historical fiction and fantasy dream of.

According to meteorological reports, most Atlantic hurricanes start to take shape when thunderstorms form along the West Coast of Africa and drift out over warm ocean waters. Many theories prevail throughout the African diaspora that hurricanes are manifestations of restless slave spirits affected by the trans–Atlantic slave trade. Further perpetuating this theory is the fact many hurricanes generate off the African coast, cross over much of the Middle Passage, which includes the Caribbean, and cause the most damage to Southern slave-holding states. Are such occurrences spiritual retribution? We may never know.

The majority of the chapters in *The Truth About Awiti* incorporate actual events that occurred in areas that played key roles in the trans–Atlantic slave trade and the institution of slavery. I encourage the reader to conduct their own research to understand the role the institution of slavery had on African, Caribbean, European, and American histories.

ACKNOWLEDGEMENTS

THERE ARE SO many people who were influential in the writing of *The Truth About Awiti*. First and foremost, I would like to honor my ancestors who endured such a sorrowful existence during the trans–Atlantic slave trade. I am so thankful for those who survived. I am forever indebted to the men and women who left us with memoirs and historical evidence of defiance and overcoming life's adversities. It is because of these stories I had enough information to invent a fictional timeline of the hardships people of African descent experienced and endured for centuries. My dear ancestors, thank you for persevering.

I would also like to thank my family, especially my husband, Joseph Patrick, and daughter, Nalah Palmer, for being patient with me as I worked endless hours to complete this novel. Thank you for allowing me to hide in my office for days and nights to achieve one of my dreams. Likewise, I thank my close friends for their sacrifices—particularly for listening to unfinished chapters (and the terrible early versions).

Thank you to my editor, Emma Simmons, who helped make *The Truth About Awiti* shine. Where would I be without someone to fix my past and present participles?

And of course, a special thank you to my readers. Thank you for taking this journey with me!

ABOUT THE AUTHOR

CHRISTINE PLATT WAS born in 1976 in West Palm Beach. After graduating from Suncoast Community High School in 1994, she obtained a B.A. in Africana Studies from the University of South Florida, M.A. in African Studies from The Ohio State University, and J.D. from Stetson University College of Law. She began writing under the moniker CP Patrick after marrying her husband, Joseph Patrick, in 2010. CP Patrick enjoys writing fiction and fantasy interwoven with the African Diasporic experience. Her work is drawn from the inspiration of many, particularly Octavia Butler. She lives in Washington, DC with her husband and daughter.

Made in the USA
Middletown, DE
09 May 2015